I0553735

The Unjust Steward by Margaret Oliphant

or The Minister's Debt

Margaret Oliphant Wilson was born on April 4th, 1828 to Francis W. Wilson, a clerk, and Margaret Oliphant, at Wallyford, near Musselburgh, East Lothian.

Her youth was spent in establishing a writing style and by 1849 she had her first novel published: Passages in the Life of Mrs. Margaret Maitland.

Two years later, in 1851 Caleb Field was published and also an invitation to contribute to Blackwood's Magazine; the beginning of a life time business relationship.

In May 1852, Margaret married her cousin, Frank Wilson Oliphant. Their marriage produced six children but, tragically, three died in infancy. When her husband developed signs of the dreaded consumption (tuberculosis) they moved to Florence, and then to Rome where, sadly, he died.

Margaret was naturally devastated but was also now left without support and only her income from writing to support the family. She returned to England and took up the burden of supporting her three remaining children by her literary activity.

Her incredible and prolific work rate increased both her commercial reputation and the size of her reading audience. Tragedy struck again in January 1864 when her only remaining daughter Maggie died.

In 1866 she settled at Windsor to be closer to her sons, who were being educated at near-by Eton School.

For more than thirty years she pursued a varied literary career but family life continued to bring problems. Cyril Francis, her eldest son, died in 1890. The younger son, Francis, who she nicknamed 'Cecco', died in 1894.

With the last of her children now lost to her, she had little further interest in life. Her health steadily and inexorably declined.

Margaret Oliphant Wilson Oliphant died at the age of 69 in Wimbledon on 20th June 1897. She is buried in Eton beside her sons.

Index of Contents

CHAPTER I

A SUDDEN ALARM

Elsie and Roderick Buchanan were the son and daughter, among a number of others, of the Rev. George Buchanan, a minister much esteemed in the city of St. Rule, and occupying a high place among the authorities and influential personages of that place. They were members of a large family, and not important members, being the youngest. It is true that they were not two boys or two girls, but a girl and boy; but being so, they were as nearly inseparable as a boy and girl could be. They were called in the family the Twins, though there was quite a year, a year and a day as in a fairy tale, between them. It was the girl who was the elder of the two, which, perhaps, accounted for the fact that they were still the same height as well as so very like each other that in their infancy it was scarcely possible to know them apart, so that the name of the Twins was quite appropriate. Elsie was fourteen, and Roderick, better known as Rodie, according to the Scotch love of diminutives, just thirteen. Up to this age, their lessons and their amusements had gone on together,—the girls in St. Rule's, from the beginning of time, having been almost as athletic as the boys, and as fond of the links and the harbour, while the old Scotch fashion of training them together had not yet given way before the advancing wave of innovation, which has so much modified education in Scotland. They were in the same class, they read the same books, they had the same lessons to prepare. Elsie was a little more diligent, Rodie more strong in his Latin, which was considered natural for a boy. They helped each other mutually, he being stronger in the grammar, she more "gleg" at construing. She went all wrong in her tenses, but jumped at the meaning of a thing in a way that sometimes astonished her brother. In this way, they were of great assistance to each other in their school life.

The other side of life, the amusements and games, were not nearly of so much importance, even with children, then as now. It was the object of his elders and masters rather to curb Rodie's enthusiasm for football than to stimulate it, notwithstanding his high promise as a player; and the gentlemen who played golf were exceedingly impatient of laddies on the links; and as for girls presuming to show their faces there, would have shown their disapprobation very pointedly; so that, except for a few "holes" surreptitiously manufactured in a corner (even the Ladies' Links being as yet non-existent), the youngsters found little opportunity of cultivating that now all-important game. They turned out, however, sometimes early, very early, of a morning, or late in the afternoon, and in their hurried performances, Elsie as yet was almost as good as her brother, and played up to him steadily, understanding his game, when they two of a summer evening, when all the club was at dinner, and nobody about to interfere, played together in a single. Lawn-tennis was still far in the future, and it had not been given to the children to do more than stand afar off and admire at the performance of the new game called croquet, which had just been set up by an exclusive society on the Castle Green. Who were the little Buchanans to aspire to take part in such an Olympian contest among the professors and their ladies? They looked on occasionally from a pinnacle of the ruins, and privately mocked between themselves at the stiffness of a great man's learned joints, or the mincing ways of the ladies, sending confusing peals of laughter over the heads of the players at any mishap, till the indignant company used the rudest language in respect to the Buchanan bairns, along, it must be allowed, with the Beaton bairns and the Seaton bairns, and several more scions of the best families, and threatened to put them out of the Castle ruins altogether: though everybody knew this was a vain threat, and impossible to carry out. It was strictly forbidden that these young people should ever adventure themselves in a boat, the coast being so dangerous, a prohibition which Elsie did not resent, having distinguished herself as a very bad sailor, but against which Rodie kicked with all his might. The reader will therefore see that they were not encouraged to spend their strength in athletics, which is so much the custom now.

Perhaps this encouraged in them the delight in books which they had shown from a very early age. It was always possible to keep the Twins quiet with a story-book, their elders said, though I confess that Rodie began to show symptoms of impatience with Elsie's books, and unless he got a story "of his own kind," was no longer so still and absorbed as in early days. The stories he loved, which were "of his own kind," were, I need not say, tales of adventure, which he was capable of reading over and over again till he knew by heart every one of the Crusoe-like expedients of his seafaring or land-louping heroes. Elsie had a weakness for girl's stories, full of devotion and self-abnegation, and in which little maidens of her own age set all the world right, which perhaps, naturally, did not appeal to Rodie. But there was one series which never failed in its attraction for both. In Mr. Buchanan's library there was a set of the Waverleys, such as formed part of the best of the plenishing for a new household in those days when they were but recent publications, as it still continues we hope to do in every house which desires to fortify itself against the tedium of the years. The children were never tired of Ivanhoe and Quentin Durward, and the Fair Maid of Perth. Indeed, there was not one of them that had not its lasting charm, though perhaps the preponderance of a lassie in the Heart of Midlothian, for instance, dulled Rodie's enthusiasm a little; while Elsie, more catholic, was as profoundly interested in Harry Bertram's Adventures, and followed Rowland Græam through all that happened in the Castle of Lochleven, with as warm interest as heart could desire. They thought, if that wildly presumptuous idea could be entertained, that Sir Walter was perhaps mistaken about bloody Claverhouse, but that, no doubt, was owing to their natural prejudices and breeding. One of their most characteristic attitudes was over one of these books (it was the edition in forty-eight volumes, with the good print and vignettes on the title-pages), spread out between them (they broke all the backs of his books, their father complained) their heads both bent over the page, with faint quarrels arising now and then that Elsie read too fast, and turned the page before Rodie was ready, or that Rodie read too slow and kept his sister waiting, which furnished a little mutual grievance that ran through all the reading, manifested now and then by a sudden stroke of an elbow, or tug at a page.

The place in which they chiefly pursued their studies was a little round corner, just big enough to hold them, which adjoined their father's study, and which, like that study, was lined with books. It was really a small turret, the relic of some older building which had been tacked to the rambling house, old-fashioned enough in its roomy irregularity, but not nearly so old as the little ashen-coloured tower, pale as with the paleness of extreme old age, which gave it distinction, and afforded a very quaint little adjunct to the rooms on that side. There was scarcely more than room enough in it for these two to sit, sometimes on an old and faded settle, sometimes on the floor, as the humour seized them. They were on the floor, as it happened, at the special moment which I am about to describe. The inconvenience of this retreat was that it was possible from that retirement to hear whatever might be said in the study, so that the most intimate concerns of the family were sometimes discussed by the father and mother in the hearing of these two little creatures, themselves unseen. There was nothing in this to blame them for, for it was well known that the turret was their haunt, and Mr. Buchanan, when reminded of it by some little scuffling or exchange of affectionate hostilities, would sometimes be moved to turn them out, as disturbing his quiet when he was busy with his sermon. But in many other cases their presence was forgotten, and there were not many secrets in the innocent household. On the other hand, Elsie and Rodie were usually far too much occupied with their book to pay any attention to what the rather tedious discussions of father and mother—usually about money, or about Willie and Marion the two eldest, who were about to be sent out in the world, or other insignificant and long-winded questions of that description—might be about.

And I cannot tell for what exquisite reason it was, that on this particular day their minds were attracted to what was going on in the study; I think they must have been reading some scene in which the predominance of lassies (probably the correspondence of Miss Julia Mannering, what I have always felt disposed to skip) had lessened Rodie's interest, but which Elsie, much distracted by the consciousness of his rebellion, but for pride of her own sex pretending to go carefully through, yet was only half occupied with, occasioned this openness of their joint minds to impression. At all events, they both heard their mother's sudden entrance, which was hurried indeed, and also flurried, as appeared a thing not quite common with her. They heard her come in with a rapid step, and quick panting breath, as if she had run up-stairs. And "William," she said, standing by the writing-table, they felt sure, which was also a usual thing for her to do—"William, have you heard that old Mr. Anderson is very bad to-day, and not expected to live?"

"Old Mr. Anderson!" he said, in a surprised and troubled tone.

"So they say. The Lord help us, what shall we do? Willie's outfit just paid for, and not a penny to the fore. Oh, my poor man!"

"It's very serious news," their father said; "but let us hope that both for his sake and our own it may not be true."

"Ill news is aye true," said Mrs. Buchanan, with a sound of something like a sob.

Why should mamma be so troubled about old Mr. Anderson, the children said to themselves, giving each other a look?

"That is just want of faith, my dear," he replied.

"Oh, I've no doubt it's want of faith! it's all in God's hands, and He can bring light out of darkness, I know; but oh! William, it's not always that He thinks fit to do that! You know as well as me. And if this time it should not be His will?"

"Mary," he said, "let us not forestall the evil; perhaps it will never come; perhaps there will be a way out of it—at the worst we must just bear it, my dear."

"Oh, I know that, I know that!" she cried, with a sound of tears in her voice. "You gave your word to pay it if he died, immediately thereafter, that there might be no talking. Wasn't that the bargain?"

"That was the bargain," he said.

"But we never thought it was to come like this, at the worst moment, just after the siller is gone for Willie's outfit."

"Mary, Mary, it is worse for him than for us."

"Do you think so, do you think so?" she cried, "and you a minister! I do not think that. He is an old man, and a good man, and if all we believe is true, it will be a happy change for him. Who has he to leave behind him? Na, he will be glad to go. But us with our young family! Oh, the power of that filthy siller; but for that, what happier folk could be, William, than just you and me?"

"We must be thankful for that, Mary," said the minister, with a quiver. "We might have had worse things than the want of money; we might have had sickness or trouble in our family, and instead of that they're all well, and doing well."

"Thank God for that!" mamma said, fervently, and then there was a pause.

"I will have to go at once to the man of business, and tell him," father said; "that was in the bargain. There was no signing of paper, but I was to go and tell; that was part of the bargain."

"And a very hard part," his wife cried, with a long sigh. "It is like sharpening the sword to cut off your own head. But, maybe," she said, with a little revival of courage, "Mr. Morrison is not a hard man; maybe he will give you time."

"Maybe our old friend will pull through," papa said, slowly.

"That would be the best of all," she said, but not in a hopeful tone. And presently they heard her shut the door of the study, and go down-stairs again, with something very different from the flying step with which she came.

The children did not stir, they did not even turn the leaf; they felt all at once that it was better that their presence there should not be known. They had heard such consultations before, and sometimes had been auditors of things they were not desired to hear; but they had never, they thought, heard anything so distinctly before, nor anything that was of so much importance. They were very much awe-stricken to hear of this thing that troubled father so, and made mother cry, without understanding very well what it was—old Mr. Anderson's illness, and Willie's outfit, and something about money, were all mixed up in their minds; but the relations between the one and the other were not sufficiently clear.

Presently they heard papa get up and begin to walk about the room. He did this often when he was deep in thought, composing his sermon, and then he would often say over and over his last sentence by way of piecing it on, they supposed to the next. So that it did not trouble, but rather reassured them, to hear him saying something to himself, which gave them the idea that he had returned to his work, and was no longer so much disturbed about this new business. When they heard him say, "no signing of papers, no signing of papers, but to go and tell," they were somewhat disturbed, for that did not sound like a sermon. But, presently, he sat down again and drew a book towards him, and they could hear him turning over the leaves. It was, there could be no doubt, the large Bible—large because it was such big print, for father's eyes were beginning to go—which always lay on his table. He turned over the leaves as they had so often heard him doing; no doubt it was some reference he was looking up for his sermon. He must have found what he wanted very soon, for there was a little silence, and then they heard him say, with great emphasis—"Then the Lord commended the unjust steward." He said it very slowly, pausing upon almost every word. It was the way he said over his text when he was pondering over it, thinking what he was to say. Then he began to read. It was to be a long text this time; Rodie tried to whisper in his sister's ear, but Elsie stopped him, quietly, with emphatic signs and frowns.

"He called every one of his Lord's debtors and said unto the first,
How much owest thou unto my Lord?
And he said an hundred measures of oil.
And he said unto him,
Take thy bill and sit down quickly and write fifty."

Then there was another pause. And again father spoke, so clearly, with such a distinct and emphatic voice that they thought he was speaking to them, and looked at each other fearfully. "The Lord commended the unjust steward." There was something awful in his tone: did he mean this for them, to reprove them? But they had done nothing, and if the Lord commended that man, surely there could be nothing to be so severe upon.

Elsie and Rodie missed everything that was pleasant that afternoon. It was thought they were on the hills, or on the sands, and nobody knew they were shut up there in the turret, now thoroughly alarmed, and terrified to change their position, or make themselves audible in any way, or to turn a leaf of their book, or to move a finger. In all their experience—and it was considerable—father had never been like this before. After a while, he began again, and read over the whole parable: and this he repeated two or three times, always ending in that terrible tone, which sounded to the children like some awful sentence, "The Lord commended the unjust steward"—then they would hear him get up again, and pace about the room, saying over and over those last words; finally, to their unspeakable relief, he opened the door, and went slowly down-stairs, so slowly that they sat still, breathless, for two minutes more, until his footsteps had died away.

Then the two children sprang up from their imprisonment, and stretched their limbs, which were stiff with sitting on the floor. They rushed out of the room as quickly as possible, and got out into the garden, from whence there was an exit toward the sea. The one thing which, without any consultation, they were both agreed upon, was to keep out of sight of father and mother, so that nobody might divine in what way they had been spending the afternoon. They did not, however, say much to each other about it. When they had got quite clear, indeed, of all possible inspection, and were out upon the east sands, which were always their resort when in disgrace or trouble, Rodie ventured to hazard an opinion on the situation.

"Papa's text is an awfu' kittle one to-day," he said. "I wonder if he'll ding it out."

"Oh, whisht!" said Elsie, "yon's not his text; he was never like that before."

"Then what is it?" said Rodie; but this was a question to which she would give no reply.

As they returned home, towards the twilight, they passed old Mr. Anderson's house, a large, old-fashioned mansion in the High Street, and gazed wistfully at the lights which already appeared in the upper windows, though it was not dark, and which looked strange and alarming to them as if many people were about, and much going on in this usually silent house.

"Does he need so many candles to die by?" said Rodie to his sister.

"Oh, perhaps he is better, and it's for joy," said Elsie, taking a more hopeful view.

Their father came out from the door, as they gazed, awe-stricken, from the other side of the street. His head was sunk upon his breast; they had never seen him so cast down before. His aspect, and the fact that he passed them without seeing them, had a great effect upon the children. They went home very quietly, and stole into the house without making any of the familiar noises that usually announced their arrival. However, it cheered them a little to find that their mother was very busy about Willie's outfit, and that their eldest sister Marion was marking all his new shirts in her fine writing, with the small bottle of marking ink, and the crow quill. The interest of this process and the pleasure of getting possession of the hot iron, which stamped that fine writing into a vivid black, gave a salutary diversion to Elsie's thoughts. As for Rodie, he was very hungry for his supper, which had an equally salutary effect.

CHAPTER II

A FRIEND IN NEED

Mr. Buchanan, the minister of St. Leonard's Church, was a member of a poor, but well-connected family in the West of Scotland, to which district, as everybody knows, that name belongs; and it is not to be supposed that he came to such advancement as a church in a university town all at once. He had married early the daughter of another minister in Fife, and it was partly by the interest procured by her family, and partly by the great reputation he had attained as a preacher, that he had been promoted to his present charge, which was much more important and influential than a mere country parish. But a succession of flittings from manse to manse, even though each new transfer was a little more important than the previous one, is hard upon a poor clergyman's purse, though it may be soothing to his self-esteem; and St. Leonard's, though St. Rule was an important port, had not a very large stipend attached to it. Everybody dwelt upon the fact that it was a most important post, being almost indeed attached to the university, and with so large a sphere of influence over the students. But influence is a privilege and payment in itself, or is supposed to be, and cannot be made into coin of the realm, or even pound notes, which are its equivalent. Mr. Buchanan himself was gratified, and he was solemnised, and felt his responsibility as a power for good over all those young men very deeply, but his wife may be forgiven, if she sighed occasionally for a few more tangible signs of the importance of his post. On the contrary, it led them into expenses to which a country minister is not tempted. They had to take their share in the hospitalities of the place, to entertain strangers, to give as seldom as possible, but still periodically, modest dinner-parties, a necessary return of courtesy to the people who invited them. Indeed, Mrs. Buchanan was like most women in her position, the soul of hospitality. It cost her a pang not to invite any lonely person, any young man of whom she could think that he missed his home, or might be led into temptation for want of a cheerful house to come to, or motherly influence over him. She, too, had her sphere of influence; it hurt her not to exercise it freely. Indeed, she did exercise it, and was quite unable often to resist the temptation of crowding the boys up at dinner or supper, in order to have a corner for some protégé. "It was a privilege," she said, but unfortunately it was an expensive one, plain though these repasts were. "Oh, the siller!" this good woman would say, "if there was only a little more of that, how smoothly the wheels would run."

The consequence of all this, however, of the frequent removals, of the lapses into hospitality, the appearances that had to be kept up, and, finally, the number of the family, had made various hitches in the family progress. Settling in St. Rule's, where there was no manse, and where a house had to be taken, and new carpets and curtains to be got, not to speak of different furniture than that which had done so very well in the country, had been a great expense; and all those changes which attend the setting out of young people in the world had begun. For Marion, engaged to another young minister, and to be married as soon as he got a living, there was the plenishing to think of, something more than the modern trousseau, a provision which included all the household linen of the new house; and, in short, as much as the parents could do to set the bride forth in a becoming and liberal manner. And Willie, as has been told, had his outfit for India to procure. These were the days before examinations, when friends—it was a kindly habit superseded now by the changed customs of life—put themselves to great trouble to further the setting out in life of a clergyman's sons. And William Buchanan had got a writership, which is equivalent, I believe, to an appointment in the Civil Service, by the exertions of one of his father's friends. The result of these two desirable family events, the provision for life of two of its members, though the very best things that could have happened, and much rejoiced over in the family, brought with them an appalling prospect for the father and mother when they met in private conclave, to consider how the preliminaries were to be accomplished. Where were Willie's outfit and Marion's plenishing to come from? Certainly not out of the straightened stipend of the Kirk of St. Leonard, in the city of St. Rule. Many anxious consultations had ended in this, that money must be borrowed in order to make the good fortune of the children available—that is to say, that the parents must put themselves under a heavy yoke for the greater part of their remaining life, in order that the son and the daughter might make a fair and equal start with their compeers. It is, let us thank heaven, as common as the day that such sacrifices should be made, so common that there is no merit in them, nor do the performers in the majority of cases think of them at all except as simple necessities, the most everyday duties of life. It was thus that they appeared to the Buchanans. They had both that fear and horror of debt which is, or was, the accompaniment of a limited and unelastic income with most reasonable people. They dreaded it and hated it with a true instinct; it gave them a sense of shame, however private it was, and that it should be betrayed to the world that they were in debt was a thing horrible to them. Nevertheless, nothing remained for them but to incur this dreadful reproof. They would have to pay it off slowly year by year; perhaps the whole of their remaining lives would be overshadowed by this, and all their little indulgences, so few, so innocent, would have to be given up or curtailed. The prospect was as dreadful to them—nay, more dreadful—than ruin and bankruptcy are to many nowadays. The fashion in these respects has very much changed. It is perhaps the result of the many misfortunes in the landed classes, the collapse of agriculture, the fall of rents; but certainly in our days the confession of poverty is no longer a shame; it is rather the fashion; and debts sit lightly on many shoulders. The reluctance to incur them, the idea of discredit involved in them is almost a thing extinguished and gone.

When Mr. Buchanan set out one black morning on the dreadful enterprise of borrowing money, his heart was very sore, and his countenance clouded. He was a man of a smiling countenance on ordinary occasions. He looked now as if disgrace had overtaken him, and nothing but despair was before him. It was not that he had an evil opinion of human nature. He had, perhaps, notwithstanding what it is now the fashion to call his Calvinistic creed, almost too good an opinion of human nature. It has pleased the literary class in all times, to stigmatise the Calvinistic creed as the origin of all evil. I, for one, am bound to say that I have not found it to be so, perhaps because dogmatical tenets hold, after all, but a small place in human hearts, and that the milk of human kindness flows independent of all the formal rules of theology. Mr. Buchanan was no doubt a Calvinist, and set his hand unhesitatingly to all the standards. But he was a man who was for ever finding out the image of God in his fellow men, and cursing was neither on his lips nor in his heart. He did not religiously doubt his fellow creature or condemn him. The tremour, the almost despair, the confusion of face with which he set out to borrow money was not because of any dark judgment on other men. It was the growth of that true sense of honour, exaggerated till it became almost a defect, which his Scotch traditions and his narrow means combined to foster in him. An honourable rich man may borrow without scruple, for there is no reason in his mind why he should not pay. But to an honourable poor man it is the thing most dreadful in the world, for he knows all the difficulties, the almost impossibility of paying, the chance of being exposed to the world in his inmost concerns, the horror of ruin and a roup, the chance of injuring another man, and dying under the shame of indebtedness, all these miseries were in Mr. Buchanan's mind when he went out on his terrible mission. He would rather have marched through a shower of bullets, or risked his life in any other way.

He went to old Mr. Anderson, who had been the head of the bank, and who was still believed to be the highest authority in any kind of financial matter. He had retired from the bank, and from all active business several years before. He was an elder of the church; and from the beginning of Mr. Buchanan's incumbency had been one of his greatest admirers and friends. He was, besides all this, a wealthy old man, and had no children nor any near relative to come after him. It was not, however, with any thought of the latter circumstance, or indeed expectation of actual help from himself that the minister sought this old gentleman. He thought of the bank, which, according to Scottish methods, gives advantages to struggling people, and intended only to ask Mr. Anderson's advice as to what should be done, perhaps if emboldened by his manner to ask him to be his surety, though the thought of making such a request to any man bathed the minister in a cold dew of mental anguish. Had he been asked by any other poor man what reception such an application would have received from Mr. Anderson, he would have bidden that other take courage.

"He is the kindest man in the world," he would have said. But when it came to be his own case the minister's heart sank within him. He could not have been more miserable had his old friend, instead of being the kindest, been the most cold-hearted man in the world.

There is, perhaps, no more wonderful sensation in life, than that complete and extraordinary relief which seems to fill the heart with a sudden flood of undreamed of ease and lightness, when a hand is held out to us all at once in our trouble, and the help which we have not believed possible, comes. Mr. Buchanan could not believe his ears when the old banker's first words fell upon him.

"Possible! oh, yes, more than possible; how could you doubt it?" he said. The poor man felt himself float off those poor feet that had plodded along the street so heavily, into an atmosphere of ease, of peace, of consolation unspeakable. The thing could be done. Instead of bringing a cold shade over his friend's face, it brought a light of kindness, even of pleasure. Yes, of pleasure, pleasure in being trusted, in being the first to whom recourse was made, in being able to give at once relief. It was so great a gleam of that sunshine which sometimes comes out of a human face, brighter than the very sun in the firmament, that poor Buchanan was dazzled, and for the moment made to think better even of himself as calling forth such friendship and kindness. A glow came into his heart, not only of gratitude but of approval. To see a man do what in one circumstance is the highest and noblest thing to do, to feel him exceed all our expectations, and play the part almost of a beneficent God to misfortune, what more delightful spectacle is there, even if it had nothing to do with ourselves. Mr. Buchanan poured forth all his soul to his old friend, who understood everything at half a word, and only hesitated to think which would be the best way of fulfilling his wishes. It was by old Anderson's advice at last that the idea of the bank was abandoned. He decided that it would be better to lend the money to the minister himself.

"We will have no fixed times or seasons," he said. "You shall pay me just as you can, as you are able to put by a little, and we'll have no signing of papers. You and me can trust each other; if I die before you, as naturally I will, you'll make it up to my heirs. If you, which God forbid, should die before me, there will be no use of paper to trouble your wife. It's just between you and me, nobody has any business to make or mell in the matter. I have no fine laddie to put out in the world, the more's the pity; and you have, and a bonnie lassie too, I wish you joy of them both. We'll just say nothing about it, my dear sir, just a shake of the hand, and that's all there's needed between you and me."

"But, Mr. Anderson, how can I accept this? You must let me give you an acknowledgment. And then the interest—"

"Toots," said the old man, "interest! what's fifteen pounds to me? I hope I can live and enjoy myself without your fifteen pounds. Nonsense, minister! are you too proud to accept a kindly service, most kindly offered and from the heart, from an old man, that you have done both good and pleasure to many a day?"

"Oh, proud, no, not proud," cried Buchanan, "unless it were proud of you, old friend, that have the heart to do such a blessed thing."

"Hoot," said the old man, "it's nothing but filthy siller, as your good wife says."

This had been the bargain, and it was a bargain which probably gave more pleasure to the lender than to the borrower. It redoubled the old gentleman's interest in the family, and indeed made him take a personal share in their concerns, which pricked the parents a little, as if he felt a certain right to know all about Willie's outfit and Marion's plenishing. He gave his advice about the boy's boxes, and his gun, and kindly criticised his clothes, and warned them not to pay too much for boots and shoes, and other outside articles, pressing certain makers upon them with almost too warm a recommendation. And he liked to see Marion's sheets and her napery, and thought the damask tablecloths almost too fine for a country manse, where, except on a presbytery meeting or the Monday's dinner after a sacramental occasion, there would be no means of showing them. But all this was very harmless, though it sometimes fretted the recipients of his bounty, who could not explain to their children the sudden access of interest on the part of old Anderson in all their concerns.

And now to think, while the first year had not more than passed, when William's outfit had just been paid off to the utmost farthing, and Marion's bill for her napery and her stock of personal linen, that the old man should die! I judge from Mr. Anderson's reference to fifteen pounds (five per cent. being the usual interest in those days, though I am told it is much less now), that the sum that Mr. Buchanan had borrowed was three hundred pounds, for I presume he had certain urgent bills to provide for as well as Willie and May. Fifty pounds was still in the bank, which was a reserve fund for Marion's gowns and her wedding expenses, etc. And to think that just at that moment, when as yet there had not been time to lay up a penny towards the repayment of the loan, that this whole house of cards, and their comfort and content in the smoothing away of their difficulties should, in a moment, topple about their ears! There seemed even some reason for the tone of exasperation which came into Mrs. Buchanan's voice in spite of herself. Had he done it on purpose it could scarcely have been worse. And indeed it looked as if it had been done on purpose to drop them into deeper and deeper mire.

Mr. Buchanan fought a battle with himself, of which no one had the faintest idea, when his wife left him that afternoon. She indeed never had the faintest idea of it, nor would any one have known had it not been for the chance that shut up those two children in the turret-room. They did not understand what they had heard, but neither did they forget it. Sometimes, the one would say to the other:

"Do you remember that afternoon when we were shut up in the turret and nobody knew?" When such a thing had happened before, they had laughed; but at this they never laughed, though they could not, till many years had passed, have told why. The boy might have forgotten, for he had a great many things to think of as the toils of education gathered round him and bound him faster and faster; but the girl, perhaps because she had not so much to do, there being no such strain of education in those days for female creatures, never forgot. She accompanied her father unconsciously in his future, during many a weary day, and pitied him when there was no one else to pity.

In the meantime, as the children saw, Mr. Buchanan went out; he went to old Mr. Anderson's house to inquire for him before he did any of his usual afternoon duties. And after he had completed all these duties, he went back again, with a restlessness of anxiety which touched all the people assembled round the dying man, his brother who had been summoned from Glasgow, and his doctors, one of whom had come from Edinburgh, while the other was the chief practitioner of St. Rule's, and his nurses, of whom there were two, for he had no one of his own, no woman to take care of him. They thought the minister must be anxious about the old gentleman's soul that he should come back a second time in the course of the afternoon, and Dr. Seaton himself went down-stairs to reply to his inquiries.

"I am afraid I cannot ask you to come up-stairs, for he is past all that," he said, in the half scornful tone which doctors sometimes assume to a clerical visitor.

"Is he so bad as that?" said the minister.

"I do not say," said Dr. Seaton, "that our patient may not regain consciousness. But certainly, for the present, he is quite unable to join in any religious exercises."

"I was not thinking of that," said Mr. Buchanan, almost humbly, "but only to take the last news home. Mr. Anderson has been a good friend to me."

"So he has been to many," said Dr. Seaton. "Let us hope that will do more for him where he is going than prayer."

"Prayer can never be out of place, Dr. Seaton," said the minister. He went away from the door angry, but still more cast down, with his head sunk on his breast as the children had seen him. He had no good news to take home. He had no comfort to carry with him up to his study, whither he went without pausing, as he generally did, to say a word to his wife. He had no word for anybody that evening. All night long he was repeating to himself the words of the parable, "Sit down quickly, and take thy bill, and write fifty." Could God lead men astray?

CHAPTER III

AFTER THE FUNERAL

"After the funeral, after the funeral will be time enough," Mr. Buchanan said, when his wife urged him to get it over, and to have his interview with Mr. Morrison, the man of business, in whose hands all Mr. Anderson's affairs were. Everybody remarked how ill the minister was looking during the week which elapsed between the old man's death and the large and solemn funeral, which filled the entire length of the High Street with black-coated men. It was a funeral d'estime. There was no active sorrow among the long train of serious people who conducted his mortal part to its long home, but there were a great many regrets. His was a figure as well known as the great old tower of St. Rule, which is one of the landmarks from the sea, and the chief distinction of the town on land, and he was a man who had been kind to everybody. He had been very well off, and he had lived very quietly, spending but little money on himself, and he had no near relation, only a distant cousin's son, to inherit what he had to leave behind him, for the brother, who was the chief mourner, was a lonely man like himself, and also rich, and without heirs. This being the case, old Mr. Anderson had used his money as few rich men do. He had behaved to many people as he had done to Mr. Buchanan. He had come to the aid of many of the poor people in St. Rule, the fisher population, and the poor shopkeepers, and many a needy family; therefore, though there were perhaps few tears shed, there was a great and universal regret in all the town. Many men put on their "blacks," and went East, which was their way of indicating the quaint burying-ground that encircled the ruins of the old cathedral, who would not have swelled any other funeral train in the neighbourhood. He was a loss to everybody; but there were few tears. An old man going home, nearer eighty than seventy as the people said, a good old man leaving the world in charity with everybody, and leaving nobody behind whom he would miss much when he got there. A woman, here and there, at her doorhead or her stairfoot, flung her apron over her head as she watched the procession defiling into the wide space before the churchyard, which was visible from the houses at the fishers' end of the lower street. But the tears she shed were for grief's sake, and not for grief—for there was no weeping, no desolation, only a kind and universal regret.

Mr. Buchanan was more blanched and pale than ever, as he walked bareheaded behind the coffin. There was one, everybody said, who had a feeling heart—and many were glad when the ceremonial— always of so very simple a kind in the Scotch church, and in those days scarcely anything at all, a short prayer and no more—was over, with the thought that the minister being evidently so much out of health and spirits, and feeling the loss of the kind old elder so deeply, was just in the condition in which some "get their death," from the exposure and chill of a funeral. Several of his friends convoyed him home after all was completed, and warned Mrs. Buchanan to take very good care of him, to give him some good, strong, hot toddy, or other restorative, and do all she could to bring back his colour and his spirit.

"We have all had a great loss," said Mr. Moncrieff, who was another leading elder, shaking his head, "but we are not all so sensitive as the minister."

Poor Mrs. Buchanan knew much better than they did what made the minister look so wae. She took all their advices in very good part, and assured his friends that the minister felt their kindness, and would soon be himself again. Alas, there was that interview still to come, which she thought secretly within herself she would have got over had she been the minister, and not have thus prolonged the agony day after day. There were a great many things that Mrs. Buchanan would have done, "had she been the minister," which did not appear in the same light to him—as indeed very commonly happens on either side between married people. But she accepted the fact that she was not the minister, and that he must act for himself, and meet his difficulties in his own way since he would not meet them in hers. She did not comfort him with hot and strong toddy, as the elders recommended; but she did all she knew to make him comfortable, and to relieve his burdened spirit, pointing out to him that Mr. Morrison, the man of business, was also a considerate man, and acquainted with the difficulties of setting out a family in the world, and impressing upon him the fact that it was a good thing, on the whole, that Willie's outfit had been paid at once, since Mr. Morrison, who would be neither better nor worse of it in his own person, would be, no doubt, on behalf of the heir, who was not of age nor capable of grasping at the money, a more patient creditor than a shop in Edinburgh, where a good discount had been given for the immediate payment of the account.

"They would just have worried us into our graves," Mrs. Buchanan said, and she added that Willie would probably be able to send home something to help in the payment before it had to be made. She said so much indeed, and it was all so reasonable, that poor Buchanan almost broke down under it, and at last implored her to go away and leave him quiet.

"Oh, Mary, my dear, that is all very just," he said, "and I admire your steadfast spirit; but there are things in which I am weaker than you are, and it is I that have to do it while you stay quiet at home."

"Let me do it, Claude," she cried. "I am not feared for Mr. Morrison; and I could tell him all the circumstances maybe as well—"

Perhaps she thought better, and had been about to say so; but would not hurt in any way her husband's delicate feelings. As for Mr. Buchanan, he raised himself up a little in his chair, and a slight flush came to his pale cheek.

"No," he said, "I will not forsake my post as the head of the house. These are the kind of things that the man has to do, and not the woman. I hope I am not come to that, that I could shelter myself from a painful duty behind my wife."

"Oh, if I had been the minister!" Mrs. Buchanan breathed, with an impatient sigh, but she said,—

"No, Claude, I know well you would never do that," and left him to his thoughts.

She had placed instinctively the large printed Bible, which he always used, on the little table beside him. He would get strength there if nowhere else. The day was gray and not warm, though it was the beginning of June, and a fire had been lighted in the study to serve the purpose, morally and physically, of the hot toddy recommended by the elder. Poor Mr. Buchanan spread his hands out to it when he was left alone. He was very much broken down. The tears came to his eyes. He felt forlorn, helpless, as if there was nothing in heaven or earth to support him. It was a question of money, and was not that a wretched thing to ask God for? The filthy siller, the root of so much evil. He could have demonstrated to you very powerfully, had you gone to ask his advice in such an emergency, that it was not money, but the love of money that was the root of all evil; but in his heart, in this dreadful emergency, he cursed it. Oh, if it were not for money how much the problems of this life would be lessened? He forgot, for the moment, that in that case the difficulties of getting Willie his outfit would have been very much increased. And, instinctively, as his wife had placed it there, he put out his hand for his Bible. Is it possible that there should be poison to be sucked out of that which should be sweeter than honey and the honeycomb to the devout reader? The book opened of itself at that parable over which he had been pondering. Oh, Mr. Buchanan was quite capable of explaining to you what that parable meant. No one knew better than he for what it was that the Lord commended the unjust steward. He had no excuse of ignorance, or of that bewilderment with which a simple mind might approach so difficult a passage. He knew all the readings, all the commentaries; he could have made it as clear as daylight to you, either in the pulpit or out of the pulpit. And he knew, none better, that in such a case the letter killeth; but the man was in a terrible strait, and his whole soul was bent on getting out of it. He did not want to face it, to make the best of it, to calculate that Willie might, by that time, be able to help, or even that Mr. Morrison was a considerate man, and the heir a minor, and that he would be allowed time, which was his wife's simple conception of the situation. He wanted to get out of it. His spirit shrank from the bondage that would be involved in getting that money together, in the scraping and sparing for years, the burden it would be on his shoulders. A thirst, a fury had seized him to get rid of it, to shake it off. And even the fact that the Bible opened at that passage had its effect on his disturbed mind. He would have reproved you seriously for trying any sortes with the Bible, but in his trouble he did this, as well as so many other things of which he disapproved. He knew very well also that he had opened at that passage very often during the past week, and that it was simple enough that it should open in the same place now. Yet, with instinctive superstition he took the book, holding it in his two hands to open as it would, and his heart gave a jump when he found this strike his eyes: "Sit down quickly, and take thy bill, and write fourscore." These were the words, like a command out of heaven. What if that was not the inner meaning, the sense of the parable? Yet, these were the words, and the Bible opened upon them, and they were the first words that caught his eye.

Suppose that this temptation had come to another man, how clearly would its fallacy have been exposed, what daylight would have been thrown upon the text by the minister? He would have almost laughed at, even while he condemned and pitied, the futile state of mind which could be so led astray. And he knew all that, but it had no effect upon the workings of his own distracted mind at that dreadful moment. He went over it again and again, reading it over aloud as he had done on the first occasion when it had flashed upon his troubled soul, and seemed to give him an occult and personal message. And thus he remained all the rest of the afternoon, with his knees close to the bars of the grate, and his white, thin hands blanched with cold. Surely he had caught a chill, as so many people do in the cold and depression of a funeral. He rather caught at that idea. It might kill, which would be no great harm; or, at least, if he had caught a bad cold, it would, at least, postpone the interview he dreaded—the interview in which he would sit down and take his bill and write fifty—or perhaps fourscore.

"I think I have caught a chill," he said, in more cheerful tones, when he went down-stairs to supper.

But the minister here had reckoned without his wife. It might not be in her province to see Mr. Morrison and arrange with him about the debt, but it certainly was quite in her province to take immediate steps in respect to a bad cold. He had his feet in hot water and mustard before he knew where he was—he was put to bed, and warmly wrapped up, and the hot toddy at last administered, spite of all remonstrances, in a potent measure.

"Mr. Moncrieff said I was to make you take it as soon as you came in; but I just gave in to your humours, knowing how little biddable you were—but not now: you must just go to your bed like a lamb, and do what I bid you now."

And there could not be a word said now as to what was or was not the woman's sphere. If anything was her business at all, decidedly it was her business to keep her family in health. Mr. Buchanan did what he was bid, a little comforted by feeling himself under lawful subjection, which is an excellent thing for every soul, and warm through and through in body, and hushed in nerves, slept well, and found himself in the morning without any chill or sign of a chill, quite well. There was thus no further excuse for him, and he perceived at once in his wife's eyes, as she brought him his breakfast before he got up—an indulgence that always followed the hot-foot bath and the hot drink over-night—that no further mercy was to be accorded to him, and that she would not understand or agree to any further postponement of so indispensable a duty. When she took away his tray—for these were duties she performed herself, the servants being few, and the work of the house great—she said, patting him upon the shoulder,—

"Now, Claude, my dear, the best time to see Mr. Morrison is about eleven o'clock; that will leave you plenty of time to get up and get yourself dressed. It is a fine morning, and your cold is better. If you like, I will send over to the office to say you are coming."

"There is no necessity for that," Mr. Buchanan said.

"No, no necessity, but it might be safer; so that he might wait for you if he should have any temptation otherwise, or business to take him out."

"If he has business, he will see to it whether he knows I am coming or not," said the minister; "and if I do not see him this morning, I can see him another day."

"Oh, Claude, my man, don't put off another day! It will have to be done sooner or later. Do not keep it hanging over you day after day."

"Well, then," said the minister, with some crossness of tone, "for goodsake, if you are so urgent, go away and let me get up. How can I get myself dressed with you there?"

Mrs. Buchanan disappeared without another word. And he had no further excuse for putting off. Even the wife of his bosom, though she knew it would be a bad moment, did not know half how bad it was. Mrs. Buchanan had made up her mind to it, however it might turn out. She had already planned out how the expenses were to be lessened after Marion's marriage. Elsie was the only other girl, and she was but fourteen. Several years must elapse before it was necessary to bring her out, and give her that share in the pleasures and advantages of youthful life which was her due. And between that time and this there was no privation that the good mother was not ready to undertake in order to pay off this debt. You would have thought to see their frugal living that to spare much from it was impossible, but the minister's wife had already made her plans, and her cheerfulness was restored. It might take them a long time to do it, but Mr. Anderson's heir was only seventeen, and had still a good many years of his minority to run. And Willie by that time would have a good salary, and would be able to help. It would be a case of sparing every sixpence, but still that was a thing that could be done. What a good thing that education was so cheap in St. Rule. John, who was going to be a clergyman, like his father, would have all his training at home in the most economical way. And Alick was to go to Mr. Beaton's, the writer, as soon as he had completed his schooling, without any premium. They might both be able to help if the worst came to the worst, but between her own economies and Willie's help, who had the best right to help, seeing it was greatly on his account the money had been borrowed, she had little doubt that in four years they would manage to repay, at least, the greater part of the three hundred pounds.

This was all straightforward, but the minister's part was not so straightforward. He read over the parable again before he went down-stairs, and made up his mind finally to take his bill and write fifty. After all, was not this what Mr. Anderson would have desired? He was an old man and took no particular interest in his heir. He would not, of course, have left his money away from him, or injured him in any way. He quite recognised his claim through his father, a cousin whom the old man had never known, but who still was his next of kin; yet, on the other hand, if it came to that, Mr. Anderson was more fully interested in the young Buchanans. He had seen them all grow up, and Willie and Marion had been a great deal more to him than young Frank Mowbray. And Mr. Buchanan was his friend. The minister was persuaded that old Mr. Anderson would far rather have pardoned him the debt than extorted it from him almost at the risk of his life. "Take thy bill, and sit down quickly, and write fifty." The words of the parable seemed more and more reasonable, more and more adapted to his own case as he read them over and over. What he was about to do seemed to him, at the end, the very right thing to do and the command of heaven.

Mrs. Buchanan met him in the hall with his hat brushed to a nicety, and his gloves laid out upon the table. She came up to him with a brush in her hand, to see if there was the faintest speck upon his broadcloth. She was his valet, and a most cheerful and assiduous one, loving the office. She liked to turn him out spotless, and to watch him sally forth with delight and pride in his appearance, which never failed her. It was one of the ways of the women of her day, and a pretty one, I think. She was pleased with his looks, as he stood in the hall ready to go out.

"But why are you so pale?" she said; "it is not an affair of life and death. I hope you are not feared for Mr. Morrison."

"I am feared for everybody," said Mr. Buchanan, "that has to do with money."

"Oh, Claude," she said, "I just hate the filthy lucre myself, but it's not a question of life or death. The bairns are all well and doing well, and will pay it off before Frank Mowbray comes of age. I promise you we will. I have it all in my eye. Do not, my dear man, do not look so cast down."

He shook his head but made no answer. He was not thinking of what she said. He was saying over to himself, "Sit down quickly, and take thy bill, and write fourscore."

CHAPTER IV

TAKE NOW THY BILL AND WRITE FIFTY

Mr. Buchanan went first to the bank, and drew out the money—the residue of the loan which had been placed there for Marion's final equipment. In those days people did not use cheques, as we do now for every purpose. When a man paid a debt, it seemed far more sure and satisfactory to pay it in actual money. To all, except to business men, the other seemed a doubtful, unsatisfactory way, and those who received a cheque made great haste to cash it as if in the meantime the bank might break, or the debtor's balance turn the wrong way. To pay with a simple bit of paper did not seem like paying at all. Mr. Buchanan received his fifty pounds in crisp new notes, pretty notes printed in blue and red. They were like a little parcel of pictures, all clean and new. He looked at them with a forlorn admiration: it was seldom he saw such a thing as a ten-pound note: and here were five of them. Ah, if that had been all! "Sit down quickly and write fourscore." This variant troubled his mind a little in his confusion! But that was measures of wheat, he said to himself, with a distracted sense that this might somehow make a difference. And then he walked up the High Street in the morning sunshine to Mr. Morrison's office; and sure enough the writer was there and very glad to see him, so that no chance of escape remained.

"I have come to speak to you," the minister said, clearing his throat, and beginning with so much difficulty—he that would read you off an hour's sermon without even pausing for a word!—"about business, Morrison—about a little—monetary transaction there was—between me and our late—most worthy friend—"

"Anderson?" said the writer. And then he added with a half laugh, tempered by the fact that "the death" had been so recent. "Half St. Rule's, I'm thinking, have had monetary transactions with our late friend—"

"He would not permit any memorandum of it to be made," said the minister.

"No: that was just like him: only his estate will be the worse for it; for we can't expect everybody to be so frank in acknowledging as you."

Mr. Buchanan turned the colour of clay, his heart seemed to stop beating. He said: "I need not tell you—for you have a family of your own—that now and then there are expenses that arise."

The lawyer waved his hand with the freemasonry of common experience. "Well I know that," he said; "it is no joke nowadays putting the laddies out in the world. You will find out that with Willie—but what a fine opening for him! I wish we were all as well off."

"Yes, it is a good opening"—if it had not been that all the joy and the pride in it was quenched by this!—"and that is precisely what I mean, Morrison. It was just Willie—ordinary expenses, of course, my wife and I calculate upon and do our best for—but an outfit—"

"My dear Mr. Buchanan," said the writer, "what need to explain the matter to me. You don't imagine I got my own lads all set out, as thank the Lord they are, without feeling the pinch—ay, and incurring responsibilities that one would wish to keep clear of in the ordinary way of life."

"Yes," said the minister, "that was how it was; but fortunately the money was not expended. And I bring you back the fifty pounds—intact."

Oh, the little, the very little lie it was! If he had said it was not all expended, if he had kept out that little article the—the fifty pounds implying there was no more. Anyhow, it was very different from taking a bill and writing fourscore. But the criminal he felt, with the cold drops coming out on his forehead, and his hand trembling as he held out—as if that were all! these fifty pounds.

"Now bide a wee, bide a wee," said the writer; "wait till I tell you—Mr. Anderson foresaw something of this kind. Put back your money into your pocket. He foresaw it, the friendly old body that he was; wait till I get you the copy of the will that I have here." Morrison got up and went to one of the boxes, inscribed with the name of Anderson, that stood on the shelves behind him, and after some searching drew out a paper, the heading of which he ran over sotto voce, while Mr. Buchanan sat rigid like an automaton, still holding out in his hand the bundle of notes.

"Here it is," said Mr. Morrison, coming back with his finger upon the place. "You'll see the case is provided for. 'And it is hereby provided that in the case of any persons indebted to me in sums less than a hundred pounds, which are unpaid at the time of my death, that such debts are hereby cancelled and wiped out as if they had never existed, and my executors and administrators are hereby authorised to refuse any payments tendered of the same, and to desire the aforesaid debtors to consider these sums as legacies from me, the testator.'

"Well, sir," said the writer, tilting up his spectacles on his forehead, "I hope that's plain enough: I hope you are satisfied with that."

For a moment the minister sat and gasped, still stretching out the notes, looking like a man at the point of death. He could not find his voice, and drops of moisture stood out upon his forehead, which was the colour of ashes. The lawyer was alarmed; he hurried to a cupboard in the corner and brought out a bottle and a glass. "Man," he said, "Buchanan! this is too much feeling; minister, it is just out of the question to take a matter of business like this. Take it down! it's just sherry wine, it will do you no harm. Bless me, bless me, you must not take it like this—a mere nothing, a fifty pounds! Not one of us but would have been glad to accommodate you—you must not take it like that!"

"Sums under a hundred pounds!" Mr. Buchanan said, but he stammered so with his colourless lips that the worthy Morrison did not make out very clearly what he said, and, in truth, had no desire to make it out. He was half vexed, half disturbed, by the minister's extreme emotion. He felt it as a tacit indictment against himself.

"One would think we were a set of sticks," he said, "to let our minister be troubled in his mind like this over a fifty pound! Why, sir, any one of your session—barring the two fishers and the farmer— Take it off, take it off, to bring back the blood—it's nothing but sherry wine."

Mr. Buchanan came to himself a little when he had swallowed the sherry wine. He had a ringing in his ears, as if he had recovered from a faint, and the walls were swimming round him, with all the names on the boxes whirling and rushing like a cloud of witnesses. As soon as he was able to articulate, however, he renewed his offer of the notes.

"Take this," he said, "take this; it will always be something," trying to thrust them into the writer's hand.

"Hoot," said Morrison; "my dear sir, will you not understand? You're freely assoilised and leeberated from every responsibility; put back your notes into your own pouch. You would not refuse the kind body's little legacy, and cause him sorrow in his grave, which, you will tell me, is not possible; but, if it were possible, would vex him sore, and that we well know. I would not take advantage and vex him because he was no longer capable of feeling it. No, no; just put them back into your pouch, Buchanan. They are no use to him, and maybe they will be of use to you."

This was how the interview ended. The minister still attempted to deposit his notes upon Mr. Morrison's table, but the lawyer put them back again, doing everything he could to restore his friend and pastor to the calm of ordinary life. Finally, Morrison declaring that he had somebody to see "up the town," and would walk with Mr. Buchanan as far as their ways lay together, managed to conduct him to his own door. He noted, with some surprise, that Mrs. Buchanan opened it herself, with a face which, if not so pale as her husband's, was agitated too, and full of anxiety.

"The minister is not just so well as I would like to see him," he said. "I would keep him quiet for a day or two, and let him fash himself for nothing," he added—"for nothing!" with emphasis.

The good man was much disturbed in his mind by this exhibition of feeling.

"Oh, why were 'writers' made so coarse, and parsons made so fine?" He would have said these words to himself had he known them, which, perhaps he did, for Cowper was a very favourite poet in those days. Certainly that was the sentiment in his mind. To waste all that feeling upon an affair of fifty pounds! The wife had more sense, Mr. Morrison said to himself, though she was frightened too, but that was probably for his sake. He went off about his own business, and I will not say that he did not mention the matter to one or two of his brother elders.

"You or me might be ruined and make less fuss about it," he said.

"When a man had just a yearly stipend and gets behindhand, it's wae work making it up," said the other.

"We must just try and see if we cannot get him a bit augmentation," said Morrison, "or get up a testimonial or something."

"You see, a testimonial could scarcely take the form of money, and what comfort would he get out of another silver teapot?" observed the second elder, prudent though kind.

It was not a much less ordeal for the minister to meet his wife than it had been to meet the lawyer. She knew nothing about his purpose of taking his bill and writing fourscore, and he dared not let her suspect that he had spoken of the "fifty," as if that fifty were his whole debt, or that the debts that were forgiven were debts under a hundred pounds. He said to himself afterwards that it was more Morrison's fault than his, that the lawyer would not let him explain that he had said "this would be something," meaning that this would be an instalment. All these things he said to himself as he sat alone for the greater part of the day, "reading a book," which was supposed to be an amusing book, and recovering from that great strain; but he did not venture to tell his wife of these particulars. What he said to Mrs. Buchanan was that Mr. Anderson had assoilised his debtors in general, and that each man was to consider the loan as a legacy, and that Morrison said he was not entitled to take a penny, and would not. His wife took this news with a burst of grateful tears and blessings on the name of the good man who had done this kind thing. "The merciful man is merciful, and lendeth and asketh not again," she said. But after this outburst of emotion and relief, her good sense could not but object.

"It is an awfu' deliverance for us, Claude; oh, my man! I had it all planned out, how we were to do it, but it would have been a heavy, heavy burden. God bless him for the merciful thought! But," she added, "I am not clear in my mind that it is just to Frank. To be sure, it was all in his own hand to do what he liked with his own, and the laddie is but a far-off heir; but still he has been trained for that, and to expect a good fortune: and if there are many as we are, Claude—"

"It is not our affair, Mary; he had full command of his faculties, and it was his own to do what he liked with it," her husband said, though with faltering lips.

"Well, that is true," she replied, but doubtfully: "I am not denying a man's right to do what he likes with his own. And if it had been only you, his minister, that perhaps he owed much more to, even his own soul, as Paul says—"

"No, no; not so much as that."

"But if there are many," Mrs. Buchanan went on, shaking her head, "it might be a sore heritage for Frank. Claude, if ever in the days to come we can do anything for that lad, mind I would think it was our duty to prefer him before our very own: for this is a great deliverance, and wrought, as you may say, at his cost but without his consent—"

"My dear, a sum like that," said Mr. Buchanan, with a faint smile and a heavy heart, "is not a fortune."

"That is true, but it is a great deliverance to us; and if ever we can be helpful to him, in siller or in kindness, in health or in sickness—"

There came a rush of tenderness to Mrs. Buchanan's heart, with the tears that filled her eyes, and she could say no more.

"Yes, yes," he said a little fretfully, "yes, yes; though he had no merit in it, and not any such great loss either that I can see."

She judged it wise to leave the minister to himself after this; for, though nerves were not much thought of in those days, she saw that irritability and a tendency to undervalue the great deliverance, which filled her with such overflowing gratitude, had taken the place of more amiable feelings in his mind. It was better to leave him quiet, to recover from his ill mood, and from the consequence of being overdone. "I have so many things to take off my mind," she said to herself. Perhaps she thought the minister's cares—though most people would have thought them so much more important—nothing to hers, which were so many, often so petty, so absorbing, leaving her no time to brood. And had she not provided him with the new Waverley, which most people thought the best anodyne for care—that is, among the comforts of this world, not, of course, to count among higher things?

But Mr. Buchanan did not, I fear, find himself capable of having his mind taken off, even by the new Waverley. He was spared, he said to himself, from actual guilt—Was he spared from actual guilt? He had not required to take his bill and write fourscore. But for that one little word the—the fifty (how small a matter!) he had said nothing: and that was not saying anything, it was merely an inference, which his next words might have made an end of; only, that Morrison would not hear my next words. If there was a fault in the matter, it was Morrison's fault. He repeated this to himself fretfully, eagerly, impatient with the man who had saved him from committing himself. Never, never would he commit any business to Morrison's hands! Such a man was not to be trusted; he cared nothing for his client's interest. All that he was intent upon was to relieve the debtor, to joke about the "friendly body," who was so kind, even in his grave. "A sore saint for his heir," Morrison had again said, as was said of the old king—instead of standing for the heir's rights as he ought to have done, and hearing what a man had to say!

And this then was the end of it all—salvation—from all the consequences, even from the very crime itself which he had planned and intended, but had not required to carry out. He had saved everything, his conscience, and his fifty pounds, not to speak of all the rest, the sum which his wife had planned by so many daily sacrifices to make up. He had not, after all, been like the unjust steward. He had said nothing, had not even written the fourscore; he had been saved altogether, even the fifty he had offered. Was this the Lord's doing, and marvellous in our eyes—or what was it? Mr. Buchanan put away the Waverley, which was given him to comfort him, and took up the Bible with the large print. It opened again at that parable; and then, with a great start of pain, he recognised his fate, and knew that henceforward it would open always at that parable, now that the parable was no longer a suggestion of deliverance to him but a dreadful reminder. A convulsive movement went through all his limbs at that thought. Mr. Buchanan had often preached of hell, it was the fashion of his time; but he had never known what he himself meant. Now he knew: this was hell where their worm dieth not, and their fire is not quenched. It lay here, not in a vague, unrealised region of fire and brimstone; but here, within the leaves of the New Testament, which was his chief occupation, inspiring all the work of his life. This was hell—to see the book open, the book of life, always at that one place. He had not to wait for it; the worm had begun to gnaw and the fire to burn.

CHAPTER V

MARION AND ELSIE

It was not till a long time after this that the Rev. Matthew Sinclair, who was the betrothed of Marion Buchanan, got a kirk, and the faithful pair were able to marry. The snowy heaps of Marion's linen, which her mother now spoke of, in the bosom of the family, as in reality a present from old Mr. Anderson, seeing that it was paid for by a loan from him, generously converted into a legacy when he died—had lain spread out, with sprigs of lavender between the folds, in the big press at the head of the nursery stairs for nearly two years, during which time Elsie grew into almost a young woman. Rodie, too, became an ever more and more "stirring" school-boy, less disposed to sit and read from the same book with his sister, and more occupied with outdoor games and the "clanjamfry," as his mother said, of school-fellows and playfellows who were always hanging about waiting for him, or coming with mysterious knockings to the door to ask him out. Some of them, Mrs. Buchanan thought, were not quite proper comrades for the minister's son, but the framework of juvenile society in St. Rule's was extremely democratic, all the classes going to school together according to Scotch precedent—the laird's son and the shoemaker's on the same bench, and Rodie Buchanan cheek by jowl with the fisher laddies from east the town. In the play hours, it was true, things equalised themselves a little; but there was certainly one fisher laddie his prompter and helper in school, who kept a great ascendancy over Rodie, and would lead him away in long tramps along the sea-shore, when he might have been at football or "at the gouff" with companions of his own standing, and when Elsie was pining for his society at home. Elsie felt the partial desertion of her brother extremely. She missed the long readings together in the turret and elsewhere, and the long rambles, in which Johnny Wemyss had become Rodie's companion, apparently so much more interesting to him than herself. Johnny Wemyss, it was evident, had a great deal of knowledge, which Elsie was inclined, in her ignorance, to be thankful she did not possess; for Rodie would come in with his pockets all full of clammy and wet things—jelly-fish, which he called by some grand name—and the queer things that wave about long fingers on the edges of the pools, and shrink into themselves when you touch them. This was before the days when sea-anemones became a fashionable pursuit, but children brought up by the sea had, of course, known and wondered at these creatures long before science took them up. But to bring them home was a different matter; filling the school-room with nasty, sticky things, which, out of their native element, decayed and made bad smells, and were the despair of the unfortunate maid who had to keep that room in order, and dared not, except in extremity, throw Rodie's hoards away. "It is not Rodie's fault; it is Johnny Wemyss that just tells him nonsense stories," Elsie said. She would have given her little finger to have gone with him on those rambles, and to have heard all about those strange living things; but already the invisible bonds that confine a woman's movements had begun to cramp Elsie's free footsteps, and the presence of Johnny Wemyss made, she was well aware, her own impossible, though it was just Johnny Wemyss's "nonsense stories" that she desired most to hear.

Rodie condescended to accompany her on her Sunday walk when all St. Rule's perambulated the links from which they were shut out on week-days; but that became the only occasion on which she could calculate on his company, and not even the new Waverley, which had failed to beguile the minister from his urgent trouble, could seduce Rodie from his many engagements with his fellows to sit with his sister in the turret, with the book between them as of old.

Elsie, it is true, gradually began to make herself amends for this desertion by forming new alliances of her own with girls of her own age, who have always abounded in St. Rule's; but these did not at all make up to her, as Johnny Wemyss seemed to make up to Rodie, for the separation from her natural companion and fellow. These young ladies were beginning already, as they approached sixteen, to think of balls and triumphs in a way which was different from the romps of old. The world, in the shape of young men older than their boyish companions, and with other intentions, began to open about them. At that time it was nothing very remarkable that girls should marry very early, a circumstance which, of itself, made a great change in their ideas, and separated them more than anything else could have done from their childish contemporaries of the other sex.

Elsie was in that hot stage of indignation and revolt against sweethearts, and all talk on the subject, which is generally a phase in a girl's development. She was angry at the introduction of this unworthy subject, and almost furious with the girls who chattered and laughed about Bobbie this and Willie that— for in St. Rule's they all knew each other by their Christian names. She could understand that you should prefer your own brother's society to that of any girl, and much wondered that Rodie should prefer any boy to herself—which was one great distinction between girls and boys which she discovered with indignation and shame. "I like Rodie better than anybody, but he likes his Johnny Wemyss better than me! Ay!" she cried, the indignation gaining upon her, "and even if Johnny Wemyss were not there, Ralph Beaton or Harry Seaton, or any laddie—whereas I would give up any lassie for him."

"That is just the way of men," said Marion, her eldest sister, who, being now on the eve of marriage, naturally knew a great deal more than a girl of sixteen.

"Not with Matthew," cried Elsie, who, if she had no experience, was not without observation; "he likes you better than all the men in the world."

"Oh, Matthew!" said Marion, with a blush—"that's different: but when he's used to me," added this discreet young woman—"Matthew, I've every reason to believe, will just be like the rest. He will play his gouff, though I may be sitting solitary at home—and he will go out to his dinner and argue among his men, and take his walks with Hugh Playfair, or whoever turns up. He will say, 'My dear, I want a long stretch that would be too far for you,' as my father says to my mother. She takes it very well, and is glad he should be enjoying himself, and leaving her at peace to look after her house and her bairns—but perhaps she was not so pleased at first: and perhaps I'll not be pleased either when it comes to that," Marion said, reflectively.

Sense was her great characteristic, and she had, in her long engagement, had much time to turn all these things over in her mind.

"I don't think it will ever come to that—for he cannot let you be for a moment," said Elsie. "I sometimes wish he were a hundred miles away."

"Ah," said Marion, "but you know that will not last; and, indeed, it is better it should not last, for how could you ever get anything done if your man was draigling after you all the day long? No, no, it is more manlike that he should keep till his own kind. You may think you would like to have Rodie at your tail for ever, as when you were little bairns, and called the twins: but you would not, any more than he does—-just wait a wee, and you will find that out for yourself: for it should surely be more so with your brother, who is bound to go away from you, when it is so with your man."

"Then I think the disciples were right," said Elsie, who was very learned in her Bible, as became a minister's daughter. "And if the case of a man be so with his wife it would be better not to marry."

"Well, it does not seem that folk think so," said Marion, with a smile, "or it would not have gone on so long. Will you get me the finest dinner-napkins, the very finest ones, out of the big napery press at the head of the stairs?—for I am not sure that they are all marked properly, and time is running on, and everything must be finished."

Marion was very great at marking, whether in white letters worked in satin stitch, or in small red ones done with engrained cotton, or finally with the little bottle of marking-ink and the hot iron with which Elsie still loved to help her—but in the case of the finest dinner-napkins, I need not say that marking-ink was not good enough, and the finest satin stitch was employed.

It need not be added that notwithstanding the reflection above stated Elsie felt a great interest in the revelations of the sister thus standing on the brink of a new life, and so soberly contemplating the prospect before her, not with any idea, as it seemed, of ideal blessedness, nor of having everything her own way.

Marion had been set thinking by the girl's questions, and was ready to go on talking when Elsie returned with the pile of dinner-napkins in her arms, as high as her chin, which reposed upon them. It had been Mrs. Buchanan's pride that no minister's wife in the whole presbytery should have more exquisite linen, and both mother and daughter were gratified to think that the table would be set out for the dinner on the Monday after the Sacrament as few such tables were. The damask was very fine, of a beautiful small pattern, and shone like white satin. Elsie had a little talent for drawing, and she it was who drew the letters which Marion worked; so that this duty afforded occupation for both.

"It is a little strange, I do not deny," said Marion, "that though they make such a work about us when they are courting and so forth, the men are more content in the society of their own kind than we are: a party that is all lassies, you weary of it."

"Not me!" cried Elsie, all aflame.

"Wait till you are a little older," said the sage Marion; "it's even common to say; though I doubt if it is true, that after dinner we weary for them, if they are too long of coming up-stairs. But they never weary for us: and a man's party is always the most joyful of all, and they like it above everything, and never wish that we were there. I must say I do not understand how this is, considering how dependent they are upon us for their comfort, and how helpless they are, more helpless than a woman ever is. Now, what my father would do if mamma did not see that he was brushed and trimmed up and kept in order, I cannot tell: and no doubt it will be just the same with Matthew. He will come to me crying, 'May, there are no handkerchiefs in my drawer,' or, 'May, the button's off my glove,' as if it was my great fault—and when he is going off to preach anywhere, he will forget his very sermon if I don't take care it's put into his portmanteau."

"Well, my dear! I am no better than my mother, and that is what she has to do: but when they get a few men together, and can gossip away, and talk, and take their glass of toddy, then is the time when they really enjoy themselves. And so it is with the laddies, or even more—you wish for them, but they don't wish for you."

"I wish for none of them, except Rodie, my own brother, that has always been my companion," Elsie said.

"And you would think he would wish for you? but no: his Johnny Wemyss and his Alick Beaton, or was it Ralph?—that's what he likes far best, except, of course, when he falls in love, and then he will run after the lassie wherever she goes, till she takes him, and it's all settled, and then he just goes back to his men, as before. It is a very mysterious thing to me," said Marion, "but I have thought a great deal about it, and it's quite true. I do not like myself," she added, with a pause of reflection, "men that are always at a woman's tails. If you never could turn round or do a thing without your man after you, it would be a great bother. I am sure mamma feels that; she is always easy in her mind when my father is set down very busy to his sermon, or when somebody comes in to talk to him, or he goes out to his dinner with Professor Grant. Then she is sure he will be happy, and it leaves her free. I will just feel the same about Matthew, and he about me. He would not be without me for all the world, but he will never want me when he gets with his own cronies. Now, we always seem to have a kind of want of them."

"You have just said that mamma was quite happy when she got papa off her hands," Elsie said.

"That is a different thing; but do you think for a moment that she would enjoy herself with a party of women as he does at Professor Grant's? That she would not; she is glad to get him off her hands because she is sure he will enjoy himself, and be no trouble to anybody. But that would be little pleasure to her, if she were to do the same: and you yourself, if you had all the Seatons and the Beatons that ever were born—"

"I want only Rodie, my own brother," Elsie said, with indignation.

"And he," said Marion, calmly reflecting, "does not want you; that is just what I say—and what is so queer a thing."

"If the case of a man is so with his wife?" said Elsie, oracularly.

"Toots—the man is just very well off," said Marion. "He gets his wife to take care of him, and then he just enjoys himself with his own kind."

"Then I would never marry," cried Elsie; "not whatever any one might say."

"That is very well for you," said Marion. "You will be the only daughter when I am away; they will be very well contented if you never marry; for, to be left without a child in the house, would be hard enough upon mamma. But even, with all my plenishing ready, and the things marked, and everything settled—not that I would like to part with Matthew, even if there was no plenishing—I would rather have him without a tablecloth than any other man with the finest napery in the world. But I just know what will happen, and I am quite pleased, and it is of no use going against human nature. For company, they will always like their own kind best. But then, on the other hand, women are not so keen about company. When there's a family, they are generally very well content to bide at home, and be thankful when their man enjoys himself without fashing anybody."

This is not a doctrine which would, perhaps, be popular with women nowadays; but, in Marion's time, it was considered a kind of gospel in its way.

Elsie was not much interested in the view of man, as husband, put forth by her sister. Her mind did not go out towards that development of humanity; but the defection of Rodie, her own brother as she said, was a more serious matter. Most girls in as large family have an own brother their natural pair, the one most near to them in age or temperament. It had once been Willie and Marion, just as it had once been Elsie and Rodie; but Elsie could not bear the thought that Rodie might become to her, by his own will, the same as Willie was to Marion—her brother, but not her own brother, with no special tie between them. Her mind was constantly occupied by the thought of it, and how it was to be averted. Marion, she thought, had done nothing to lead Willie back when he first began to go after, what Marion called, his own kind, and to jilt his sister: so far from that, she had brought in a stranger into the family, a Matthew, to re-open and widen the breach, so that it was natural that Willie should go out of nights, and like his young men's parties, and come in much later than pleased father. This was not a thing that Elsie would do—she would bring in no strange man. All the Matthews in the world might flutter round her, but she would never give Rodie any reason to think that there was anybody she wanted but her brother—no, whatever might happen, she would be faithful to Rodie, even if it were true, as Marion said, that men (as if Rodie were a man!) liked their own kind best. Why, she was his own kind; who could be so near him as his sister, his own sister, the one that was next in the family?

Elsie went seriously into this question, as seriously as any forsaken wife could do, whose husband was being led astray from her, as she took a melancholy ramble by herself along the east sands, where Rodie never accompanied her now. She asked herself what she could do to bring him back, to make him feel that, however his Johnnys and his Alicks might tempt him for the moment, it was Elsie that was his true friend: she must never scold him, nor taunt him with liking other folk better, she must always be kind, however unkind he might be. With these excellent resolutions warm in her mind, it happened to Elsie to see, almost straight in front of her, hanging on the edge of a pool among the rocks, Rodie himself, in company with Johnny Wemyss, the newly-chosen friend of his heart. Johnny was up to his elbows in the pool, digging out with his hands the strange things and queer beasts to be found therein; and half to show the charity of her thoughts, half out of curiosity and desire to see what they were about, Elsie hurried on to join them. Johnny Wemyss was a big boy, bigger than Rodie, as old as Elsie herself—roughly clad, with big, much-mended nailed boots, clouted shoon, as he would himself have called them, and his rough hair standing out under the shabby peak of his sailor's cap.

"What are you doing—oh, what are you finding? Let me see," cried Elsie, coming up behind them with noiseless feet on the wet but firm sand.

Johnny Wemyss gave a great start, and raised himself up, drawing his bare and dripping arms out of the water, and standing confused before the young lady, conscious that he was not company for her, nor even for her brother, the minister's son, he who came of mere fisher folk.

But Rodie turned round fierce and threateningly, with his fists clenched in his pockets.

"What are you wanting?" he cried. "Can you not let a person abee? We are no wanting any lassies here."

"Rodie," cried his sister, flushed and almost weeping, "do you say that to me?"

"Ay do I!" cried Rodie, red with wrath and confusion. "What are you wanting? We just want no lassies here."

Elsie gave him but one look of injured love and scorn, and, without saying another word, turned round and walked away.

Oh, May was right! she was only a lassie to her own brother, and he had insulted her before that Johnny, who was the cause of it all—she only hoped they were looking after her to see how firm she walked, and that she was not crying—no, she would not cry—why should she cry about him, the hard-hearted, unkind boy? and with that, Elsie's shoulders heaved, and a great sob rent her breast.

She had indeed mourned his desertion before: yet this was practically her first revelation of the hollowness of life.

Meanwhile, Rodie was far from comfortable on his side; all the more that Johnny Wemyss gave him a kick with his clouted shoe, and said, with the frankness of friendship:

"Ye little cankered beast—how dare ye speak to her like that? How can she help it if she is a lassie?—it's no her blame!"

CHAPTER VI

A HOUSEHOLD CONTROVERSY

Notwithstanding the great sobriety of her views, as disclosed above, Marion, on the eve of her marriage, was no doubt the most interesting member of the Buchanan family; and, if anything could have "taken off" the mind of Elsie from her own misfortune, it would have been the admiring and wondering study she was quite unconsciously making of her sister, who had come to the climax of a girl's life, and who regarded it with so staid and middle-aged a view. Marion had always been a very steady sort of girl all her life, it was common to say. There was no nonsensical enthusiasm about her. Even when in love— that is, in the vague and gaseous period, before it has come to anything, when most girls have their heads a little pardonably turned, and the excitement of the new thing runs strong in their veins—even then, her deportment had been everything that could be desired in a minister's daughter, and future minister's wife. There had been no contrivings of meetings, no lingering on the links or the sands. Never once, perhaps, in that period when even a lassie is allowed to forget herself a little, had Marion failed to be at home in time for prayers, or forgot any of her duties. She was of the caste of the Scotch minister, in which the woman as well as the man belongs more or less to a sacred profession, and has its character to keep up. But, no doubt, it was owing to the sober tone of her own mind that she took at so early an age, and so exciting a moment of her career, the very sensible and unexalted views which she expressed so clearly. The Rev. Matthew Sinclair was neither cold nor negligent as a lover; he was limited by duty, and by a purse but indifferently filled. He could only come to see her after careful arrangement, when he could afford it, and when he could secure a substitute in his work. He could not shower presents upon her, even daily bouquets or other inexpensive luxuries. In those days, if you had a garden at your hand, you might bring your beloved "a flower"—that is, a bunch of flowers—roses and southernwood, and bachelor's buttons and gilly-flowers, with a background of the coloured grasses, called gardener's garters in Scotland, tightly tied together; but there were no shops in which you could find the delicate offerings, sweet smelling violets, and all the wonders of the South—which lovers deal in nowadays. But he did his part very manfully, and Marion had nothing to complain of in his attentions. Yet, as has been made apparent, she was not deceived. She did not expect, or even wish, to attach him to her apron strings. She was quite prepared to find that, in respect of "company," that is society, he would prefer, as she said, his own kind. And she did not look forward to this with any prevision of that desolate sense of the emptiness of the world and all things, which was in the mind of Elsie when her brother told her that he wanted no lassies there. Marion knew that if she went into her husband's study when two or three of the brethren were gathered together, her entrance would probably stop a laugh, and her husband would look up and say, "Well, my dear?" interrogatively, with just the same meaning, though less roughly than that of Rodie. She had seen it in her mother's case; she accepted it as quite natural in her anticipations of her own. This curious composure made her, perhaps, all the more interesting—certainly a more curious study—to Elsie, who had fire and flame in her veins incomprehensible to the elder sister. Elsie followed her about with that hot iron to facilitate the marking, and drank in her words with many a protest against them. Let it not be supposed that Marion marked her own "things" with the vulgarity of marking-ink; but she marked the dusters and the commoner kinds of napery, the coarser towels and sheets, all the inferior part of her plenishing in this common way, an operation which occupied a good many mornings, during which there went on much edifying talk. Sometimes, while they sat at one end of the large dining-table in the dining-room,—for it was not permitted to litter the drawing-room with this kind of work,—Mrs. Buchanan would be seated at the other, with her large basket of stockings to darn, or other domestic mendings, and, in that case, the talk was more varied, and went over a wider field. Naturally, the mother was not quite philosophic or so perfectly informed as was the young daughter on the verge of her life.

"I hear," said Mrs. Buchanan, "that old Mr. Anderson's house in the High Street is getting all prepared and made ready for young Frank Mowbray and his mother. She is not a very wise woman, and very discontented. I fear that the old man left much less than was expected. When I think how good he was to us, and that Willie's outfit and your plenishing are just, so to speak, gifts of his bounty, I feel as if we were a kind of guilty when I hear of his mother's complaint. For, if he had not given us, and other people as well as much as he did, there would have been more for her, or at least for her Frank."

"But she had nothing to do with it, mother," said Marion; "and he had a good right to please himself, seeing it was all his own."

"All that is quite true," said Mrs. Buchanan; "I made use of the very same argument myself when your father was so cast down about it, and eager to pay it back, and James Morrison would not listen to him. I just said, 'It's in the very Scripture—Shall I not do what I like with my own?' And then your father tells me that you must not always take the words of a parable for direct instruction, and that the man who said that was meaning—but if you ask him, he will tell you himself what we were to understand."

"Was it the one about the unjust steward?" asked Elsie, suddenly looking up, with the heated iron in her hand.

"What would the unjust steward have to do with it?" said Mrs. Buchanan, astonished. "Neither your father nor Mr. Anderson would go for instruction to the unjust steward. Your father had a fine lecture on that, that he delivered about a year and a half ago. You never mind your father's best things, you bairns, though one would think you might be proud of them."

"I mind that quite clearly," said Marion; "and, mother, if you'll no be angry, I would like to say that it did not satisfy my mind. You would have thought he was excusing yon ill man: and more than that, as if he thought our Lord was excusing him: and, though it was papa that said it, that was what I could not bide to hear."

It may be supposed how Elsie, with her secret knowledge, pricked up her ears. She sat with the iron suspended in her hand, letting Marion's initials grow dry upon the linen, and forgetting altogether what she was about.

"I am astonished that you should say that," said the mother, giving a little nod; "that will be some of Matthew's new lights—for, I am sure, he explained as clear as could be that it was the man's wisdom, or you might say cunning, that the Lord commended, so to speak, as being the best thing for his purpose, though his purpose was far from being a good one. Your father is not one that, on such a subject, ever gives an uncertain note."

"It is an awfu' difficult subject for an ordinary congregation," said Marion. "Matthew is just as little a man for new lights as papa; but still he did say, that for a common congregation—"

"I thought it would be found that Matthew was at the bottom of it," said Mrs. Buchanan, with a laugh; "though it would set a young man better to hold his peace, and make no comments upon one that has so much more experience than himself."

"You are a little unjust to Matthew," said Marion, nodding in her turn; "he made no more comment than any of the congregation might have done—or than I did myself. He is just very careful what he says about papa. He says that theology, like other things, makes progress, and that there's more exegesis and—and other things, since my father's time—which makes a difference; but he has always a great opinion of papa's sermons, and says you may learn a great deal from them, even when—"

"I am sure we are much beholden to him," said Mrs. Buchanan, holding her head high. "It's delicate of him to spare your feelings; for, I suppose, however enlightened you may be beyond your fellows, you must still have some kind of objection to hear your father criticised."

"Oh, mother, how can you take it like that?" said Marion; "there was no criticism. If anything was said, it was more me than him. I said I could not bide to hear a word, as if our Lord might have approved such an ill man. And he said it was dangerous for a mixed congregation, and that few considered the real meaning of a parable, but just took every word as if it was instruction."

"And that was just your father's strong point. He said it was like taking another man's sail to fill up a leak in a boat. You would praise the man for getting the first thing he could lay his hands on to save himself and his crew, but not for taking his neighbour's sail—that was just his grand point; but there are some folk that will always take things in the matter-of-fact way, to the letter, and cannot understand what's expounded according to the spirit. That, however, has always just been your father's special gift," said the minister's wife, de facto. She, who was only a minister's wife in expectation, ought to have bowed her head; but, being young and confident, even though so extremely reasonable, Marion could not subdue herself to that better part.

"That was just what Matthew said—dangerous for a mixed congregation," she repeated; "the most of them just being bound by nature to the letter, and very matter-of-fact—"

"No doubt Matthew is a great authority," said Mrs. Buchanan, with a violent snap of her big scissors.

"Well, mamma," said Marion, with the soft answer that does not always take away wrath, "you'll allow that he ought to be to me—"

And there then ensued a deep silence; a whole large hole in the heel of Rodie's stocking filled up, as by magic, in the mother's hands, quickened by this contrariety, and the sudden absorption in her work which followed, and Marion marked twelve towels, one after the other, so quickly that Elsie could scarcely follow her with the iron in time to make them all shine. It was she who took up the thread of the conversation again, but not wisely. Had she been a sensible young person, she would have introduced a new subject, which is the bounden duty of a third party, when the other two have come to the verge of a quarrel. But Elsie was only sixteen, and this discussion had called back her own strange experience in the turret-room.

"It must have given papa a great deal of thinking," she said. "Once me and Rodie were in the turret as—as he never comes now—" This was very bad grammar, but Elsie's heart was full of other things. "We were reading Quentin Durward, and very, very taken up with all that was going on at Liege, if you mind." Liége had no accent in Elsie's mind or her pronunciation. "And then you came into the study, mother, and talked. And after he began again with his sermon. It was a long time ago, but I never forgot, for it was strange what he said. It was as if he was learning the parable off by heart. 'Take now thy bill, and sit down quickly, and write fourscore'—or 'write fifty.' He said it over and over, just those words—sometimes the one and sometimes the other. It was awfu' funny. We both heard it; both me and Rodie, and wondered what he could be meaning. And we dared not move, for though he knew we were there, we did not like to disturb him. We thought he had maybe forgotten us. We were so stiff, we could scarcely move, and that was always what he said, 'Take now thy bill, and sit down—'"

Mrs. Buchanan had dropped her work and raised her head to listen; a puzzled look came over her face, then she shook her head, slightly, unable to solve the problem which she dimly felt to be put before her. She said, at last, with a change of countenance:

"I came into the study and talked?—and you there? What was I talking about? do you mind that?"

"Oh, nothing," said Elsie. "Old Mr. Anderson; it was just before he died."

"And you were there, Rodie and you, when I came in to talk private things with your father! Is that the kind of conduct for children in a decent house?"

Mrs. Buchanan had reddened again, and wrath, quite unusual, was in her tone.

"Mamma, when it was raining, and we had a book to read, we were always there, and father knew, and he never said a word!"

"You knew too, mother," said Marion; "the two little things were always there."

"Little things!" cried Mrs. Buchanan, almost with a snort—Rodie's heel, stretched out upon her hand, and now filled up with a strong and seemly web of darning in stout worsted, was quite as big as his father's. And Elsie was taller than either of the two women by her side. "They were little things with muckle lugs," she said, with a rather fierce little laugh; "if you think, Elsie, it was right to spy upon the private conversation of your father and mother, that is not my opinion. Do you think I would have spoken to him as I did if I had known you two were there?"

"Mother, about old Mr. Anderson?" cried Marion, meditating; "there could be nothing so private about that."

She gave them both a look, curious and anxious; Marion took it with the utmost composure, perhaps did not perceive it at all. Elsie, with a wistful but ignorant countenance, looked at her mother, but did not wince. She had no recollection of what that conversation had been.

"Oh, mamma," she said, "we spying!" with big tears in her eyes.

"I am not saying you meant it," said her mother; "it was a silly habit, but I must request, Elsie, that it never may happen again."

"Oh!" cried Elsie, the big tears running over, "he never will come now! He is not caring neither for me nor the finest book that ever was written. There is no fear, mother. It breaks my heart to sit there my lane, and Rodie never will come now!"

"You are a silly thing," said Mrs. Buchanan; "it is not to be expected, a stirring laddie. Far better for him to be out stretching his limbs than poring over a book. But I can understand, too, it's a disappointment to you."

"Oh, a disappointment!" Elsie cried, covering her face with her hands: the word was so inadequate.

To be disappointed was not to get a new frock when you want it, or something else, unworthy of a thought: but to be forsaken by your own brother! You wanted for that a much bigger word.

"All the same," the mother said, "I have often things to say to your father that are between me and him alone, and not for you. You must not do this again, Elsie. Another time, if you hear me go in to speak to your papa, you must give warning you are there. You must not sit and hold your breath, and listen. There are many things I might say to him that were never intended for you. Now, mind what I say. I forgive you because I am sure you did not mean it; but another time—"

"There will never be another time, mother," said Elsie, with a quivering lip.

"Well, I am sure I hope so," said her mother, and she finished her stockings carefully, made them into round balls, and carried them away to put them into their respective drawers. At this particular moment, with all that was going on, and all that was being prepared in the house, she had very little time to spend with her daughters in the pleasant exercise of sewing, virtuous and most necessary as that occupation was.

"Do you remember what they were saying about old Mr. Anderson?" said Marion; "for I have always thought there was something about that—that was—I don't know what word to say. He died, you know, when they were in his debt, and he freely forgave them; and that was why I got such a good plenishing, and Willie the best of outfits, and I would like to know what they said."

"I do not mind what they said," said Elsie; "and, if I did mind, I would not tell you, and you should not ask me. Rodie and me, we were not heeding about their secrets. It was just after, when my father went on and on about that parable, that we took any notice what he said."

"And what was he saying about the parable?"

"Oh, I have told you already. He just went on and on—'Take thy bill, and write fourscore'—you know what it says—till a person's head went round and round. And we dared never move, neither me nor Rodie, and very glad we were when he went down-stairs."

"Poor bit things, not daring to move," said Marion. "But that was a strange thing to say over and over: he said nothing about that in his sermon, but just how clever the man was for his purpose, though it was not a good purpose. But Matthew is of opinion that it's a dangerous thing to treat the parables in that way."

"And how should Matthew know better than my father?" cried Elsie, in indignation. "He may just keep his opinion; I'm of the same opinion as papa."

"It is not of much consequence what your opinion is," said Marion, imperturbably; "but Matthew has been very well instructed, and he has all the new lights upon things, and the exegesis and all that, which was not so advanced in my father's day. But it was a fine sermon," she added, with an approving nod, "though maybe dangerous to the ignorant, which was all we ever said."

As for Elsie, she ceased altogether to think of the mystery of that afternoon, and the sound of her father's voice—which was such as she had never heard before—in her hot indignation against Matthew, who dared to be of a different opinion from papa.

CHAPTER VII

THE FIRST MARRIAGE IN THE FAMILY

Marion's marriage took place in the summer, at the very crown of the year. And it was a very fine wedding in its way, according to the fashion of the times. Nobody in Scotland thought of going to church for this ceremony, which took place in the bride's home, in the drawing-room upstairs, which was the largest room in the house, and as full as it could be with wedding-guests. There were two bridesmaids, Elsie and a sister of Matthew's, whose mission, however, was unimportant in the circumstances, unless, indeed, when it happened to be the duty of one of them to accompany the bride and bridegroom, with the aid of the best man, upon their wedding-tour. This curious arrangement had never been thought of in Marion's case, for no wedding-tour was contemplated. The wedding pair were to proceed at once to their own quiet manse, somewhere in the centre of Fife, where they could travel comfortably in a post-chaise; and there they were disposed of for life, with no further fuss. There were many things, indeed, wanting in this wedding which are indispensable now. There were, for example, no wedding-presents, or at least very few, some pieces of silver of the massive order, a heavy tea-service, which was indeed a "testimonial" from those who had profited by the Rev. Matthew's services, in his previous sphere, and a number of pretty things sent by Willie, such as used to be sent from India by all the absent sons, pieces of Indian muslin, embroidered and spangled (over which Mrs. Buchanan had held up her hands, wondering what in the world Marion could do with them), and shawls, one of them heavy with gold embroidery, about which the same thing might be said. Willie had been by this time about eighteen months in India, and was already acquainted with all the ways of it, his mother believed. And he sent such things as other young men sent to their families, without considering whether they would be of any use. He also sent various beautiful things in that mosaic of ivory and silver, which used to adorn so many Scotch houses, and which made the manse parlour glorious for years to come. On the whole, "every justice" was done to Marion. Had she come from Mount Maitland itself, the greatest house in the neighbourhood, or even from the Castle at Pittenweem, or Balcarres, she could not have been better set out.

It was at this great festivity that there were first introduced to the society at St. Rule's two figures that were hereafter to be of great importance to it, and to assume an importance beyond what they had any right to, according to ordinary laws. These were Frank Mowbray and his mother, who had very lately come to St. Rule's, from a country vaguely called the South, which was not, after all, any very distant or different region, but perhaps only Dumfrieshire, or Northumberland, in both of which they had connections, but which do not suggest any softness of climate or exuberance of sunshine to our minds nowadays. They had led, it was believed, a wandering life, which was a thing very obnoxious to the public sentiment of St. Rule's, and almost infallibly meant minds and manners to correspond, light-headedness and levity, especially on the part of the woman, who could thus content herself without a settled home of her own. It was naturally upon Mrs. Mowbray that all the criticism centred; for Frank was still very young, and, of course, as a boy had only followed his mother's impulse, and done what she determined was to be done. She was not in outward appearance at all unlike the rôle which was given her by the public. She gave for one thing much more attention to her dress than was then considered right in St. Rule's, or almost even decent, as if desirous of attracting attention, the other ladies said, which indeed was probably Mrs. Mowbray's design. In the evening, she wore a scarf, gracefully draped about her elbows and doing everything but cover the "bare neck," which it was intended to veil: and though old enough to wear a cap, which many ladies in those days assumed, however young they might be—as soon as they married, did not do so, but wore her hair in large bows on the top of her head, with stray ringlets upon either cheek, which, for a woman with a grown-up son, seemed almost an affront to public morality. And she used a fan with much action and significance, spreading it out, and shutting it up as it suited her conversation, with little gestures that were like nothing in the world but a foreigner, one of the French, or persons of that kind, that thought of nothing but showing themselves off. It was perhaps an uncharitable judgment, but there was so much truth in it, that Mrs. Mowbray's object was certainly to make the most of herself, and do herself justice which is what she would have said.

And Frank at this period was what was then called a young "dandy;" and also thought a great deal of his own appearance, which was even more culpable or at least more contemptible on the part of a young man than on that of a lady. He wore a velvet collar to his coat, which came up to his ears, and sometimes a stock so stiff that he could look neither to the right hand nor the left, and his nankeen trousers and flowered waistcoats were a sight to behold. Out of the high collar, and voluminous folds of muslin which encircled his neck, a very young, boyish face came forth, with a small whisker on either cheek, to set forth the rosy colour of his youthful countenance, which was quite ingenuous and simple, and had no harm in it, notwithstanding the scoffs and sneers which his contemporaries in St. Rule's put forth against his airs and graces, and the scent on his handkerchief "like a lassie," which was the last aggravation, and called forth roars of youthful laughter, not unmingled with disgust. The pair together made a great commotion in the society of St. Rule's. Mr. Anderson's house, which was old-fashioned but kindly, with old mahogany, so highly polished that you could see your face in it, and old dark portraits hanging on the panelled walls, underwent a complete revolution to please what St. Rule's considered the foreign tastes. She had one of those panelled rooms covered with wall-paper, to the consternation of the whole town. I am obliged to allow that this room is the pride of the house now, for the paper— such things as yet being scarce in the British Islands—was an Oriental one, of fine design and colour, which has lasted over nearly a century, and is as fresh now as when it was put up, and the glory of the place; but in those days, Scotch taste was all in favour of things dark and plain, without show, which was a wicked thing. To please the eye at all, especially with brightness and colour, was tacitly considered wicked, at that day, in all circumstances. It was not indeed a crime in any promulgated code, but it certainly partook of the nature of vice, as being evidently addressed to carnal sentiments, not adapted for confidence or long duration, or any other recognised and virtuous purpose, but only to give pleasure which was by its very nature an illegitimate thing. It was not indeed that these good people did not love pleasure in their hearts. There was far more dancing in those days than has ever been since, and parties for the purpose, at which the young people met each other, and became engaged to each other and made love, and married with a general persistency and universalness no longer known among us; and there was much more drinking and singing of jovial songs and celebration of other kinds of pleasure. But a bright wall-paper, or a cheerful carpet, or more light in a room than was absolutely necessary, these were frivolities almost going the length of depravity that were generally condemned.

The new-comers were among the wedding-guests, and Mrs. Mowbray came in a white Indian shawl, and a white satin bonnet, adorned with roses inside its cave-like sides, as if she had been the bride herself: while Frank had already a flower in his coat before the wedding-favour was added which made him, in the estimation of his compeers, a most conspicuous figure, and more "like a lassie" than ever. When the time came for Marion and her husband to go away, it was he who drew from his pocket the white satin slipper which landed on the top of the post-chaise, and made the bridal pair also "so conspicuous"—to their great wrath, when they discovered by the cheers that met them in every village what an ensign they were carrying with them, though they had indeed a most sober post-chaise from the old Royal: and Matthew had taken care that the postillion took off his favour as soon as they were out of the town. To throw an old shoe for luck was a well-understood custom, but satin slippers were not so common in St. Rule's in those days that they should be used in this way, and Marion never quite forgave this breach of all decorum, pointing her out to the world just on the day of all others when she most desired to escape notice. But the Mowbrays did not understand how you ever could desire to escape notice, which, for their part, they loved. The young people who crowded about the door to see the bride go off, the girls laughing and crying in their excitement, the lads cheering and shouting, were, I need not say, augmented by half the population of St. Rule's, all as eager and as much interested as if they too had been wedding-guests. The women about, though they had no occasion to be specially moved, laughed and cried too, for sympathy, and made their comments at the top of their voices, with the frankness of their class.

"She is just as bonnie a bride as I ever saw, as I aye kent she would be; but he's but a poor creature beside her," said one of the fishwives.

"Hoot, woman," said another, "the groom, he's aye the shaddow on the brightness, and naithing expected from him."

"But he's not that ill-faured either," said another spectator.

"She's a bonnie creature, and he's a wise-like man." Elsie, who had always an ear for what was going on, took in all these comments, and the aspect of affairs generally without really knowing what she heard and saw. But there was one episode which, above all, caught that half attention which imprints a scene on the memory we cannot tell how. At the house door, Frank Mowbray, with the slipper in his hand, very proud of that piece of fashion and prettiness, stood stretching himself to his full height (which was not great), and preparing for his throw. While at the same moment she caught sight of a very different figure close to the chaise watching the crowd, which was Johnny Wemyss, the friend for whom Rodie her own brother had deserted her, and whom, consequently, she regarded with no favourable eyes. He was a tall weedy boy, with long arms growing out of his jacket-sleeves, and that look of loose-jointed largeness which belongs to a puppy in all varieties of creation. He was in his Sunday clothes and bareheaded, and as Marion walked across the pavement, he stooped down and laid before the steps of the chaise a large handful of flowers. The bride gave an astonished look, and then a nod and a smile to the rough lad, who rose up, red as fire with the shamefacedness of his homage, and disappeared behind the crowd. It was only the affair of a moment, and probably very few people noticed it at all. But Elsie saw it, and her face burned with sympathetic excitement. She was pushed back at almost the same moment by the sudden action of Frank, throwing his missile, and then, amid laughter, crying, and cheers, the post-chaise drove away.

"My dear," said Mr. Buchanan, a few minutes after, "some bairn has dropped its flowers on the pavement, or perhaps it was Marion that let them fall. Send one of the women out to clear them away; it has a disorderly look before the door," the minister said.

Elsie did not know what made her do it, but she darted out in her white frock among the dispersing crowd, and gathered up, with her own hands, the flowers on which Marion had set her foot. She took a rose from among them and put it into her own belt. They were, I fear, dusty and soiled, and only fit, as Mr. Buchanan said, to be swept away, but it was to Elsie the only touch of poetry in the whole business. Bride and bridegroom were very sober persons, scarcely worthy, perhaps, to tread upon flowers, which, indeed, Mr. Matthew Sinclair had avoided by kicking them (though gently) out of his way. But Elsie felt the unusual tribute, if no one else did. She gave a glance round for Johnny Wemyss, and caught him as he cast back a furtive glance from behind the shadow of a burly fisherman. And again the boy grew red, and so did she. They had a secret between them from that day, and everybody knows, who has ever been sixteen, what a bond that is, a bond for life.

"Take out that dirty flower out of your belt," said Rodie, putting out his hand for it; "if you want a flower, you can get a fresh one out of the garden. All the folk in the street have tramped upon it." This word is constantly used in Scotland, with unnecessary vehemence of utterance, for the simpler syllable trod.

"I'll not take it out," said Elsie, "and only Marion put her foot upon it. It is the bonniest thing of all that has happened; and it was your own friend Johnny Wemyss that you are so fond of."

"I am not fond of him," said Rodie, ingenuously; "do you think me and him are like a couple of lassies? Throw it away this minute."

"No for you, nor all the fine gentlemen in the world!" cried Elsie, holding her rose fast; and there would probably have been a scuffle over it, Rodie at fifteen having no sense as yet that a lassie's whims were more to be respected than any other comrade's, had not Mrs. Buchanan suddenly appeared.

"Elsie," she said half severely, "are you forgetting already that you're now the only girl in the house? and nobody to look after the folk upstairs—oh, if they would only go away! but you and me."

"I'm going, mamma," cried Elsie, and then, though embraces were rare in this reserved atmosphere, she threw her arms round her mother and gave her a kiss. "I'm not so good as May, but I will try my best," she said.

"Oh my dear, but I am tired, tired! both body and mind," said Mrs. Buchanan; "and awfu' thankful to have you, to be a comfort. Rodie, run away and divert yourself and leave her alone; there's plenty about of your own kind."

It gave Elsie a pang, yet a thrill of satisfaction to see her brother, who had deserted her, thus summarily cleared off the scene. Marion had said regretfully, yet dispassionately, that they liked their own kind best, which had been a revelation and a painful one to the abandoned sister. But to have him thus sent off rather contemptuously than otherwise to his own kind, as by no means a superior portion of the race, gave her a new light on the subject, as well as a new sensation. Boys, she remembered, and had always heard were sent to divert themselves, as the only thing they were good for, when a lassie was useful in many ways. In this manner she began to recover from the bitter sense of the injury which the scorn of the laddies had inflicted upon her. They might scorn away as they pleased. But the other folk, who had more experience than they, thought otherwise; this helped Elsie to recover her balance. She almost began to feel that even if Rodie were lost, all would not be lost. And her exertions were great in the tired and wavering afternoon party, which had nothing to amuse itself with, and yet could not make up its mind to break up and go away, as the hosts, quite worn out with the long strain, and feeling that everything was now over, most fondly desired them to do.

"Will you come and see me?" said Mrs. Mowbray. "I have taken a great fancy to this child, Mrs. Buchanan. She has such pretty brown eyes and rosy cheeks."

"Will you come and see me, Elsie? I have got no pretty daughters. Oh! how I wish I had one to dress up and play with; Frank is all very well, he is a good boy—but a girl would make me quite happy."

Elsie was much disgusted with this address: to be told to her face that she had pretty brown eyes and rosy cheeks was unpardonable! In the first place, it was not true, for Elsie was well aware she was freckled, and thought red cheeks very vulgar and common. In those days heroines were always of an interesting paleness, and had black or very dark hair, "raven tresses" in poetry. And alas, Elsie's locks were more ruddy than raven. She was quite aware that she was not a pretty daughter, and it was intolerable that anyone should mock her, pretending to admire her to her face!

Mrs. Buchanan took it much more sweetly. She looked at Elsie with caressing eyes. "She is the only girlie at home now," she said, with a little sigh, "and she will have to learn to be a woman. Marion was always the greatest help—my right hand—since she was little more than a baby. And now Elsie will have to learn to take her place."

"I don't care so much for them being useful when they are ornamental," said Mrs. Mowbray, "for that is the woman's part in the world is it not? The men may do all the hard work, but they can't do the decoration, can they? We want the girls for that."

"Dear me," said Mrs. Buchanan, "I am not sure that I ever looked upon it in that light. There is a great deal to be done, when there is a family of laddies; you cannot expect them to do things for themselves, and when there is only one sister, it is hard work."

"Oh, I do not hold with that," said the other lady. "I turn all that over to my maid. I would not make the girls servants to their brothers: quite the contrary. It is the boys that should serve the girls, in my opinion. Frank would no more let a young lady do things for him!—I consider it quite wrong for my part."

Mrs. Buchanan was a little abashed.

"When you have plenty of servants and a small family, it is of course quite different, but you know what the saying is, 'a woman's work is never done'—"

"My dear Mrs. Buchanan, you are simply antediluvian," said her visitor.

(Oh, if she would only go away, instead of standing havering there!) The minister's wife was more tired than words could say. "Claude," she said, clutching at her husband's arm as he passed her, "Mrs. Mowbray has not seen our garden, and you know we are proud of our garden. Perhaps she would like to take a turn and look at the view."

"I am so glad to get you for a little to myself, Mr. Buchanan," said Mrs. Mowbray. "Oh yes, let us go to the garden. I have been so longing to speak to you. There are so many things about poor Mr. Anderson's estate, and other matters, that I don't understand."

CHAPTER VIII

A NEW FACTOR

Mrs. Mowbray took the minister's arm with a little eagerness. "I am so glad," she said, "so very glad to have an opportunity of speaking to you alone. I want so much to consult you, Mr. Buchanan. I should have ventured to come over in the morning to ask for you, if I had not this opportunity; but then your wife would have had to know, and just at first I don't want anyone to know—so I am more glad of this opportunity than words can say—"

"I am sure," said Mr. Buchanan, steadily, "that I shall be very glad if I can be of any use to you. I am afraid you will not find much to interest you in our homely garden. Vegetables on one side, and flowers on the other, but at the east corner there is rather a pretty view. I like to come out in the evening, and see the lighthouses in the distance slowly twirling round. We can see the Bell Rock—"

"Oh, yes," said Mrs. Mowbray, "I have no doubt it is very fine, but take me to the quietest corner, never mind about the view—other people will be coming to see the view, and to talk is what I want."

"I don't think anyone will be coming," said the minister, and he led her among the flower-beds, and across what was then, in homely language, called not the lawn, but the green, to the little raised mound upon which there was a little summer-house, surrounded with tall lilac bushes—and the view. Mrs. Mowbray gave but a passing glance at the view.

"Oh, yes," she said, "the same as you see from the cliffs, the Forfarshire coast and the bay. It is very nice, but not remarkable—whereas what I have got to say to you is of the gravest importance—at least to Frank and me. Mr. Buchanan, as the clergyman, you must know of everything that is going on—you knew the late Mr. Anderson, my husband's uncle, very well, didn't you? Well, you know Frank has always been brought up to believe himself his great-uncle's heir. And we believed it would be something very good. My poor husband, in his last illness, always said, 'Uncle John will provide for you and the boy.' And we thought it would be quite a good thing. Now you know, Mr. Buchanan, it is really not at all a good thing."

In the green shade of the foliage, Mr. Buchanan's face looked gray. He said, "Indeed, I am sorry," in a mechanical way, which seemed intended to give the impression that he was not interested at all.

"Oh, perhaps you think that is not of much importance," said the lady. "Probably you imagine that we have enough without that. But it is not really so—it is of the greatest importance to Frank and me. Oh, here are some people coming! I knew other people would be coming to see this stupid view—when they can see it from the road just as well, any time they please."

It was a young pair of sweethearts who came up the little knoll, evidently with the intention of appropriating the summer-house, and much embarrassed to find their seniors in possession. They had, however, to stay a little and talk, which they all did wildly, pointing out to each other the distant smoke of the city further up, and the white gleam of the little light-house opposite. Mrs. Mowbray said scarcely anything, but glared at the intrusive visitors, to whom the minister was too civil. Milly Beaton, who was one of these intruders, naturally knew every point of the view as well as he did, but he pointed out everything to her in the most elaborate way, at which the girl could scarcely restrain her laughter. Then the young people heard, or pretended to hear, some of their companions calling them, and hurried away.

"I knew," said Mrs. Mowbray, "that we should be interrupted here—"

"No, I don't think so: there will be no more of it," said the minister.

He was not so unwilling to be interrupted as she was. Then it occurred to her, with a knowledge drawn from other regions than St. Rule's, that she was perhaps compromising the minister, and this idea gave her a lively pleasure.

"They will be wondering what we have to say to each other," she cried with a laugh, and she perceived with delight, or thought she perceived, that this idea discomposed Mr. Buchanan. He changed colour, and shuffled from one foot to the other, as he stood before her. She had placed herself on the garden-seat, within the little chilly dark green bower. She had not contemplated any such amusement, but neither had she time to indulge in it, which might have been done so very safely with the minister. For it was business that was in her mind, and she felt herself a business woman before all.

"Fortunately," she went on, "nobody can the least guess what I want to consult you about. Oh! here is another party! I knew how it would be. Take me to see your cabbages, Mr. Buchanan, or anywhere. I must speak to you without continual interruptions like this."

Her tone was a little imperative, which the minister resented. He was not in the habit of being spoken to in this way, and he was extremely glad of the interruption.

"It is only a parcel of boys," he said, "they will soon go." Perhaps he did not perceive that the carefully-attired Frank was among the others, led by his own older son John, who, Mr. Buchanan well knew, would not linger when he saw how the summer-house was occupied. Frank, however, came forward and made his mother a satirical bow.

"Oh, this is where you are, mater?" he said. "I couldn't think where you had got to. My compliments, I wouldn't interrupt you for the world."

"You ridiculous boy!" Mrs. Mowbray said; and they both laughed, for what reason neither Mr. Buchanan nor his serious son John could divine.

"So you have come up, too, to see the view," said the lady; "I never knew you had any love for scenery and the beauties of nature."

"Do you call this scenery?" said Frank, who, in his mother's presence, felt it necessary to be superior as she was. "If you could only have the ruins in the foreground, instead of this great bit of sea, and those nasty little black rocks."

"They may be little," said John, with all the sudden heat of a son of St. Rule's, "but they're more dangerous than many that are far bigger. I would not advise you to go near them in a boat. Father, isn't that true?"

"It is true that it is a dangerous coast," said Mr. Buchanan, "that is the reason why no ship that can help it comes near the bay."

"I don't care for that kind of boating," said Frank. "Give me a wherry on the river."

"Give you a game—a ball, or something," said his mother, exasperated. "You ought to get up something to amuse the young ladies. Doesn't Mrs. Buchanan allow dancing? You might teach them, Frank, some of the new steps."

"We want you for that, mater," said the lad.

"Oh, I can't be bothered now. I've got some business to talk over with Mr. Buchanan."

Frank looked malicious and laughed, and Mrs. Mowbray laughed, too, in spite of herself. The suggestion that she was reducing the minister to subjection was pleasant, even though it was an interruption. Meanwhile, Mr. Buchanan and his son stood gazing, absolutely unable to understand what it was all about. John, however, not used to badinage, seized with a firm grip the arm of the new-comer.

"Come away, and I'll take you into the Castle," he said, giving a drag and push, which the other, less vigorous, was not able to resist.

"I cannot stand this any longer," cried Mrs. Mowbray, "take me please somewhere—into your study, Mr. Buchanan, where I can talk to you undisturbed. I am sure for once your wife will not mind."

"My wife!" the minister said, in great surprise, "why should my wife mind?" But it was certain, that he did himself mind very much, having not the faintest desire to admit this intruder into his sanctum. But it was in vain to resist. He took her among the cabbages as she had suggested, but by this time the garden was in the possession of a young crowd penetrating everywhere, and after an ineffectual attempt among those cabbages to renew the conversation, Mrs. Mowbray so distinctly declared her desire to finish her communication in the study, that he could no longer resist. Mrs. Mowbray looked about her, before she had taken her seat, and went into the turret-room with a little curiosity.

"I suppose you never admit anyone here," she said.

"Admit! No, but the two younger children used to be constantly here," said Mr. Buchanan. "They have left some of their books about still. There was a great alliance between them a few years ago, but since Rodie grew more of a school-boy, and Elsie more of a woman—"

"Elsie! why, she is quite grown-up," said the visitor. "I hope you don't let her come here to hear all your secrets. I shouldn't like her to hear mine, I am sure. Is there any other door?"

"There is neither entrance nor exit, but by my study door," Mr. Buchanan said, somewhat displeased.

"Well, that is a good thing. I hope you always make sure when you receive your penitents that there is nobody there."

The minister made no reply. He thought her a very disagreeable, very presuming and impertinent woman; but he placed a chair for her with all the patience he could muster. He had a faint feeling as if she had lodged an arrow somewhere in him, and that he felt it quivering, but did not inquire into his sensations. The first thing seemed to be to get rid of her as quickly as he could.

"Now we can talk at last," she said, sinking down into the arm-chair, stiff and straight as it was—for the luxury of modern days had scarcely yet begun and certainly had not come as far as St. Rule's—which Mrs. Buchanan generally occupied when she came upstairs to talk over their "whens and hows" with her husband.

"It is very serious indeed, and I am very anxious to know if you can throw any light upon it. Mr. Morrison, the man of business, tells me that old Mr. Anderson had lent a great deal of money to various people, and that it proved quite impossible to get it back. Was that really the case? or is this said merely to cover over some defalcations—some—"

"Morrison," cried the minister, almost angrily, "is as honourable a man as lives; there have been no defalcations, at least so far as he is concerned."

"It is very satisfactory to hear that," said Mrs. Mowbray, "because of course we are altogether in his hands; otherwise I should have got my English solicitor to come down and look into matters. But you know one always thinks it must be the lawyer's fault—and then so many men go wrong that have a very good reputation."

Mr. Buchanan relieved his heart with a long painful breath. He said:

"It is true; there are such men: but Morrison is not one of them."

"Well, that's satisfactory at least to hear," she said doubtfully, "but tell me about the other thing. Is it true that our old uncle was so foolish, so mad—I really don't know any word sufficiently severe to use— so unjust to us as to give away his money on all hands, and lend to so many people without a scrap of acknowledgment, without so much as an I.O.U., so that the money never could be recovered; is it possible this can be true?"

Mr. Buchanan was obliged to clear his throat several times before he could speak.

"Mr. Anderson," he said, "was one of the men who are so highly commended in Scripture, though it is perhaps contrary to modern ideas. The merciful man is merciful and lendeth. He was a providence to many troubled persons. I had heard—"

"But, Mr. Buchanan," cried the lady, raising herself up in her chair, "you cannot think that's right; you cannot imagine it is justifiable. Think of his heirs."

"Yes," he replied, "perhaps at that time he did not think of his heir. If it had been his own child—but we must be fair to him. Your son was not a very near relation, and he scarcely knew the boy."

"Not a near relation!" exclaimed Mrs. Mowbray, "but he was the nearest relation. There was no one else to count at all. A man's money belongs to his family. He has no right to go and alienate it, to give a boy reason to expect a good fortune, and then to squander the half of it, which really belonged to Frank more than to him."

"You must remember," said the minister, with a dreadful tightening at his throat, feeling that he was pleading for himself as well as for his old benefactor, "you must remember that the money did not come from the family—in which case all you say might be true—but from his own exertions; and probably he believed what is also written in Scripture, that a man has a right to do what he will with his own."

"Oh, Mr. Buchanan!" cried Mrs. Mowbray, "that I should hear a clergyman speak like this. Who is the widow and the orphan to depend upon, if not on the clergy, to stand up for them and maintain their rights? I should have thought now that instead of encouraging people who got round this old man—who probably was not very clear in his head at the end of his life—and got loans from him, you would have stood up for his heirs and let them know—oh! with all the authority of the church, Mr. Buchanan—that it was their duty before everything to pay their debts, all the more," cried the lady, holding up an emphatic finger, "all the more if there was nothing to show for them, no way of recovering them, and it was left to their honour to pay."

The minister had been about to speak; but when she put forth this argument he sat dumb, his lips apart, gazing at her almost with a look of terror. It was a full minute before he attempted to say anything, and that in the midst of a discussion of this sort seems a long time. He faltered a little at last, when he did speak.

"I am not sure," he said, "that I had thought of this: but no doubt you are right, no doubt you are right."

"Certainly I am right," she cried, triumphant in her victory. "I knew you would see the justice of it. Frank has always been brought up to believe that he would be a rich man. He has been brought up with this idea. He has the habits and the notions of a man with a very good fortune; and now that I am here and can look into it, what is it? A mere competence! Nothing that you could call a fortune at all."

Oh, what it is to be guilty! The minister had not a word to say. He looked piteously in her face, and it seemed to him that it was an injured woman who sat before him, injured by his hand. He had never wronged any one so far as he knew before, but this was a woman whom he had wronged. She and her son, and her son's children to all possible generations,—he had wronged them. Though no one else might know it, yet he knew it himself. Frank Mowbray's fortune, which was not a fortune, but a mere competence, had been reduced to that shrunken measure by him. His conscience smote him with her voice. There was nothing to show for it, no way of recovering it; it was a debt of honour, and it was this that he refused to pay. He trembled under her eye. He felt that she must be able to read to the bottom of his soul.

"I am very sorry," he said; "I am afraid that perhaps none of us thought of that. But it is all past—I don't know what I could do, what you would wish me to do."

"I would wish you," cried Mrs. Mowbray, "to talk to them about it. Ah! I knew I should not speak in vain when I spoke to you. It is a shameful thing, is it not, to defraud a truthful, inexperienced boy, one that knows nothing about money nor how to act in such circumstances. If he had not his mother to speak for him, what would become of Frank? He is so young and so peace-making. He would say don't bother if he heard me speaking about it. He would be content to starve himself, and let other people enjoy what was his. I thought you would tell me perhaps who were the defaulters."

"No, I certainly could not do that," he said harshly, with a sound in his voice which made him not recognise it for his. He had a momentary feeling that some one else in the room, not himself, had here interposed and spoken for him.

"You could not? you mean you would not. And you the clergyman, the minister that should protect the orphan! Oh, Mr. Buchanan, this is not what I expected when I braced up my nerves to speak to you. I never thought but that you would take up my cause. I thought you would perhaps go round with me to tell them they must pay, and how badly my poor boy had been left: or that at least you would preach about it, and tell the people what was their duty. He must have lent money to half St. Rule's," cried Mrs. Mowbray; "those people that all look so decent and so well-dressed on Sunday at church. They are all as well-dressed (though their clothes are not well made) as any one need wish to be: and to think they should be owing us hundreds, nay, thousands of money! It is a dreadful thing for my poor Frank."

"Not thousands," said the minister, "not thousands. A few hundreds perhaps, but not more."

"I beg your pardon," said Mrs. Mowbray. "I have heard there was one that got four hundred out of him; at interest and compound interest, what does that come to by this time? Not much short of thousands, Mr. Buchanan, and there may be many more."

"Did Morrison tell you that?" he asked hastily.

"No matter who told me. How am I to get at that man? I should make him pay up somehow, oh trust me for that, if I could only make out who he was."

"There was no such man," said the minister. There breathed across his mind, as he spoke, the burden of the parable: "Take now thy bill, and sit down quickly, and write fourscore." "I have not heard of any of Mr. Anderson's debtors who had got so large a loan as that: but Morrison expressly said that it was in the will he had freely forgiven them all."

"I should not forgive them," cried the lady, harshly. "Get me a list of them, Mr. Buchanan, give me a list of them, and then we shall see what the law will say. Get me a list of them, Mr. Buchanan! I am sure that you must know them all."

"I don't know that I could tell you more than one of them."

"That will be the four hundred man!" cried Mrs. Mowbray. "Tell me of him, tell me of him, Mr. Buchanan, and I shall always be grateful to you. Tell me the one you know."

"I must first think it over—and—take counsel," the minister said.

CHAPTER IX

MAN AND WIFE

"What did that woman want with you, Claude?" said Mrs. Buchanan, coming in with panting breath, and depositing herself in the chair from which Mrs. Mowbray had risen but a little while before.

The minister sat with his head in his hands, his face covered, his aspect that of a man utterly broken down. He did not answer for some time, and then:

"I think she wants my life-blood," he said.

"Your life-blood! Claude, my man, are you taking leave of your senses—or what is it you mean?"

Once more there was a long pause. His wife was not perhaps so frightened as she might have been in other circumstances. She was very tired. The satisfaction of having got rid of all her guests was strong in her mind. She had only just recovered her breath, after toiling upstairs. Lastly, it was so absurd that any one should want the minister's life-blood; last of all, the smiling and flattering Mrs. Mowbray, that she was more inclined to laugh than to be alarmed.

"You may laugh," said Mr. Buchanan, looking up at her from below the shadow of his clasped hands, with hollow eyes, "but it is death to me. She wants me to give her a list of all old Anderson's debtors, Mary. I told her I only knew one."

"Goodness, Claude! did you say it was yourself?"

"Not yet," he said, with a deep sigh.

"Not yet! do you mean that after the great deliverance we got, and the blessed kindness of that old man, you are going to put your head under the yoke again? What has she to do with it? He thought nothing of her. He let the boy get it because there was nobody else, but he never took any interest even in the boy. He never would have permitted—Claude! those scruples of yours, they are ridiculous; they are quite ridiculous. What, oh! what do you mean? To ruin your own for the sake of that little puppy of a boy? God forgive me; it is probably not the laddie's fault. He is just the creation of his silly mother. And they are well off already. If old Anderson had left them nothing at all, they were well off already. Claude, if she has come here to play upon your weakness, to get back what the real owner had made you a present of—"

"Mary, I have never been able to get it out of my mind that it was the smaller debtors he wanted to release, but not me."

"Had you any reason to mistrust the old man, Claude?"

He gave her a look, still from under his clasped hands, but made no reply.

"Which of them were more to him than you," said Mrs. Buchanan, vehemently; "the smaller debtors? Joseph Sym, the gardener, that he set up in business, or the Horsburghs, or Peter Wemyss? Were they more to him than you?—was this woman, with her ringlets, and her puffed sleeves more to him than you? Or her silly laddie, no better than a bairn, though he may be near a man in years? I have reminded you before what St. Paul says: 'Albeit, I do not say to thee how thou owest me thine own self besides.' He was not slow to say that, the old man, when you would let him. And you think he was more taken up with that clan-jamfry than with you?"

"No—no; I don't say that, Mary. I know he was very favourable to me, too favourable; but I have never felt at rest about this. Morrison would not let me speak; perhaps he thought I had got less than I really had. This has always been in my head." The minister got up suddenly and began to walk about the room. "Take now thy bill, and sit down quickly, and write fourscore," he said, under his breath.

"What is that you are saying, Claude? That is what Elsie heard you saying the day of Mr. Anderson's death. She said, quite innocent, it gave you a great deal of trouble, your sermon, that you were always going over and over—"

"What?" said Mr. Buchanan, stopping short in his walk, with a scared face.

"Dear me, Claude! no harm, no harm, only that, that you are saying now—about writing fourscore. Oh, Claude, my dear, you give it far more thought than it deserves. We could have almost paid it off by this time, if it had been exacted from us. And when that good, kind, auld man said—more than saying—when he wrote down in his will—that it was to be a legacy, God bless him! when I heard that, with thanksgiving to the Lord, I just put it out of my mind—not to forget it, for it was a great deliverance—but surely not to be burdened by it, or to mistrust the good man in his grave!"

The eyes of the minister's wife filled with tears. It was she who was the preacher now, and her address was full of natural eloquence. But, like so many other eloquent addresses, her audience paid but little attention to it. Mr. Buchanan stopped short in his walk; he came back to his table and sat down facing her. When she ceased, overcome with her feelings, he began, without any pretence of sharing them, to question her hastily.

"Where was Elsie, that she should hear what I said? and what did she hear? and how much does she know?" This new subject seemed to occupy his mind to the exclusion of the old.

"Elsie? oh, she knows nothing. But she was in the turret there, where you encouraged them to go, Claude, though I always thought it a dangerous thing; for the parents' discussions are not always for a bairn's ears, and you never thought whether they were there or not. I have thought upon it many a day."

"And she knows nothing?" said Mr. Buchanan. "Well, I suppose there is no harm done; but I dislike anyone to hear what I am saying. It is inconvenient; it is disagreeable. You should keep a growing girl by your own side, Mary, and not let her stray idle round about the house."

He had not heard her complain against himself as encouraging the children to occupy the turret. His wife was well enough accustomed with his modes of thought. He ignored this altogether, as if he had no responsibility. And the thought of Elsie thus suggested put away the other and larger thought.

"I should like exactly to know how much she heard, and whether she drew any conclusions. You can send her to me when you go down down-stairs."

"Claude, if you will be guided by me, no—do not put things into the bairn's head. She will think more and more if her thoughts are driven back upon it. She will be fancying things in her mind. She will be—"

"What things can she fancy in her mind? What thoughts can she have more and more, as you say? What are you attributing to me, Mary? You seem to think I have been meditating—or have done—something—I know not what—too dark for day."

He looked at her severely, and she looked at him with deprecating anxiety.

"Claude," she said, "my dear, I cannot think what has come over you. Am I a person to make out reproaches against you? I said it was a pity to get the bairns into a habit of sitting there, where they could hear everything. That was no great thing, as if I was getting up a censure upon you, or hinting at dark things you have done. I would far easier believe," she said, with a smile, laying her hand upon his arm, "that I had done dark deeds myself."

"Well, well," he said, "I suppose I am cranky and out of sorts. It has been a wearying day."

"That it has," cried Mrs. Buchanan, with warm agreement. "I am not a woman for my bed in the daytime; but, for once in a way, I was going to lie down, just to get a rest, for I am clean worn out."

"My poor Mary," he said, with a kind smile. When she felt her weakness, then was the time when he should be strong to support her. "Go and lie down, and nobody shall disturb you, and dismiss all this from your mind, my dear; for, as far as I can see, there is nothing urgent, not a thing for the moment to trouble your head about."

"It is not so easy to dismiss things from your mind," she said, smiling too, "unless I was sure that you were doing it, Claude; for when you are steady and cheery in your spirits, I think there is nothing I cannot put up with, and you may be sure I will not make a fuss, whatever you may think it a duty to do. And it is not for me to preach to you; but mind, there are many things that look like duty, and are not duty at all, but just infatuation, or, maybe, pride."

"You have not much confidence in the clearness of my perceptions, Mary."

"Oh, but I have perfect confidence." She pronounced this word "perfitt," and said it with that emphasis which belongs to the tongue of the North. "But who could ken so well as me that your spirit's a quick spirit, and that pride has its part in you—the pride of aye doing the right thing, and honouring your word, and keeping your independence. I agree with it all, but in reason, in reason. And I would not fly in that auld man's face, and him in his grave, Claude Buchanan, not for all the women's tongues in existence, or their fleeching words!"

He had been standing by the table, from which she had risen too, with an indulgent smile on his face; but at this his countenance changed, and, as Mrs. Buchanan left the room, he sat down again hastily, with his head in his hands.

Was she right? or was his intuition right? That strong sense, that having meant wrong he had done wrong, whether formally or not. Many and many a day had he thought over it, and he had come to a moral conviction that his old friend had intended him to have the money, that he was the last person in the world from whom Anderson would have exacted the last farthing. Putting one thing to another he had come to that conviction. Of all the old man's debtors, there was none so completely his friend. It was inconceivable that all the other people should be freed from the bonds, and only he kept under it. He had quite convinced himself rather that it was for his sake the others had been unloosed, than that it was he alone who was exempt from relief. But it only required Mrs. Mowbray's words to overset this carefully calculated conclusion. His conscience jumped up with renewed force, and, as his wife had divined, his pride was up in arms. That this foolish woman and trifling boy had a right to anything that had been consumed and alienated by him, was intolerable to think of. Mary was right. It was an offence to his pride which he could not endure. His honest impulses might be subdued by reason, but his pride of integrity—no, that was not to be subdued.

The thought became intolerable to him as he pondered seriously, always with his head between his hands. He began once more to pace up and down the room heavily, but hastily—with a heavy foot, but not the deliberate quietness of legitimate thought. Such reflections as these tire a man and hurry him; there is no peace in them. Passing the door of the turret-room, he looked in, and a sudden gust of anger rose. A stool was standing in the middle of the room, a book lying open on the floor. I do not know how they had got there, for Elsie very seldom now came near the place of so many joint readings and enjoyments. The minister went in, and kicked the stool violently away. It should never, at least, stand there again to remind him that he had betrayed himself; and then it returned to his mind that he desired to see Elsie, and discover how much she knew or suspected. Her mother had said no, but he was not always going to yield to her mother in everything. This was certainly his affair. He went down-stairs immediately to find Elsie, walking very softly on the landing not to disturb his wife, who had, indeed, a good right to be tired, and ought to get a good rest now that everybody was gone; which was quite true. He never even suggested to himself that her door was open; that she might hear him, and get up and interrupt him. There was nobody to be found down-stairs. The rooms lay very deserted, nothing yet cleared from the tables, the flowers drooping that had decorated the dishes (which was the fashion in those days); the great white bride-cake, standing with a great gash in it, and roses all round it. There was nothing, really, to be unhappy about in what had taken place to-day. Marion was well, and happily provided for. That was a thing a poor man should always be deeply thankful for, but the sight of "the banquet-hall deserted" gave him a pang as if it had been death, instead of the most living of all moments, that had just passed over his house. He went out to the garden, where he could see that some of the younger guests were still lingering; but it was only Rodie and the boys who were his boon companions that were to be seen. Elsie was not there.

He found her late in the afternoon, when he was returning from a long walk. Walks were things that neither he himself nor his many critics and observers would have thought a proper indulgence for a minister. He ought to be going to see somebody, probably "a sick person," when he indulged in such a relaxation; and there were plenty of outlying invalids who might have afforded him the excuse he wanted, with duty at the end. But he was not capable of duty to-day, and the sick persons remained unvisited. He turned his face towards home, after treading many miles of the roughest country. And it was then, just as he came through the West Port, that he saw Elsie before him, in her white dress, and fortunately alone. The minister's thoughts had softened during his walk. He no longer felt disposed to take her by the shoulders, to ask angrily what she had said to her mother, and why she had played the spy upon him; but something of his former excitement sprang up in him at the sight of her. He quickened his pace a little, and was soon beside her, laying his hand upon her shoulder. Elsie looked up, not frightened at all, glad to be joined by him.

"Oh, father, are you going home?" she said, "and so am I."

"We will walk together, then; which will be a good thing, as I have something to say to you," he said.

Elsie had no possible objection. She looked up at him very pleasantly with her soft brown eyes, and he discovered for the first time that his younger daughter had grown into a bonnie creature, prettier than Marion. To be angry with her was impossible, and how did he know that there was anything to be angry about?

"Elsie," he said, "your mother has been telling me of something you heard me say in my study a long time ago, something that you overheard, which you ought not to have overheard, when you were in the turret, and I did not know you were there."

Elsie grew a little pale at this unexpected address.

"Oh, father," she said, "you knew we were always there."

"Indeed, I knew nothing of the kind. I never supposed for a moment that you would remain to listen to what was said."

"We never did. Oh, never, never!" cried Elsie, now growing as suddenly red.

"It is evident you did on this occasion. You heard me talking to myself, and now you have remembered and reported what I said."

"Oh, father!" cried Elsie, with a hasty look of remonstrance, "how can you say I did that?"

"What was it, then, you said?"

He noticed that she had no need to pause, to ask herself what it was. She answered at once.

"It was about the parable. They said you had preached a sermon on it, and I said I thought your mind had been very full of it; because, when Rodie and me were in the turret, we heard you."

"Oh, there were two of you," said Mr. Buchanan, with a pucker in his forehead.

"There were always, always two of us then," said Elsie, with a sudden cloud on hers; "and what you said was that verse about taking your bill and writing fourscore. I did not quite understand it at the time."

"And do you understand it now?"

"No, father, for it was a wrong thing," said Elsie, sinking her voice. "It was cheating: and to praise a man for doing it, is what I cannot understand."

"Oh, I'll tell you about that; I will show you what it means," he said, with the instinct of the expositor, "but not at this moment," he added, "not just now. Was that all that you thought of, when you heard me say those words to myself?"

Elsie looked up at him, and then she looked all round; a sudden dramatic conflict took place in her. She had thought of that, and yet she had thought of something more than that, but she did not know what the something more was. It had haunted her, but yet she did not know what it was. She looked up and down the street, unconsciously, to find an answer and explanation, but none came. Then she said, faltering a little:—

"Yes, father, but I was not content; for I did not understand: and I am just the same now."

"I will take an opportunity," he said, "of explaining it all to you" and then he added, in a different tone, "it was wrong to be there when I did not know you were there, and wrong to listen to what I said to myself, thinking nobody was near; but what would be most wrong of all, would be to mention to any living creature a thing you had no right to overhear. And if you ever do it again, I will think you are a little traitor, Elsie, and no true child of mine. It would set you better to take care not to do wrong yourself, than to find fault with the parable."

He looked at her with glowing, angry eyes, that shone through the twilight, while Elsie gazed at him with consternation. What did he mean? Then and now, what did he mean?

CHAPTER X

BROTHER AND SISTER

All that evening Elsie tried in vain to secure the attention of Rodie, her brother, her own brother, whom life had already swept away from her, out of her feminine sphere. To be so intimately allied as that in childhood, which is a thing which doubles every joy, at least for the girl, and probably at that early age for the boy also—generally involves the first pang of existence to one at least of these sworn companions. It is, I think, always the girl who suffers, though sometimes no doubt the girl is carried away on the wave of new friendships, especially if she goes to school, and is swept up into the whirl of feminine occupations, before the boy is launched into the circle of contemporaries, who are more absorbing still. But Rodie among "his laddies," had left his sister more completely "out of it" than any boy in possession of all his faculties can ever be. He was always busy with something, always wandering somewhere with the Seatons, or the Beatons, when he was not in the still more entrancing company of Johnny Wemyss. And they never seemed to be tired of each other's company, day or night. There were times when he did not even come in to his meals, but went along with his cronies, in the freedom of his age, without invitation or preparation; even he had been known to sit down to the stoved potatoes in the Wemyss's cottage, though they were not in a class of life to entertain the minister's son; but what did Rodie care? When he brought in Johnny Wemyss in his turn to supper, Mrs. Buchanan could not shame the rules of hospitality, by giving the fisher lad a bad reception, but her notice of him was constrained, if kind, so that none of the young ones were very comfortable. But Alick Seaton and Ralph Beaton were frequent visitors, taken as a matter of course, and would sit at the end of the table, with Rodie between them, making their jokes, and shaking with convulsions of private laughter, which broke out now and then into a subdued roar, making the elders ask "what was the fun now?" John in special, who was "at the College," and sported a red gown about the streets, being gruff in his critical remarks: for he had now arrived at an age when you are bound to behave yourself, and not to "carry on" like the laddies. This being the state of affairs, however, it was very difficult to long hold of Rodie, who often "convoyed" his friends home, and came back at the latest moment practicable, only escaping reprimand by a rush up-stairs to bed. It was not therefore till the Sunday following that Elsie had any opportunity of seeing her brother in private, which even then was not with his will: but there was an interval between breakfast and church, which Rodie, with the best will in the world, could not spend with "his laddies," and which consequently lay undefended, liable to the incursions of his sister. This moment was usually spent in the garden, and often in calculating strokes by which, teeing at a certain spot, he might make sure or almost sure, as sure as the sublime uncertainty of the game permitted, of "holeing" his ball. Naturally, to have taken out a club on Sunday morning, even to the hole in the garden, would have been as good as devoting one's self to the infernal gods: but thought is free. Rodie had a conviction that Elsie would come bouncing along, through the lilac bushes, to spoil his calculations, as she usually did; but this did not lessen the frown with which he perceived that his anticipation had come to pass. "What are you wantin' now?" he said gloomily, marking imaginary distances upon the grass.

"Oh, nothing—if you are so deep engaged," said Elsie, with a spark of natural pride.

"I'm no deep engaged!" said Rodie, indignantly; for he knew father would not smile upon his study, neither would it be appreciated by Alick or Ralph (though they were probably engaged in the same way themselves), that he should be studying the strokes which it was their pride to consider as spontaneous or, indeed, almost accidental. He threw down the cane he had in his hand, and turned away towards the summer-house, whither Elsie followed him.

"I want awfully to speak to you, Rodie—"

"You are always wanting to speak to me," said the ungrateful boy.

"I'm nothing of the kind; and if I were, want would be my master," cried Elsie, "for there's never a moment when you're free of these laddies. You're just in their arms and round their necks every moment of your life."

"I'm neither in their arms nor round their necks," cried Rodie furious, being conscious that he was not weaned from a certain "bairnly" habit of wandering about with an arm round his cronies' shoulders. Elsie, however, not sorry for once in a way to find him at a disadvantage, laughed.

"It's Ralph and Alick, Ralph and Alick, just day and night," she cried, "or else Johnny Wemyss—but you're not so keen about Johnny Wemyss because they say he's not a gentleman; but I think he's the best gentleman of them all."

"It's much you ken!" cried Rodie. His laddies had made him much more pronounced in his Fife sing-song of accent, which the minister, being from the West Country (though it is well known in Fife that the accent of the West Country is just insufferable), objected to strongly.

"I ken just as well as you—and maybe better," said Elsie. Then she remembered that this passage of arms, however satisfactory in itself, was not quite in accordance with the object of the interview which she desired. "I am not wanting to quarrel," she said.

"It was you that began," said Rodie, with some justice. They had by this time reached the summer-house, with its thick background of lilac bushes. The bay lay before them, in all that softened splendour of the Sabbath morning, concerning which so many of us hold the fond tradition that in its lustre and its glory there is something distinct from all other days. The Forfarshire coast lay dim and fair in a little morning haze, on the other side of the blue and tranquil sea, with faint lines of yellow sand, and here and there a white edge of foam, though all was so still, lighting up the distance. The hills, all soft with light and shadow, every knowe and howe visible under the caress of the mild and broad sunshine, the higher rocks upon the near shore half-draped with the intense greenery of the delicate sea-weed, the low reefs, lying dark in leathery clothing of dulse, like the teeth of some great sea monster, half hidden in the ripples of the water, the horizon to the east softening off into a vague radiance of infinity in the great breadth of the German Ocean. I have always thought and often said, that if there is a spot on earth in which one can feel the movement of the great round world through space, though reduced by human limitations to a faint rhythm and swaying, it is there under the illimitable blue of the northern sky, on the shores and links of St. Rule's.

The pair who came thus suddenly in sight of this landscape, were not of any sentimental turn, and were deeply engaged in their own immediate sensations; but the girl paused to cry, "Oh, how bonnie, how bonnie!" while the boy sat down on the rough seat, and dug his heels into the grass, expecting an ordeal of questioning and "bothering," in which the sky and the sea could give him but little help. Elsie was much of the mind of the jilted and forsaken everywhere. She could not keep herself from reproaches, sometimes from taunts. But the sky and sea did help Rodie after all, for they brought her back by the charm of their aspect, an effect more natural at sixteen than at fifteen, and to a girl rather than a boy.

"I am not wanting to quarrel, and it's a shame and a sin on the Sabbath, and such a bonnie day as this. Oh, but it's a bonnie day! there is the wee light-house that is like a glow-worm at night; it is nothing but a white line now, as thin as an end of thread: and muckle Dundee nothing but a little smoke hanging above the Law—"

"I suppose," said Rodie, scornfully, "you have seen them all before?"

"Oh, yes, I have seen them all before: but that is not to say that they are not sometimes bonnier at one time than another. Rodie, you and me that are brother and sister, we never should be anything less than dear friends."

"Friends enough," said Rodie, sulkily. "I am wanting nothing but just that you'll let me be."

"But that," said Elsie, with a sigh, "is just the hardest thing! for I'm wanting you, and you're no wanting me, Rodie! But I'll say no more about that; Marion says it's always so, and that laddies and men for a constancy they like their own kind best."

"I didna think Marion had that much sense," the boy said.

"Oh, dinna anger me over again with your conceit," cried Elsie, "and me in such a good frame of mind, and the bay so bonnie, and something so different in my thoughts."

Rodie settled himself on the rude bench, as though preparing to endure the inevitable: he took his hands out of his pockets and began to drum a faint tune upon the rustic table. The attitude which many a lover, many a husband, many a resigned male victim of the feminine reproaches from which there is no escape, has assumed for ages past, came by nature to this small boy. He dismissed every kind of interest or intelligence from his face. If he had been thirty, he could not have looked more blank, more enduring, more absolutely indifferent. Since he could not get away from her, she must have her say. It would not last for ever, neither could it penetrate beyond the very surface of the ear and of the mind. He assumed his traditional attitude by inheritance from long lines of forefathers. And perhaps it was well that Elsie's attention was not concentrated on him, or it is quite possible that she might have assumed the woman's traditional attitude, which is as well defined as the man's. But she was fortunately at the visionary age, and had entered upon her poetry, as he had entered into the dominion of "his laddies." Her eye strayed over the vast expanse spread out before her, and the awe of the beauty, and the vast calm of God came over her heart.

"Rodie, I want to speak to you of something. It's long past, and it has nothing to do with you or me. Rodie, do you mind yon afternoon, when we were shut up in the turret, and heard papa studying his sermon?"

"What's about that? You've minded me of it many a time: but if I was to be always minding like you, what good would that do?"

"I wanted to ask you, Rodie—sometimes you mind better than me, sometimes not so well. Do you mind what he was saying? I want to be just sure for once, and then never to think upon it again."

"What does it matter what he was saying? It was just about one of the parables." I am afraid the parables were just "a thing in the Bible" to Rodie. He did not identify them much, or think what they meant, or wherein one differed from another. This, I need not say, was not for want of teaching: perhaps it was because of too much teaching, which sometimes has a similar effect. "I mind," he said with a laugh, "we were just that crampit, sitting so long still, that we couldn't move."

"Yes, yes," said Elsie, "but I want to remember quite clear what it was he said."

"It did not matter to us what he said," said Rodie. "Papa is sometimes a foozle, but I am not going to split upon him." This was the slang of those days, still lingering where golf is wont to be played.

"Do you think I would split upon him?" cried Elsie with indignation.

"I don't know, then, what you're carrying on about. Yes, I mind he said something that was very funny; but then he often does that. Fathers are so fond of saying things, that you don't know what they mean, and ministers worse than the rest. There's the first jow of the bell, and it's time to get your bonnet on. I'm not for biding here havering; and then that makes us late."

"You're keen about being in time this morning, Rodie!"

"I'm always keen for being in time. When you come in late, you see on all their faces: 'There's the minister's family just coming in—them that ought to set us an example—and we've been all here for a quarter of an hour.'"

"We are never so late as that," cried Elsie, indignantly.

"You will be to-day, if you do not hurry," he said, jumping up himself and leading the way.

And it was quite true, Elsie could not but allow to herself, that the minister's family were sometimes late. It had originated in the days when there were so many little ones to get ready; and then, as Mrs. Buchanan said, it was a great temptation living so near the church. You felt that in a minute you could be there; and then you put off your time, so that in the end, the bell had stopped ringing, and you had to troop in with a rash, which was evidently a very bad example to the people. And they did look up with that expression on their faces, as if it were they who were the examples! But the fact that Rodie was right, did not make what he said more agreeable. It acted rather the contrary way. She had wished for his sympathy, for his support of her own recollections, perhaps for surer rectification of her impressions; and she found nothing but high disapproval, and the suggestion that she was capable of splitting upon papa. This reproach broke Elsie's heart. Nothing would have induced her to betray her father. She would have shielded him with her own life, she would have defended him had he been in such danger, for instance, as people, and especially ministers, were long ago, in Claverhouse's time—or dug out with her nails a place to hide him in, like Grizel Home. But to fathom the present mystery, and remember exactly what he said, and find out what it meant, had not seemed to her to be anything against him. That it was none of her business, had not occurred to her. And she did not for the moment perceive any better sense in Rodie. She thought he was only perverse, as he so often was now, contrary to whatever she might say, going against her. And she was very sure it was no enthusiasm for punctuality, or for going to church, which made him hasten on before to the house, where his Sunday hat, carefully brushed, was on the hall-table, waiting for him. That was a thing that mother liked to do with her own hands.

The thought of Rodie in such constant opposition and rebellion, overshadowed her through all the early service, and it was not really till the middle of the sermon that a sudden perception caught her mind. Was that what Rodie meant? "He may be a foozle, but I will never split on him." But papa was no foozle. What was he? A good kind man, doing nobody any wrong. There was nothing to say against him, nothing for his children to betray. Even Elsie's half-developed mind was conscious of other circumstances, of children whose father might have something to betray. And, in that dreadful case, what would one do? Oh, decline to hear, decline to know of anything that could be betrayed, shut your ears to every whisper, believe not even himself to his own undoing! This idea leapt into her mind in the middle of the sermon. There was nothing in the sermon to make her think of that. It was not Mr. Buchanan who was preaching, but the other minister, his colleague, who did not preach very good sermons, not like father's! And Elsie's attention wandered in spite of herself. And then, all in a moment, this thought leapt into her mind. In these circumstances, so different from her own, that would have been the only thing for a child to do. Oh, never to listen to a word against him, not even if it came from himself. Elsie's quick mind sprang responsive to this thought. This was far finer, far higher than her desire to remember, to fathom what he had meant. And from whence was it that this thought had come? From Rodie, her brother, the boy whom she had been accusing in her mind, not only of forsaking her, but of becoming more rough, more coarse, less open to fine thoughts. This perception surprised Elsie so, that it was all she could do, not to jump up in her place, to clap her hands, to cry out: "It was Rodie." And she who had never known that Rodie was capable of that! while all St. Rule's, and the world besides, had conceived the opinion of him that he was a foolish callant. Elsie's heart swelled full of triumph in Rodie. "He may be a foozle"—no, no, he was no foozle—well did Rodie know that. But was not Elsie's curiosity a tacit insult to papa, as suggesting that he might have been committing himself, averring something that was wrong? Elsie would have condemned herself to all the pangs of conscience, to all the reproaches against the ungrateful child, who in her heart was believing her father guilty of some unknown criminality, if it had not been that her heart was flooded with sudden delight, the enchantment of a great discovery that Rodie had chosen the better part. There was a true generosity in her, notwithstanding her many foolishnesses. That sudden flash of respect for Rodie, and happy discovery that in this one thing at least he was more faithful than she, consoled her for appearing to herself by comparison in a less favourable light.

And the effect was, that she was silenced even to herself. She put no more questions to Rodie, she tried to put out of her own mind her personal recollections, and every attempt to understand. Did not Rodie say it was not their business, that it did not matter to them what papa said? Elsie could not put away her curiosity out of her heart, but she bowed her head to Rodie's action. After all, what a grand discovery it was that Rodie should be the one to see what was right.

CHAPTER XI

THE GROWING UP OF THE BAIRNS

This was the last incident in the secret history of the Buchanan family for the moment. The sudden, painful, and unexpected crisis which had arisen on Marion's wedding day ceased almost as suddenly as it arose. The Mowbrays, after staying a short time in St. Rule's, departed to more genial climes, and places in which more amusement was to be found—for though even so long ago, St. Rule's had become a sort of watering-place, where people came in the summer, it was not in the least a place of organised pleasure, or where there was any whirl of gaiety; nothing could be more deeply disapproved of than a whirl of gaiety in these days.

There were no hotels and few lodgings of the usual watering-place kind. People who came hired houses and transported themselves and all their families, resuming all their usual habits with the sole difference that the men of the family, instead of going out upon their usual avocations every day, went out to golf instead: which was then a diversion practised only in certain centres of its own, where most of the people could play—a thing entirely changed nowadays, as everybody is aware, when it is to be found everywhere, and practised by everybody, the most of whom do not know how to play.

Mrs. Mowbray did not find the place at all to her mind. Mr. Anderson's house, to which her son had succeeded, was old-fashioned, with furniture of the last century, and large rooms, filled with the silence and calm of years. Instead of being surrounded by "grounds," which were the only genteel setting for a gentleman's house, it had the ruins of the cathedral on one hand, and on the other the High Street. The picturesque was not studied in those days: unless it might be the namby-pamby picturesque, such as flourished in books of beauty, keepsakes, and albums, when what was supposed to be Italian scenery was set forth in steel engravings, and fine ladies at Venetian windows listened to the guitars of their lovers rising from gondolas out of moonlit lakes. To look out on the long, broad, sunny High Street, with, perhaps, the figure of a piper in the distance, against the glow of the sunset, or a wandering group, with an unhappy and melancholy dancing bear—was very vulgar to the middle-class fine lady, a species appropriate to that period, and which now has died away; and, to look out, on the other hand, upon the soaring spring of a broken arch in the ruins, gave Mrs. Mowbray the vapours, or the blues, or whatever else that elegant malady was called. We should say nerves, in these later days, but, at the beginning of the century, nerves had scarcely yet been invented.

For all these reasons, Mrs. Mowbray did not stay long in St. Rule's—she complained loudly of everything she found there, of the house, and the society which had paid her so little attention: and of the climate, and the golf which Frank had yielded to the fascination of, staying out all day, and keeping her in constant anxiety! but, above all, she complained of the income left by old Mr. Anderson, which was so much less than they expected, and which all her efforts could not increase. She said so much about this, as to make the life of good Mr. Morrison, the man of business, a burden to him: and at the same time to throw upon the most respectable inhabitants of St. Rule's a sort of cloud or shadow, or suspicion of indebtedness which disturbed the equanimity of the town. "She thinks we all borrowed money from old Anderson," the gentlemen said with laughter in many a dining-room. But there were a few others, like Mr. Buchanan, who did not like the joke.

"The woman is daft!" they said; but it was remarked by some keen observers that the minister gave but a sickly smile in response. And it may be supposed that this added to the contempt of the ladies for the pretensions of a woman of whom nobody knew who was her father or who her mother, yet who would fain have set herself up as a leader of fashion over them all. In general, when the ladies disapprove of a new-comer, in a limited society like that of St. Rule's, the men are apt to take her part—but, in this case, nobody took her part; and, as there was nothing gay in the place, and no amusement to be had, even in solemn dinner-parties, she very soon found it was not suitable for her health.

"So cold, even in summer," she said, shivering—and everybody was glad when she went away, taking that little mannikin, Frank—who, perhaps, might have been made into something like a man on the links—with her, to the inanity of some fashionable place. To like a fashionable place was then believed to be the very top, or bottom, of natural depravity in St. Rule's.

This had been a very sore ordeal to Mr. Buchanan: his conscience upbraided him day by day—he had even upon him an aching impulse to go and tell somebody to relieve his own mind, and share the responsibility with some one who might have guided him in his sore strait. Though he was a very sound Presbyterian, and evangelical to his finger-tips, the wisdom of the Church of Rome, in the institution of confession, and of a spiritual director to aid the penitent, appeared to him in a far clearer light than he had ever seen it before. To be sure, in all churches, the advantage of telling your difficulties to an adviser conversant with the spiritual life, has always been recognised: but there was no one whom Mr. Buchanan could choose for this office—they were all married men, for one thing, and who could be sure that the difficulty might not ooze out into the mind of a faithful spouse, in no way bound to keep the secrets of her husband's penitents—and whom, at all events, even though her lips were sealed by strictest honour, the penitent had no intention of confiding his secret to. No; the minister felt that his reverend brethren were the last persons to whom he would like to confide his hard case. If there had been some hermit now, some old secluded person, some old man, or even woman, in the sanctuary of years and experience, to whom a man could go, and, by parable or otherwise, lay bare the troubles of his soul. He smiled at himself even while the thought went through his mind: the prose part of his being suggested an old, neglected figure, all overgrown with beard and hair, in the hollow of St. Rule's cave, within the dashing of the spray, the very place for a hermit, a dirty old man, hoarse and callous, incapable of comprehending the troubles of a delicate conscience, though he might know what to say to the reprobate or murderer: no, the hermit would not do, he said to himself, with a smile, in our days.

To be sure, he had one faithful confidant, the wife of his bosom; but, least of all, would Mr. Buchanan have poured out his troubles to his wife. He knew very well what she would say—"You accepted an indulgence that was not meant for you; you took your bill and wrote fourscore when it was hundreds you were owing; Claude, my man, that cannot be—you must just go this moment and tell Mr. Morrison the whole truth; and, if I should sell my flannel petticoat, we'll pay it off, every penny, if only they will give us time." He knew so well what she would say, that he could almost hear the inflections of her voice in saying it. There was no subtlety in her—she would understand none of his hesitations. She would see no second side to the question. "Own debt and crave days," she would say; she was fond of proverbs—and he had heard her quote that before.

There are thus difficulties in the way of consulting the wife of your bosom, especially if she is a practical woman, who could, in a manner, force you to carry out your repentance into restitution, and give you no peace.

During this time of reawakened feeling, Mr. Buchanan had a certain distant sentiment, which he did not know how to explain to himself, against his daughter Elsie. She had a way of looking at him which he did not understand—not the look of disapproval, but of curiosity, half wistful, half pathetic—as if she wanted to know something more of him, to clear up some doubt in her own mind. What cause could the girl have to want more knowledge of her own father? She knew everything about him, all his habits, his way of looking at things—as much as a girl could know about a man so much older and wiser than herself. It half amused him to think that one of his own family should find this mystery in him. He was to himself, always excepting that one thing, as open as the day—and yet the amusement was partial, and mingled with alarm. She knew more of that one thing than any one else; could it be that it was curiosity and anxiety about this that was in the girl's eyes?

Sometimes he thought so, and then condemned himself for entertaining such a thought, reminding himself that vague recollections like that of Elsie do not take such shape in a young mind, and also that it was impossible that one so young, and his affectionate and submissive child, should entertain any such doubts of him.

The curious thing was that, knowing all he did of himself, and that he had done—or intended to do, which was the same—this one thing which was evil, he still felt it impossible that any doubt of him should lodge in his daughter's mind.

In this way the years which are, perhaps, most important in the development of the young, passed over the heads of the Buchanans. From sixteen, Elsie grew to twenty, and became, as Marion had been, her mother's right hand, so that Mrs. Buchanan, more free from domestic cares than formerly, was able to take an amount of repose which, perhaps, was not quite so good for her as her former more active life; for she grew stout, and less willing to move as her necessities lessened. John was now in Edinburgh, having very nearly obtained the full-fledged honours of a W.S. And Rodie, nearly nineteen, was now the only boy at home. Perhaps, as the youngest, and the last to be settled, he was more indulged than the others had been; for he had not yet decided upon his profession, and still had hankerings after the army, notwithstanding that all the defects of that service had been put before him again and again—the all but impossibility of buying him a commission, the certainty that he would have to live on his pay, and many other disadvantageous things.

Rodie was still not old enough to be without hopes that something might turn up to make his desires possible, however little appearance of it there might be. Getting into the army in those days was not like getting into the army now. With us it means, in the first place, examinations, which any boy of moderate faculties and industry can pass: but then it meant so much money out of his father's pocket to buy a commission: to put the matter in words, the present system seems the better way—but it is doubtful whether the father's pocket is much the better, seeing that there is often a great deal of "cramming" to be done before the youth gets through the ordeal of examinations, and sometimes, it must be allowed, boys who are of the most perfect material for soldiers do not get through that narrow gate at all.

But there was no cramming in Roderick Buchanan's day; the word had not been invented, nor the thing. A boy's education was put into him solidly, moderately, in much the same way as his body was built up, by the work of successive years—he was not put into a warm place, and filled with masses of fattening matter, like the poor geese of Strasburg.

Rodie's eyes, therefore, not requiring to be for ever bent on mathematics or other abstruse studies, were left free to search the horizon for signs of anything that might turn up; perhaps a cadetship for India, which was the finest thing that could happen—except in his mother's eyes, who thought one son was enough to have given up to the great Moloch of India: but, had the promise of the cadetship arrived any fine morning, I fear Mrs. Buchanan's scruples would have been made short work with. In the meantime, Rodie was attending classes at the College, and sweeping the skies with the telescope of hope.

Rodie and his sister had come a little nearer with the progress of the years. From the proud moment, when the youth felt the down of a coming moustache upon his upper lip, and began to perceive that he was by no means a bad-looking fellow, and to feel inclinations towards balls and the society of girls, scorned and contemned so long as he was merely a boy, he had drawn a little closer to his sister, who had, as it were, the keys of that other world. It was a little selfish, perhaps; but, in a family, one must not look too closely into motives; and Elsie, faithful to her first affection, was glad enough to get him back again, and to find that he was, by no means, so scornful of mere "lassies," as in the days when his desertion had made her little heart so sore. Perhaps it had something to do with his conversion, that "his laddies," the Alicks and Ralphs of his boyish days, had all taken (at least, as many as remained of them, those who had not yet gone off to the army, or the bar, or the W.S.'s office) to balls also, and now danced as vigorously as they played.

One of the strangest things, however, in all that juvenile band, was the change which had come over Johnny Wemyss, who, the reader will remember, was only a fisherman's son, and lived east the town in a fisher's cottage, and was not supposed the best of company for the minister's son. Johnny, the romantic, silent boy, who had put down his flowers on the pavement that the bride's path might be over them, had taken to learning, as it was easy for the poorest boy, in such a centre of education, to do. As was usual, when a lad of his class showed this turn, which was by no means extraordinary, it was towards the Church that the parents directed their thoughts, and Johnny had taken all his "arts" classes, his "humanities," the curriculum of secular instruction, and was pondering doctrine and exegesis in the theological branch, on his way to be a minister, at the moment in their joint history at which we have now arrived. I am not sure that even then he was quite sure that he himself intended to be a minister; for, being a serious youth by nature, he had much loftier views of that sacred profession than, perhaps, it was possible for a minister's son, trained up in over-much familiarity with it, to have. But his meaning was, as yet, not very clear to himself; he was fonder of "beasts," creatures of the sea-coast, fishes, and those half-inanimate things, which few people, as yet, had begun to think of at all, than of anything else in the world, except.... I will not fill in this blank; perhaps the young reader will guess what was the thing Johnny Wemyss held in still higher devotion than "his beasts;" at all events, if he follows the thread of this story, he will in time find out.

Johnny was no longer kept outside the minister's door. In his red gown, as a student of St. Rule's, he was as good as anyone, and the childish alliance, which had long existed between him and Rodie, was still kept up, although Rodie's fictitious enthusiasm for beasts, which was merely a reflection from his friend's, had altogether failed, and he was as ready as any one to laugh at the pottering in all the sea-pools, and patient observation of all the strange creatures' ways, which kept Wemyss busy all the time he could spare from his lectures and his essays, and the composition of the sermons which a theological student at St. Mary's College was bound, periodically, to produce. Those tastes of his were already recognised as very absurd and rather amusing, but very good things to keep a laddie out of mischief, Mrs. Buchanan said; for it was evident that he could not be "carrying on" in any foolish way, so long as he spent his afternoons out on the caller sands, with his wee spy-glass, examining the creatures, how they were made, and all about them, though it was a strange taste for a young man. Several times he had, indeed, brought a basin full of sea-water—carrying it through the streets, not at all put out by the amusement which surrounded him, the school-boys that followed at his heels, the sharp looks which his acquaintances gave each other, convinced now that Johnny Wemyss had certainly a bee in his bonnet—to the minister's house, that Miss Elsie might see the wonderful white and pink creatures, like sea-flowers, the strange sea-anemones, rooted on bits of rock, and waving their tentacles, or shutting them up in a moment at a rude touch.

Elsie, much disposed to laugh at first, when the strange youth brought her this still stranger trophy, gradually came to admire, and wonder, and take great notice of the sea-anemones, which were wonderfully pretty, though so queer—and which, after all, she began to think, it was quite as clever of Johnny Wemyss to have discovered, as it was of the Alicks and Ralphs to shoot the wild-fowl at the mouth of the Eden. It was even vaguely known that he wrote to some queer scientific fishy societies about them, and received big letters by the post, "costing siller," or sometimes franked in the corner with long, sprawling signatures of peers, or members of parliament. People, however, would not believe that these letters could be about Johnny Wemyss's beasts; they thought that this must simply be a pretence to make himself and his rubbish of importance, and that it must be something else which procured him these correspondents, though what, they could not tell.

Wemyss was the eldest of the little society. He was three-and-twenty, and ought to be already settled in life, everybody thought. He had, for some time, been making his living, which was the first condition of popular respect, and had already been tutor to a number of lads before he had begun his theological course. This age was rather a late age in Scotland for a student of divinity—most of those who had any interest were already sure of a kirk, and even those who had none were exercising their gifts as probationers, and hoping to attract somebody's notice who could bestow one. But Johnny somehow postponed that natural consummation: he went on with his tutor's work, and made no haste over his studies, continuing to attend lectures, when he might have applied to the Presbytery for license. It was believed, and not without truth, that not even for the glory of being a placed minister, could he make up his mind to give up his beloved sea-pools, where he was always to be found of an afternoon, pottering in the sea-water, spoiling his clothes, and smelling of the brine, as if he were still one of the fisher folk among whom he had been born. He no longer dwelt among them, however, for his father and mother were both dead, and he himself lived in a little lodging among those cheap tenements frequented by students near the West, out at the other end of the town. He did not go to the balls, nor care for dancing like the others,—which was a good thing, seeing he was to be a minister,—but, notwithstanding, there were innumerable occasions of meeting each other, common to all the young folk of the friendly, little, old-fashioned town.

CHAPTER XII

THE MOWBRAYS

Mrs. Mowbray and her son had reappeared for a short time on several occasions during these silent years. They had come at the height of the season for "the gowff," which Frank, not having been a St. Rule's boy, nor properly brought up to it, played badly like an Englishman. It must be understood that this was generations before golf had penetrated into England, and when it was, in fact, thought of contemptuously by most of the chance visitors, who considered it a game for old gentlemen, and compared it scornfully with cricket, and called the clubs "sticks," to the hot indignation of the natives. Since then "the gowff" has had its revenges, and it is now the natives who are scornful, and smile grimly over the crowds of the strangers who are so eager, but never can get over the disabilities of a childhood not dedicated to golf. Not only Rodie, and Alick, and Ralph, but even Johnny Wemyss, who, though he rarely played, had yet a natural understanding of the game, laughed at the attempts of Frank, and at his dandyism, and his "high English," and many other signs of the alien, who gave himself airs, or was supposed to do so. But, at the period of which I am now speaking, Frank had become a man, and had learned several lessons in life. He was, indeed, older than even Johnny Wemyss; he was nearly twenty-five, and had been at an English University, and had had a large pair of whiskers, and was no longer a dandy. The boys recognised him as a fellow-man, even as a man in an advanced stage, who knew some things they did not, but no longer gave himself airs. He had even learned that difficult lesson, which many persons went through life without ever learning, that he could not play golf. And when he settled himself with his mother in the old house which belonged to him, in the beginning of summer, and addressed himself seriously to the task of making up his deficiencies, his youthful acquaintances rallied round him, and forgot their criticisms upon his neckties, and his spats, and all the ornamental particulars of "the fashion," which he brought with him; nay, they began secretly to make notes of these points, and shyly copied them, one after another, with a great terror of being laughed at, which would have been completely justified by results, but for the fact that they were all moved by the same temptation. When, however, Rodie Buchanan and Alick Seaton, both stepping out, with much diffidence, on a fresh Sunday morning, in their first spats, red with apprehension, and looking about them suspiciously, with a mingled dread of and desire to be remarked, suddenly ran upon each other, they both paused, looked at each other's feet, and, with unspeakable relief, burst into a roar of laughter, which could be heard both east and west to the very ends of the town; not very proper, many people thought, on the Sunday morning, especially in the case of a minister's son. They were much relieved, however, to find themselves thus freed from the terror of ridicule, and when all the band adopted the new fashion, it was felt that the High Street had little to learn from St. James's, as well as—which was always known—much that it could teach that presumptuous locality. Johnny Wemyss got no spats, he did not pretend to follow the fashion; he smiled a little grimly at Frank, and had a good hearty roar over the young ones, when they all defiled before him on the Sunday walk on the links, shamefaced, but pleased with themselves, and, in the strength of numbers, joining in Johnny's laugh without bitterness. Frank was bon prince, even in respect to Johnny; he went so far as to pretend, if he did not really feel, an interest in the "beasts," and never showed any consciousness of the fact that this member of the community had a different standing-ground from the others, a fact, however, which, I fear, Mrs. Mowbray made very apparent, when she in any way acknowledged the little company of young men.

Mrs. Mowbray herself had not improved in these years. She had a look of care which contracted her forehead, and gave her an air of being older than she was, an effect that often follows the best exertions of those who desire to look younger than they are. She talked a good deal about her expenses, which was a thing not common in those days, and about the difficulty of keeping up a proper position upon a limited income, with all Frank's costly habits, and her establishment in London, and the great burden of keeping up the old house in St. Rule's, which she would like to sell if the trustees would permit her. By Mr. Anderson's will, however, Frank did not come of age, so far as regarded the Scotch property, till he was twenty-five, and thus nothing could be done. She had become a woman of many grievances, which is not perhaps at any time a popular character, complaining of everything, even of Frank; though he was the chief object of her life, and to demonstrate his superiority to everybody else, was the chief subject of her talk, except when her troubles with money and with servants came in, or the grievance of Mr. Anderson's misbehaviour in leaving so much less money than he ought, overwhelmed all other subjects. Mrs. Mowbray took, as was perhaps natural enough, Mr. Buchanan for her chief confidant. She had always, she said, been in the habit of consulting her clergyman; and though there was a difference, she scarcely knew what, between a clergyman and a minister, she still felt that it was a necessity to have a spiritual guide, and to lay forth the burden of her troubles before some one, who would tell her what it was her duty to do in circumstances so complicated and trying. She learned the way, accordingly, to Mr. Buchanan's study, where he received all his parish visitors, the elders who came on the business of the Kirk session, and any one who wished to consult him, whether upon spiritual matters, or upon the affairs of the church, or charitable institutions. The latter were the most frequent, and except a poor widow-woman in search of aid for her family, or, with a certificate for a pension to be signed, or a letter for a hospital, his visitors were almost always rare. It was something of a shock when a lady, rustling in silk, and with all her ribbons flying, was first shown in by the half-alarmed maid, who had previously insisted, to the verge of ill-breeding, that Mrs. Buchanan was in the drawing-room: but as time went on, it became a very common incident, and the minister started nervously every time a knock sounded on his door, in terror lest it should be she.

In ordinary cases, I have no doubt Mr. Buchanan would have made a little quiet fun of his visitor, whose knock and step he had begun to know, as if she had been a visitor expected and desired. But what took all the fun out of it and prevented even a smile, was the fact that he was horribly afraid of her all the time, and never saw her come in without a tremor at his heart. It seemed to him on each repeated visit that she must in the interval since the last have discovered something: though he knew that there was nothing to discover, and that the proofs of his own culpability were all locked up in his own heart, where they lay and corroded, burning the place, and never permitting him to forget what he had done, although he had done nothing. How often had he said to himself that he had done nothing! But it did him no good, and when Mrs. Mowbray came in with her grievances, he felt as if each time she must denounce him, and on the spot demand that he should pay what he owed. Oh, if that only could be, if she had denounced him, and had the power to compel payment, what a relief it would have been! It would have taken the responsibility off his shoulders, it would have brought him out of hell. There would then have been no possibility of reasoning with himself, or asking how it was to be done, or shrinking from the shame of revealing even to his wife, what had been his burden all these years. He had in his imagination put the very words into her mouth, over and over again. He had made her say: "Mr. Buchanan, you were owing old Mr. Anderson three hundred pounds." And to this he had replied: "Yes, Mrs. Mowbray," and the stone had rolled away from his heart. This imaginary conversation had been repeated over and over again in his mind. He never attempted to deny it, never thought now of taking his bill and writing fourscore. Not an excuse did he offer, nor any attempt at denial. "Yes, Mrs. Mowbray:" that was what he heard himself saying: and he almost wished it might come true.

The condition of strange suspense and expectation into which this possibility threw him, is very difficult to describe or understand. His wife perceived something, and perhaps it crossed her mind for a moment that he liked those visits, and that there was reason of offence to herself in them: but she was a sensible woman and soon perceived the folly of such an explanation. But the mere fact that an explanation seemed necessary, disturbed her, and gave her an uncomfortable sensation in respect to him, who never had so far as she knew in all their lives kept any secret from her. What was it? The most likely thing was, that the secret was Mrs. Mowbray's which she had revealed to him, and which was a burden on his mind because of her, not of himself. That woman—for this was the way in which Mrs. Buchanan began to describe the other lady in her heart—was just the sort of woman to have a history, and what if she had burdened the minister's conscience with it to relieve her own? "I wonder," she said to Elsie one day, abruptly, a remark connected with nothing in particular, "what kind of mind the Catholic priests have, that have to hear so many confessions of ill folks' vices and crimes. It must be as if they had done it all themselves, and not daring to say a word."

"What makes you think of that, mother?" said Elsie.

"It is no matter what makes me think of it," said Mrs. Buchanan, a little sharply. "Suppose you were told of something very bad, and had to see the person coming and going, and never knowing when vengeance might overtake them by night or by day."

"Do you mean, mother, that you would like to tell, and that they should be punished?" Elsie said.

"It would not be my part to punish her," said the mother, unconsciously betraying herself. "No, no, that would never be in my mind: but you would always be on the outlook for everything that happened if you knew—and specially if she knew that you knew. Whenever a stranger came near, you would think it was the avenger that was coming, or, at the least, it was something that would expose her, that would be like a clap of thunder. Bless me, Elsie, I cannot tell how they can live and thole it, these Catholic priests."

"They will hear so many things, they will not think much about them," Elsie said, with philosophy.

"No think about them! when perhaps it is life or death to some poor creature, and her maybe coming from time to time looking at you very wistful as if she were saying: 'Do you think they will find me out? Do you think it was such a very bad thing? do you think they'll kill me for it?' I think I would just go and say it was me that did it, and would they give me what was my due and be done with it, for ever and ever. I think if it was me, that is what I would do."

"But it would not be true, mother."

"Oh, lassie," said Mrs. Buchanan, "dinna fash me with your trues and your no trues! I am saying what I would be worked up to, if my conscience was bowed down with another person's sin."

"Would it be worse than if it was your own?" asked Elsie.

"A great deal worse. When you do what's wrong yourself, everything that is in you rises up to excuse it. You say to yourself, Dear me, what are they all making such a work about? it is no so very bad, it was because I could not help it, or it was without meaning any harm, or it was just—something or other; but when it is another person, you see it in all its blackness and without thinking of any excuse. And then when it's your own sin, you can repent and try to make up for it, or to confess it and beg for pardon both to him you have wronged, and to God, but especially to him that is wronged, for that is the hardest. And in any way you just have it in your own hands. But you cannot repent for another person, nor can you make up, nor give her the right feelings; you have just to keep silent, and wonder what will happen next."

"You are meaning something in particular, mother?" Elsie said.

"Oh, hold your tongue with your nonsense, everything that is, is something in particular," Mrs. Buchanan said. She had been listening to a rustle of silk going past the drawing-room door; she paused and listened, her face growing a little pale, putting out her hand to hinder any noise, which would prevent her from hearing. Elsie in turn watched her, staring, listening too, gradually making the strange discovery that her mother's trouble was connected with the coming of Mrs. Mowbray, a discovery which disturbed the girl greatly, though she could not make out to herself how it was.

Mrs. Buchanan could not refrain from a word on the same subject to her husband. When she went to his room after his visitor was gone, she found him with his elbows supported on his table and his face hidden in his hands. He started at her entrance, and raised his head suddenly with a somewhat scared countenance towards her: and then drawing his papers towards him, he began to make believe that he had been writing. "Well, my dear," he said, turning a little towards her, but without raising his eyes.

"Claude, my dear, what ails you that you should start like that—when it's just me, your own wife, coming into the room?"

"Did I start?" he said; "no, I don't think I started: but I did not hear you come in." Then with a pretence at a smile he added, "I have just had a visit from that weariful woman, Mrs. Mowbray. It was an evil day for me when she was shown the way up here."

"But surely, Claude," said Mrs. Buchanan, "it was by your will that she ever came up here."

"Is that all you know, Mary?" he said, with a smile. "Who am I, that I can keep out a woman who is dying to speak about herself, and thinks there is no victim so easy as the minister. It is just part of the day's duty, I suppose."

"But you were never, that I remember, taigled in this way before," Mrs. Buchanan said.

"I was perhaps never brought face to face before with a woman determined to say her say, and that will take no telling. My dear, if you will free me of her, you will do the best day's work for me you have ever done in your life."

"There must be something of the first importance in what she has to say."

"To herself, I have no doubt," said the minister, with a deep sigh. "I am thinking there is no subject in the world that has the interest our own affairs have to ourselves. She is just never done: and all about herself."

"I am not a woman to pry into my neighbour's concerns: but this must be some sore burden on her conscience, Claude, since she has so much to say to you."

"Do you think so?" he cried. "Well, that might perhaps be an explanation: for what I have to do with her small income, and her way of spending her money, and her house, and her servants, I cannot see. There is one thing that gives it a sting to me. I cannot forget that we have something to do with the smallness of her income," Mr. Buchanan said.

"We to do with smallness of her income! I will always maintain," said Mrs. Buchanan, "that the money was the old man's, and that he had the first right to give it where he pleased; but, dear Claude, man, you that should ken—what could that poor three hundred give her? Fifteen pound per annum; and what is fifteen pound per annum?—not enough to pay that English maid with all her airs and graces. If it had been as many thousands, there might have been some justice it."

"That is perhaps an idea," said the harassed minister, "if we were to offer her the interest, Mary? My dear, what would you say to that? It would be worse than ever to gather together that money and pay it back; but fifteen pounds a year, that might be a possible thing; you might put your shoulder to the wheel, and pay her that."

"Claude," said Mrs. Buchanan, "are you sure that is all the woman is wanting? I cannot think it can be that. It is just something that is on her conscience, and she wants to put it off on you."

"My dear," said the minister, "you're a very clever woman, but you are wrong there. I have heard nothing about her conscience, it is her wrongs that she tells to me." The conversation had eased his mind a little, and his wife's steady confidence in his complete innocence in the matter, and the perfect right of old Anderson to do what he liked with his own money, was always, for the moment at least, refreshing to his soul: though he soon fell back on the reflection that the only fact of any real importance in the matter was the one she never knew.

Mrs. Buchanan was a little disconcerted by the failure of her prevision, but she would not recede. "If she has not done it yet, she will do it sometime. Mind what I am saying to you, Claude: there is something on her conscience, and she wants to put it off on you."

"Nonsense, Mary," he said. "What should be on the woman's conscience? and why should she try to put it upon mine? Dear me, my conscience would be far easier bearing the weight of her ill-doing than the weight of my own. We must get this beam out of our own eye if we can, and then the mote in our neighbour's—if there is a mote—will be easy, oh, very easy, to put up with. It is my own burden that troubles me."

"Toot," said Mrs. Buchanan, "you are just very exaggerated. It was most natural Mr. Anderson should do as he did, knowing all the circumstances—and you, what else should you do, to go against him? But you will just see," she added, confidently, "that I will prove a true prophet after all. If it has not been done, it will be done, and you will get her sin to bear as well as your own."

CHAPTER XIII

PLAINTIFF OR PENITENT?

Meanwhile, the reader shall judge by the turn of one of these conversations whether Mrs. Buchanan was, or was not, justified in her prevision. Mrs. Mowbray came tripping up the long stair, which was of stone, and did not creak under foot, though she was betrayed by the rustle of her silk dress, which was in those days a constant accompaniment of a woman's movements. When she approached nearer, there were other little sounds that betrayed her,—a little jingle of bracelets and chains, and the bugles of her mantle. She was naturally dressed in what was the height of the fashion then, though we should think it ridiculous now, as we always think the fashions that are past. When Mr. Buchanan heard that little jingle and rattle, his heart failed him. He put down his pen or his book, and the healthful colour in his cheek failed. A look of terror and trouble came into his face.

"Here is that woman again," he said to himself. Mrs. Mowbray, on her side, was very far from thinking herself that woman; she rather thought the minister looked forward with pleasure to her visits, that she brought a sort of atmosphere of sunshine and the great world into that sombre study of his, and that the commonplace of his life was lighted up by her comings and goings. There are a great many people in the world who deceive themselves in this way, and it would have been a shock to Mrs. Mowbray if she had seen the appalled look of the minister's face when his ear caught the sound of her coming, and he looked up to listen the better, with a gesture of impatience, almost despair, saying to himself, "that woman again."

She came in, however, all smiles, lightly tapping at the door, with a little distinctive knock, which was like nobody else's, or so at least she thought. She liked to believe that she did everything in a distinctive way, so that her touch and her knock and all her movements should be at once realised as hers. She had been a pretty woman, and might still indeed have been so, had she not been so anxious to preserve her charms that she had undermined them for a long time, year by year. She had worn out her complexion by her efforts to retain it and make it brighter, and frizzed and tortured her hair till she had succeeded in making it of no particular colour at all. The effort and wish to be pretty were so strong in her, and so visible, that it made her remaining prettiness almost ridiculous, and people laughed at her as an old woman struggling to look young when she was not really old at all. Poor Mrs. Mowbray! looking at her from one point of view, her appearance was pathetic, for it was as much as to say that she felt herself to have no recommendation at all but her good looks, and therefore would fight for them to the death—which is, if you think of it, a kind of humility, though it gets no credit for being so. She came in with a simper and jingle of all the chains and adornments, as if she felt herself the most welcome of visitors, and holding out her hand, said:

"Here I am again, Mr. Buchanan. I am sure you must be getting quite tired of me." She expected him to contradict her, but the minister did not do so. He said:

"How do you do, Mrs. Mowbray?" rising from his chair, but the muscles of his face did not relax, and he still held his pen in his hand.

"I am so afraid you are busy, but I really will not detain you above a few minutes. It is such a comfort amid all the troubles of my life to come to this home of peace, and tell you everything. You don't know what a consolation it is only to see you, Mr. Buchanan, sitting there so calm, and so much above the world. It is a consolation and a reproach. One thinks, Oh, how little one's small troubles are in the light that comes from heaven!"

"I am afraid you are giving me credit for much more tranquillity than I can claim," said the minister. "I am not without my cares, any more than other men."

"Ah, but what are those cares?" cried the lady. "I know; the care of doing what you can for everybody else, visiting the poor and widows in their affliction, and keeping yourself unspotted from the world. Oh, how different, how different from the things that overwhelm us!"

What could the poor minister do? It seemed the most dreadful satire to him to be so spoken to, conscious as he was of the everlasting gnawing at his heart of what he had done, or at least left undone. But if he had been ever so anxious to confess his sins, he could not have done it to her; and accordingly he had to smile as best he could, and say that he hoped he might preserve her good opinion, though he had done so very little to deserve it. Perhaps if he had been less conscious of his own demerits, he would have perceived, as his wife had done, that there was a line in Mrs. Mowbray's forehead which all her little arts could not conceal, and which meant more than anything she had yet told him. Mrs. Buchanan had divined this, but not the minister, who was too much occupied with his own purgatory to be aware that amid all her rustlings and jinglings, and old-fashioned coquetries, there was here by his side another soul in pain.

"You cannot imagine," said Mrs. Mowbray, spreading out her hands, "what it is to me to think of my poor Frank deceived in his hopes, and instead of coming into a fortune, having next to no money when he comes of age. Oh, that coming of age, I am so frightened, so frightened for it! It is bad enough now to deny him so many things he wants."

"Do you deny him many things he wants?" said the minister. The question was put half innocently, half satirically, for Frank indeed seemed a spoilt child, having every possible indulgence, to the sturdy sons of St. Rule's.

Mrs. Mowbray laughed, and made a movement as of tapping the minister's arm with a fan.

"Oh, how unkind of you," she said, "to be so hard on a mother's weakness! I have not denied him much up to this time. How could I, Mr. Buchanan, my only child? And he has such innocent tastes. He never wants anything extravagant. Look at him now. He has no horse, he is quite happy with his golf, and spends nothing at all. Perhaps his tailor's bill is large, but a woman can't interfere with that, and it is such a nice thing that a boy should like to be well dressed. I like him to take a little trouble about his dress. I don't believe he ever touches a card, and betting over his game on the links is nothing, he tells me: you win one day and lose the next, and so you come out quite square at the end. Oh, it all goes on smooth enough now. But when he comes of age! It was bad enough last time when he came of age, for his English money and everything was gone over. Do you think it just, Mr. Buchanan, that a mere man of business, a lawyer, an indifferent person that knows nothing about the family, should go over all your expenses, and tell you you shouldn't have done this, and you shouldn't have done that, when he has really nothing to do with it, and the money is all your own?"

"I am afraid," said Mr. Buchanan, "that the business man is a necessity, and perhaps is better able to say what you ought to spend than you are yourself."

"Oh, how can you say so? when perhaps he is not even a gentleman, and does not understand anything about what one wants when one is accustomed to good society. This man Morrison, for instance—"

"Morrison," said the minister, "is a gentleman both by blood and breeding, although he is a simple man in his manners: his family—"

"Oh, I know what you mean," said Mrs. Mowbray, "a small Scotch squire, and they think as much of their family as if they were dukes. I know he is Morrison of somewhere or other, but that does not teach a man what's due to a lady, or what a young man wants who is entitled to expect his season in town, and all his little diversions. Morrison, Mr. Buchanan, would have put Frank to a trade. He would, it is quite true. I don't wonder you are surprised. My Frank, with so much money on both sides! He spoke to me of an office in Edinburgh. I assure you he did—for my boy!"

"I am not in the least surprised," said the minister; "we are all thankful to put our sons into offices in Edinburgh, and get them something to do."

"I am sure you won't think I mean anything disagreeable," said Mrs. Mowbray, "but your sons, Mr. Buchanan, pardon me—you have all so many of them. And I have only one, and money, as I say, on both sides. I had quite a nice fortune myself. I never for a moment will consent that my Frank should go into an office. It would ruin his health, and then he is much too old for anything of that sort. The folly of postponing his majority till he was twenty-five! And oh, Mr. Buchanan," she cried, clasping her hands, "the worst of it all is, that he will find so little, so very little when he does come into his property at last."

There was a look almost of anguish in the poor lady's face, her eyes seemed full of tears, her forehead was cut across by that deep line of trouble which Mrs. Buchanan had divined. She looked at the minister in a sort of agony, as if asking, "May I tell him? Dare I tell him?" But of this the minister saw nothing. He did not look at her face with any interest. He was employed in resisting her supposed efforts to penetrate his secret, and this concealed from him, under impenetrable veils, any secret that she might have of her own. It was not that he was dull or slow to understand in general cases, but in this he was blinded by his own profound preoccupation, and by a certain dislike to the woman who thus disturbed and assailed his peace. He could not feel any sympathy with her; her little airs and graces, her efforts to please, poor soul, which were intended only to make her agreeable, produced in him exactly the opposite sensation, which often happens, alas, in our human perversity. Neither of them indeed understood the other, because each was occupied with himself.

"I don't think," said Mr. Buchanan, roused to resistance, "that you will find things nearly so bad as you seem to expect. I am sure the estate has been very carefully administered while in my friend Morrison's hands. You could not have a more honourable or a more careful steward. He could have no interest but to do the best he could for you, and I am sure he would do it. And property has not fallen in value in Fife so far as I know. I think, if you will permit me to say so, that you are alarming yourself without cause."

All this time, Mrs. Mowbray had been looking at him through the water in her eyes, her face contracted, her lips a little apart, her forehead drawn together. He glanced at her from time to time while he was speaking, but he had the air of a man who would very gladly be done with the business altogether, and had no ear for her complaints. The poor lady drew from the depths of her bosom a long sigh, and then her face changed from the momentary reality into which some strong feeling had forced it. It was a more artificial smile than ever which she forced upon her thin lips, in which there was a quiver of pain and doubt.

"Ah, Mr. Buchanan, you always stand up for your own side. Why is it I cannot get you to take any interest in mine?"

"My dear lady," said the minister with some impatience, "there are no sides in the matter. It is simple truth and justice to Morrison."

Here she suddenly put her hand on his arm. "And how about the defaulters?" she said.

"The defaulters!" She was as ignorant wherein the sting lay to him as he was of the gnawing of the serpent's tooth in her. It was now his under lip that fell, his cheek that grew pale. "I don't know what you mean by defaulters," he said, almost roughly, feeling as if she had taken advantage when he was off his guard and stabbed him with a sharp knife.

"Oh, dear Mr. Buchanan, the men who borrowed money, and never paid it! I am sure you could tell me about them if you would. The men who cheated my poor Frank's old uncle into giving them loans which they never meant to pay."

"Mrs. Mowbray," he said, slowly, "I remember that you have spoken to me on this subject before."

"Yes, yes, I have spoken on this subject before. Isn't it natural I should? You as good as acknowledged it, Mr. Buchanan. You acknowledged, I remember, that you knew one of them: of course you know all of them! Didn't he tell you everything? You were his minister and his spiritual guide. He did nothing without you."

"Mr. Anderson never asked any advice from me as to his secular business. Why should he? He understood it much better than I did. His spiritual guide in the sense in which you use the words, I never was, and never could have been."

"Oh!" cried the lady, waving her hands about in excitement, "what does it matter about words? If you only knew how important a little more money would be to us, Mr. Buchanan! It might make all the difference, it might save me from—from—oh, indeed, I do not quite know what I am saying, but I want you to understand. It is not only for the money's sake. I know, I am certain that you could help me; only tell me who these men are, and I will not trouble you any more."

"I do not know what you mean," he said, "when you talk of those men."

"Mr. Buchanan, you said you knew one."

"Perhaps I said I knew one; that was only one, it was not many. And if I did know, and knew that they had been forgiven, do you think it would be right for me to bring those poor men into trouble, and defeat the intentions of my friend—for what, for what, Mrs. Mowbray? I don't know what you suppose my inducement would be."

She bent towards him till she almost seemed to be on her knees, and clasping her hands, said:

"For me, Mr. Buchanan, for me!"

There was no doubt that it was genuine feeling that was in her face, and in the gaze of the eager eyes looking out from their puckered lids; but the poor woman's idea of pleasing, of overcoming by her personal charms was so strong in her, that underneath those puckered and beseeching eyes which were so tragically real, there was a smile of ingratiating blandishment on her mouth, which was like the stage smile of a ballet dancer, set and fictitious, appealing to heaven knows what of the man's lower nature. She meant no harm, nor did she think any harm, but those were the days when feminine influence was supposed to lie in blandishment, in flattery, and all the arts of persuasion. Do this for me because I am so pretty, so helpless, so dependent upon your help, but chiefly because I am so pretty, and so anxious that you should think me pretty, and be vanquished by my beauty! This was the sentiment on part of Mrs. Mowbray's face, while the other was full of eager pain and trouble, almost desperation. That smile and those blandishments might perhaps have moved the man had she been indeed beautiful and young, as she almost thought she was while making that appeal. But Mr. Buchanan's eyes were calm, and they turned from the ballet-dancer's smile and ingratiating looks with something more like disgust than yielding. Alas! these feminine arts which were then supposed to be quite independent of common sense, or reason or justice, and to triumph over them all, required real beauty at least and the charms of youth! To attempt to exercise them when the natural spell had failed, was almost an insult to a man's intelligence. The minister was not conscious of this feeling, but it made him angry in spite of himself.

"For you, Mrs. Mowbray?" he said, "think what you are saying. You would like me to betray my old friend, and balk his intentions, and to disturb a number of families and snatch from them what they have been accustomed to consider as a free gift, and probably in no circumstances expected to refund— for you. For you, for what? that your son, having a great deal already, should have a little more," (here she attempted to interrupt him to say, "No, no, not having had a great deal, never having had much!" which his stronger voice bore down and penetrated through), "that you should add some luxuries to your wealthy estate. No, Mrs. Mowbray, no. I am astonished that you should ask it of me. If I could do it, I should despise myself."

What high ground he took! and he felt himself justified in taking it. He was buoyed up over all personal motives of his own by a lofty realisation of the general question. There were many others concerned as well as he. What right would he have to betray the fact that poor Horsburgh, for instance, had received a loan from Mr. Anderson to establish him in business? If Mr. Anderson's heirs proceeded against Horsburgh, who was still painfully keeping his head above water, the result would be ruin—all to put another hundred pounds, perhaps, in Frank Mowbray's pocket, an idle lad who already had plenty, and never did a hand's turn. And she thought to come over him and make him do that by the glamour of a pair of middle-aged eyes, and the flatteries of an antiquated smile? The man was angry with the woman's folly and revolted by her pretensions. No, he would not betray poor Horsburgh. Was not this the meaning after all, and a nobler meaning than he had ever thought of, of the proceedings of the unjust steward? Take thy bill, and sit down quickly, and write fourscore. Thy bill; not mine, did not that make all the difference in the world? Not for me, but for poor Horsburgh. The woman was mad to think that for her, a woman who wanted nothing, he would sacrifice a struggling family: not to say that, even now, poor Horsburgh was, as it were, looking ruin in the face.

CHAPTER XIV

ANOTHER AGENT

Mrs. Mowbray had put off all sign of agitation when in the evening she sat down with her son Frank, at the hour of seven, which, in those days, was a pretentiously late, even dissipated hour for dinner, at all events in St. Rule's, where most people dined early or at least at varying hours in the afternoon, such as four o'clock, five o'clock, the very height of discomfort, but supposed by some reasoning I am unable to account for, to be virtuous and respectable hours, while anything later than six was extravagant and almost wicked. Mrs. Mowbray dined at seven by way of waving a flag of superiority over the benighted town. It was reported commonly, that in London people were beginning to dine at eight, an hour when honest folk were thinking of getting ready for bed, or, at all events, were taking their supper as honest folk ought. I am not able to explain why one hour should be considered more innocent than another; but so it was. Frank Mowbray, half-influenced by his mother, and half-drawn away into different modes of thinking by the young society of St. Rule's, which thought every way ridiculous that was not its own way, was half-proud of the fashionable peculiarities of his mother's economy, and half-abashed to find himself held to habits which were so different to those of the others. As the nights began to lengthen he was impatient of being kept in at what the others thought the most agreeable time of the evening, when all the young fellows were clustering about the club, making up their matches for the next day. But he had not yet reached the moment of revolt.

Mrs. Mowbray had put off, so far as she could, all appearance of agitation. She was very nicely dressed according to the fashion of the times. Her ringlets were flowing, her smiles freely dispensed, though only her son was present to admire her. But she thought it was part of her duty to make herself as agreeable to Frank as to any other member of society. She listened quite patiently to all his talk about his young men. She was indeed interested in this talk and pleased to hear about everybody, who and what they were, and even whether they were first-class or second-class players: and their special deeds of prowess at the heathery hole or any other of the long list which Frank had at his finger-ends. She liked to hear all the details with which Frank could furnish her of their families as well as their golf. But that was less interesting to him, and helped her but little in her researches.

"You see a great deal of the Buchanans, don't you, Frank?" she said, in the course of the conversation, not meaning much more by the question than by many others.

But here Mrs. Mowbray instantly perceived a difference in her son's manner, which betrayed something quite new and unexpected.

Frank made a pause, which, though only for a moment, was noted by her fine and vigilant spirit of observation, looked at her furtively, coloured, and said: "Oh, the Buchanans! Yes, I see them now and then," in a tone quite different from that in which he had been discoursing about the Seatons and the Beatons, and all the rest of the tribe.

"You see them now and then? Yes, that is all I expected: they are not precisely of our monde," his mother said.

"Why not of our monde?" cried Frank, "they are the best people in St. Rule's, and that is their monde; and it is our monde, I suppose, as long as we stay here."

"Yes, dear boy," said his mother, "but, fortunately, you know we don't belong to it, and it is only a question of how long we stay here."

Upon this, Frank cleared his throat, and collecting all his courage, launched forth a suggestion which he had long desired, but, up to this moment, had never had the bravery to make.

"Mother," he said, "this is a very nice house, don't you think? The rooms are large, and I know you like large rooms. Just think what a wretched little place the house in Chapel Street was in comparison. And we were nobody there, and you always said you were not appreciated."

"That is true enough; when you have no title, and are not rich, it is hard, very hard, to get a footing in society," Mrs. Mowbray said, with a sigh.

"But we are somebody here," said Frank, "you are looked up to as the glass of fashion and the mould of form, that sort of thing, don't you know? All the ladies say to me, 'What does Mrs. Mowbray do?' or 'What is your mother going to do?' They see your superiority and make you their example."

"Frank," said his mother, pleased but a little doubtful, "you are flattering me. I don't know why you should flatter me."

"I am not flattering you a bit, mother. It is quite true. Now, what I mean to say is, why should we go back again to Chapel Street, where there is not a single thing for a man to do, and the women are so disagreeable to you, because you have no title—when we can be the first people in the place, and so much thought of here."

"Here!" said Mrs. Mowbray, with a little shriek of dismay.

"You know, mother, you always say how disappointing it is to go through the world, and never know anybody who takes you at your true value," said Frank. "People are always—I have heard you say it a hundred times—inquiring who we are, and what relation we are to Lord Mowbray, and all that: as if we were not fit to be visited because we are not related to Lord Mowbray."

"It is quite true," said Mrs. Mowbray with indignation, "but I never knew before that you had taken any notice of it, Frank."

"Oh, I have taken great notice of it," he said. "I never said anything, for what was the use when I couldn't do anything; but you don't suppose it didn't hurt me very much to see that you were not receiving proper attention, mother? Of course I took notice of it! but words never do any good."

"What a dear boy you are, Frank!" said his mother, kissing the tips of her fingers to him. It was not very often that she was flattered in this way. The flatter was usually done by herself. She was so well acquainted with it, that she was not so easily convinced of its sincerity, as others might have been; but still, sincere or not, there was no doubt that these were very nice things for Frank to say.

"But here it is your notice that everybody would seek, mother," he continued. "It is you who would set the example, and everybody would follow. Nobody thinks of asking whether we are related to Lord Mowbray, here. We are just what we are, and the objects of respect. We are the best people in the place," Frank said.

"That is what you have just said of the Buchanans, Frank—and I told you before—they are not of our monde."

"What is our monde?" cried the young man. "It is not Lord Mowbray's monde, nor the monde of the Rashleighs and those sort of people, mother, whom we used to run after. I am sure they said just what you are doing about us. They used to twist round their necks and thrust out their heads, and screw up their noses, don't you remember?"

"Oh, and bow with their eyelids and smile with the edge of their lips," cried Mrs. Mowbray. "I remember! How could I help remembering people not fit to tie our shoes, but with an odious little baronetcy in the family!"

"But nobody could do that here," said Frank, with a feeling that he had conducted his argument very cleverly, and had carried her with him all along the line.

Mrs. Mowbray burst into a laugh. "Is it all for my benefit, to see me respected, that you would like to shut me up in this little hole for life," she said.

Poor Frank was very much startled by this issue of his argument. He looked up at her half-piteous, half-angry.

"I don't call it a little hole," he said.

"But I do," said his mother, "a dreadful little hole! where you have to make yourself agreeable to all sorts of people whom you would never speak to, nor look at in society! Why, Frank, there is nobody here in society. Not one that you would like to walk along Bond Street with. Think of going along Rotten Row with any one of those girls on your arm."

"I should be very proud," cried Frank, very red, "to go anywhere with one of them on my arm."

"My poor dear boy," cried Mrs. Mowbray, "I knew that was what you meant all the time. I always forget that you have come to the age for that sort of thing. Only think how you would look if you were to meet Lady Marion, and she were to begin to ask her questions. 'Who was the young lady, and who were her friends in town?' 'Oh, she doesn't know anybody in town.' 'Where did she come from?' 'Oh, not a place you ever heard of in your life, a little town in Scotland.' 'Yes, Lord Laidlaw lives near, of course she knows the Laidlaws?' 'Oh, no, she never heard of them; oh, no, she knows nobody. She is only a minister's daughter, and except that she is prettyish—'"

Mrs. Mowbray had the art of a mimic; and she had made her sketch of the Lady Marion who asked questions, very amusing to her son, who had been in his little way cross-examined by Lady Marion many times: but when she described the young lady as prettyish, the young man bounded from his chair.

"Take care, mother! no one, not even you, shall speak so of Elsie. I won't have it," he cried.

"You would be obliged to have it, dear, if you had her," his mother said, composedly. "And as for speaking so, I have no wish to speak so. I think she's a very nice little girl, for St. Rule's; you could never take her into society, but for St. Rule's she would do very well."

"Then, mother," said Frank, "you understand me, for you make me speak very plain. We've got a good house here, and we're rich enough to be about the first people in the place; and I wish to settle in St. Rule's."

"My poor boy," cried Mrs. Mowbray, "rich, oh, my poor boy!"

And here, without any warning, she suddenly burst into a torrent of tears. This was, perhaps, a proceeding to which her son was not wholly unaccustomed; for he maintained, to a certain extent, his equanimity. He walked up and down the room, striking the backs of the chairs with a paper-knife he held in his hand for some seconds. And then he came back to her, and asked, with a little impatience:

"Why am I a poor boy? and why is it so wonderful that we should be rich? I am—I suppose we are rich—more or less—able at all events to take our place among the best people in St. Rule's." He laughed, and went on striking his little ivory toy against the chairs sharply. "It isn't so great a brag, after all," he said, laughing, "among the best people in St. Rule's."

"Oh," cried Mrs. Mowbray, "how am I to tell him? Oh, how am I to tell him? Frank, we have always said, when we came into the Scotch money, all would be well. I thought it was such a fine sum, that we should throw off all our debts, and be really rich as you say. Oh, that is only a dream, Frank, like so many things we have trusted in! There will be scarcely any money. You may well start and stare at me. Oh, Frank, I that thought as soon as it came, all our difficulties would be over, and we should be quite right."

"What difficulties?" said Frank, "what difficulties, mother? I always thought we were well off."

"This has been the aim of my life," said Mrs. Mowbray, "that you should never find out any difficulties, that everything should go as if it were on velvet; and then when the Scotch money came, that all would be right. I did not think then that all Mr. Anderson's fine fortune had been frittered away—I did not tell you that, Frank—by defaulters."

She liked the word: there was something vague and large in it: it meant something more than debtors: "defaulters," she said again, and shook her head.

"What in the world do you mean, mother? Who are the defaulters, and what have they to do with me?"

"Mr. Anderson's money has been frittered away," she said. "He lent it to everybody; and instead of preserving their notes, or their bills, or whatever it was, he threw them into the fire, I suppose. And nobody paid. I believe half St. Rule's is built on old Mr. Anderson's money, the money that ought to be yours. But he never kept the papers, and none of them have been so honourable as to pay."

Frank stared at his mother with a bewildered face. He had never managed his own affairs. For a year or two past, he had begun to think that this was foolish, and that he might perhaps, if he tried, learn to understand business as well as his mother; but he had never had the strength of mind to assert himself. He had received an ample allowance from her hands, and he had tacitly agreed that until the Scotch property became his, everything should go on as before. But it had always been understood, that when he attained his Scotch majority, there was to be a change. His Scotch majority was to be a great day. All the hoards of his old uncle were then to come into his hands. Retarded manhood, independence, and wealth were all to be his. And now what was this he heard, that these hoards of money were frittered away? He could not at once understand or grasp what it meant. He stared at his mother with bewildered eyes.

"I wish you would tell me what you mean," he said. "What has happened? Is it something you have found out? Is there anything that can be done? I cannot believe that all the property is lost."

"There is one thing that can be done, Frank. If we can find out the defaulters, we can still make them pay up. But we must make haste, for in another year the Statute of Limitations will come in, and they will be beyond our reach."

"What is the Statute of Limitations? and how can we make them pay up? And what does it mean altogether?" said the disturbed young man. "Mother, you should not have let me go on like this, knowing nothing about it. I ought to have known. And how am I to find them out and make them pay up? You that have always managed everything, you ought to have done it."

"My son, whom I have always spared and saved from all trouble," she said, throwing up her hands, "he tells me I should have done that! Oh, Frank, it isn't very pretty of you to upbraid me, when I have always done everything for the best."

"Mother, I don't want to upbraid you. I daresay you have done everything that was right," he said, "but this is rather a dreadful thing to find out all at once. And there must be something that can be done—tell me whether there isn't something I could do."

"Oh, yes," she said, with a sudden laugh, "there is one thing to be done, and that is to find out who are the defaulters. There is one man I am sure that knows, and you are, I suppose, in favour with the family, Frank, considering your intentions which you have just been telling me of. The one man is Dr. Buchanan. If you are going, as you say, to be his son-in-law, perhaps he will tell you. I am sure he is one of them himself."

"Mother, if all this is to set me against—"

"It is not to set you against any one," said Mrs. Mowbray. "I like Dr. Buchanan myself. I think he is one of them. If you can find out from him who they are, perhaps we may yet be saved."

"He is one of them! This is nonsense, nonsense! You don't know what you are saying, mother."

"I wish everybody were as clear and composed as I am. I believe he is one of them. But make use of your interest with the boy and the girl, and get him to tell you who they are. And then perhaps we may be saved."

The young man went round and round the room, striking the backs of the chairs with his paper-knife, solemnly, as if he expected to find some hollow place and make a discovery so.

"I don't understand it. I don't know what you mean. I can't believe that this is possible," he said; and he gave a louder crack to an old armchair, and stood before it, pondering, as if the secret must be out at last.

CHAPTER XV

FRANK'S OPERATIONS

Frank Mowbray was one of the young men, fitly described by the unenthusiastic, but just populace, as "no an ill callant." He was not very wise, not very clever, but he was also not "ill," in any sense of the word; a good-hearted, good-tempered, easy-going young man, willing to save himself trouble, by letting others, and especially his mother, manage his affairs for him, but no grumbler, accepting the consequences of that situation with great equanimity, allowing himself to be more or less governed, and obeying all the restrictions of his mother's house, as if he had been the most dependent of sons. This may seem to indicate a want of spirit on his part; but it was rather a spirit of justice and fair dealing, as well as the result of a gentle and contented temperament.

Frank had no desire whatever to revolt. His mother's sway had been very light upon him: had he been what he was not, inclined towards dissipation, so long as it had been carried on among what she called "the right sort of people," I am inclined to believe that Mrs. Mowbray would rather have liked it than otherwise; but that would have been perhaps because she did not know what it was, and liked to see her son's name among the names of the great, on whatsoever excuse. She would rather have had Frank conspicuous by the side of a young duke, than known to the world in the most virtuous circumstances, as the companion of lesser men; but Frank did not accept, nor was he even aware of, this tacit license to do evil, so long as it was fashionably done. He had not the slightest leaning towards dissipation—he was one of those young men whom perhaps we undervalue in theory, though in action they are the backbone of the race, who seem to be inaccessible to the ordinary temptations. Had he been offered the choice of Hercules, he would certainly, by inclination, have offered his arm to Madam Virtue, and waved away dishevelled Pleasure, however pretty, with the most unfeigned indifference: he did not care for that sort of thing, he would have said: and this insensibility was better than coat armour to him. It is common to believe that a boy, brought up as he had been, at the apron-strings of his mother, is open to every touch of temptation, and apt to find the fascination of a disorderly life irresistible; but, howsoever Frank had been brought up, the issue would have been the same—he was "no an ill callant"—he was not led away by fancies, either for good or evil, quite disposed to be kind, but never lavish in generosity; not prodigal in anything, able to balance the pros and the cons, and to accept the disadvantages with the advantages. Perhaps it was not a character to excite any great enthusiasm, but it was one that was very easy to live with, and could not have inspired any serious anxiety in the most fanciful and susceptible of minds.

Frank went out that evening to meet some of his daily companions with a great deal in his mind, but not any panic or dismay. He would not believe that the "Scotch property" could have been all frittered away by the loans which his old uncle had made, however imprudent or foolish the old man might have been in that way. He had, indeed, so just and calm a mind, that he did not harshly condemn Mr. Anderson for making these loans as his mother did; he was even willing to allow that a man had a right to do what he liked with his own, even if he had a grand-nephew to provide for, especially one who was not entirely dependent upon him, but had already a comfortable provision of his own. As he went out into the evening air, and strolled towards the club of which he was a member, and where, as I have said, the young men, who were not yet members, had a way of meeting outside, and under the verandah, arranging their matches for next day, and talking out their gossip like their elders within—he turned over the matter in his mind, and reconciled himself to it. It is foolish, he said to himself, to lend your money without interest, and without a proper certainty of one day getting it back—but still the old gentleman had no doubt his reasons for doing this, and might have had his equivalent or even been paid back without anybody knowing, as nobody knew who the borrowers were: and at the worst, if the money was lost, it was lost, and there was an end of it, and no need to upbraid poor old uncle, who probably thought himself quite entitled to do what he liked with his own. He did not believe that the estate could have been seriously impoverished in any such manner; but he thought that he might perhaps make inquiries in his own way, and even consult Mr. Buchanan, who probably would be willing enough to help him, though he might not perhaps feel disposed to respond to Mrs. Mowbray's more urgent appeals. Frank, of course, knew his mother's weak points, as all our children do, with an unerring certainty produced by the long unconscious study of childhood of all we say and do. His affection for her was quite unimpaired, but he knew exactly how she would address herself to the minister, with a vehemence and an indignation against Uncle Anderson, which Frank was impartial enough to feel, was not deserved. He would approach him quite differently—as a man to a man, Frank said to himself—and if there was really anything to be done in that way, any bloated debtor, as his mother supposed, who had grown fat on Uncle Anderson's bounty, and was not honourable enough to pay back what had been the origin of his fortune—why, the minister would probably tell him, and that would be so much gained.

When he thought, however, of thus meeting the minister in private session, Frank's orderly and steady heart beat a little higher. Before all questions of Uncle Anderson's debtors, there was one of much more importance—and that was the question of Elsie, which meant far more to Frank than money, or even the whole of the Scotch property—at least he thought so for the moment: but things were by no means so far advanced as to justify him in asking an interview with Mr. Buchanan on that subject. Alas! no, Elsie was never in the same mind (he thought) for any two meetings. Sometimes she was delightful to him, accepting his attentions; which, however, were no more than were paid to her by several other admirers as if she liked them, and giving him dances, almost as many as he asked, and allowing him to walk by her side in the weekly promenade on the Links, and talking to him sweetly, whatever his company might be: but next time they met, Elsie would be engaged for every dance, she would be flanked by other competitors on each side, and if she gave Frank a bow and a smile in passing, that would be all he obtained from her—so that if he were sometimes high in hope, he was at others almost in despair. Should he ever be allowed to see Mr. Buchanan on the subject, to ask his daughter from him? Ah, that depended! not upon Frank, but upon Elsie, who was no longer a little girl, but at the height of her simple sway, one of the prettiest girls in St. Rule's, and enjoying the position, and with no intention of cutting it short. Frank breathed a sigh, that almost blew out the lamps in the High Street, lamps already lighted, and shining in the lingering daylight, like strange little jewelled points, half green, half yellow. The electric light shines white in that street now, and makes the whole world look dead, and all the moving people like ghosts. But the lamps then were like jewels, with movement and consciousness in them, trembling in the colourless radiance of the long evening: for it was now summer weather, and already the days were long.

When the assembly outside the club dispersed, it happened to be Frank's luck to walk up the town with Rodie Buchanan, whose way was the same as his own. They went round by the West Port, though it was out of their way, to convoy Johnny Wemyss to his lodgings. Johnnie did not make matches for next day, except at rare intervals, for he was busy, either "coaching" his pupils (but that word had not then been invented), or working (as he called it) on the sands with his net and his "wee spy-glass," playing himself, the natives called it: or else he was reading theology for the next examination; but he allowed himself to walk down to the club in the evening, where all the young men met.

Johnny was not much younger than Frank, but he was paternal to the others, having the airs and aims of a man, and having put, chiefly by necessity, but a little also by inclination, boyish things from him; he was as much in advance of Frank as he was of Rodie, who had not yet attained his twentieth year.

The night was lovely, clear, and mild, and they made the round by the West Port very pleasantly together, and stood for a long time at the stairfoot of Johnny's humble lodging, which was in one of the old-fashioned square two-storied houses at that end of the town, which still retained the picturesque distinction of an outside stair. It was not thought picturesque then, but only old-fashioned, and a mark of poverty, everybody's ambition being to have a more modern and convenient house. The young men continued to discuss the matches past and present, and how Alick Seaton was off his game, and Bob Sinclair driving like fire, and the Beatons in force playing up to each other, so that they were awfully hard to beat in a foursome. Johnny took the interest of a born golfer in these particulars, though he himself played so little; and Frank, on ordinary occasions, had all the technicality of a neophyte, and outdid his more learned companions in all the terms of the game.

But when they had left Johnny at his stairfoot, and, looking back, had seen the light of his candles leap into the darkness of the window, and wondered for a moment how he could sit down to work at this hour, they proceeded along the long line of the High Street for a minute or two in silence. Rodie was taller, stronger, and heavier than Frank, though so much younger, and had a little compassionate sympathy for the fellow, who, at his antiquated age, four-and-twenty, was still only a beginner at golf.

The big youth was considering how to break down certain well considered advices for future play into terms adapted for the intellect of his elder, when Frank suddenly took the word, and began thus:

"I say, Rodie! do you remember my old Uncle Anderson, and do you know anything about him? he must have been a queer old chap, if what my mother has been telling me is true about him."

"Ten to one—" said Rodie: but paused in time—he was about to say "ten to one it isn't true"—for he heard of Mrs. Mowbray's paint and powder (which at the worst was only powder), and knew her over-civility and affectations, and therefore concluded frankly, as became his age, that nothing about her could be true. But he remembered in time that this could not fitly be said to her son. "Ten to one it's just stories," Rodie said; "there's stories about everybody; it is an awful town for stories, St. Rule's."

"I daresay that is true enough," said Frank; "but it seems that this is more than stories. They say he lent money to everybody, and never took any note or acknowledgment: and the people have never paid. They certainly should have paid; especially as, having no acknowledgment, it became, don't you see, a debt of honour. There is something which I don't quite understand about some Statute of Limitations that makes it impossible to recover money after a certain number of years. I don't know much about the law myself; but my mother's a great hand. Do you know anything about the Statute of Limitations, you that are going to be a W. S.?"

"Who said I was going to be a W. S.?" cried Rodie, red with indignation. "Nothing of the sort: I'm going into the army. It's John that is the W. S.; but I think I've heard of it," he added sulkily, after a moment, "sometimes he tells us about his cases. If you're not asked for the money for so many years, it's considered that you have been forgiven: but on the other hand if they asked for it, you're still bound; I've heard something like that from John."

"Oh, then I suppose," cried Frank, "it is rather urgent, and we ought to ask for it to preserve our claim."

There is a universal sentiment in the human heart against a creditor wishing to recover, and in favour of the debtor who is instinctively understood not to be able to pay. Especially strong is this sentiment in the bosom of the young; to lend is a fine thing, but to ask back again is always a mean proceeding. Rodie instinctively hardened himself against the legal rights of his friend.

"There's men," he said, "I've heard, that are constantly dunning you to pay them. I would rather never borrow a penny if it was to be like that."

"I would rather never borrow a penny whether it was like that or not," said the virtuous Frank.

"Oh, it's easy speaking for you, that have more money than you know what to do with; but if you think of my commission, and where the money is to come from."

"Most likely," said Frank, without any special meaning, merely as a conjecture, "if my Uncle Anderson had been living, your father would have got it from him."

Rodie grew redder than ever under this suggestion. "It might be so," he said; "but I hope you are not meaning that my father would not have paid the money back, whoever it came from: for if that is what you are meaning, you're a—"

"I was meaning nothing of the kind," cried Frank in a hurry; for to have the word leear, even though it is a mild version of liar, flung in his face by Rodie Buchanan, the brother of Elsie, was a thing he did not at all desire. "I hope I know better: but I wish I could speak to your father about my affairs, for I know that he was Uncle Anderson's great friend, and he is sure to know."

"To know what?" said Rodie.

"Oh, to know the people that borrowed from my uncle, and did not pay. I hope you don't think I ought to let them off when they have behaved like that."

"Behaved like what?" Rodie asked again.

"What is the matter with you, Rodie? I am saying nothing that is wrong. If my uncle lent them money, they ought to pay."

"And do you think," cried Rodie, in high indignation, "that my father would betray to you the names of the poor bodies that got a little money from Mr. Anderson to set them up in their shops, or to buy them a boat? Do you think if you were to talk to him till doomsday, that my father would do that?"

"Why shouldn't he?" said Frank, whose intellect was not of a subtle kind. "People should pay back the money when they have borrowed it. It is not as if it had been given to them as a present; Mr. Buchanan has been very kind to me, and I shouldn't ask him to do anything that was not right, neither would I be hard on any poor man. I was not told they were very poor men who had got my old uncle's money; and surely they had not so good a right to it as I have. I don't want to do anything that is cruel; but I will have my money if I can get it, for I have a right to it," Frank said, whose temper was gradually rising; yet not so much his temper as a sensation of justice and confidence in his own cause.

"You had better send in the sheriff's officers," said Rodie, contemptuously, "and take their plenishing, or the stock in the shop, or the boat. But if you do, Frank Mowbray, mind you this, there is not one of us will ever speak to you again."

"One of you!" cried Frank, "I don't want to quarrel with you, Rodie; but you are all a great deal younger than I am, and I am not going to be driven by you. I'll see your father, and ask his advice, and I shall do what he says; but if you think I am going to be driven by you, from anything that is right in itself, you're mistaken: and that's all I have got to say."

"You are a prig, and a beast, and a cruel creditor," cried Rodie. "Not the kind for us in St. Rule's: and good-night to you, and if you find nobody to play with to-morrow, you will just mind that you've chosen to put yourself against us, and it's your own fault."

Saying which, Rodie made a stride against the little garden gate which led to the Buchanan's front door, flung it inwards with a clang, and disappeared under the shadow of the dark elder-tree which overshadowed the entrance.

It was not until that moment that Frank realised what the consequence might be of quarrelling with Elsie's brother. He called after him, but Rodie was remorseless, and would not hear; and then the young man went home very sadly. Everybody knew that Rodie was Elsie's favourite brother; she liked him better than all the rest. If Rodie asked anything of her, Elsie was sure to grant almost everything to his request: and Frank had been such a fool as to offend him! He could not think how he could have been so foolish as to do it. It was the act of a madman, he said to himself. What was a few hundreds, or even thousands in comparison with Elsie, even if he recovered his money? It would be no good to him if he had to sacrifice his love.

Frank was not a young man who despised either hundreds or thousands, and probably, later, if all went well with him, he might think himself a fool to sacrificing good money for any other consideration; but he certainly was not in this state of feeling now. Elsie and Rodie, and the Statute of Limitations, and the money that Uncle Anderson had strewed about broadcast, jumbled each other in his mind. What did it matter to him if he lost the favour of his love? and on the other hand the pity it would be to lose the money for want of asking for it, and knowing who the man was who had got it, and had not had the honesty to pay. He grew angrier and angrier at these people as he went along, seeing that in addition to this fundamental sin against him, they were also the cause of his quarrel with Rodie, and terrible dismissal by Elsie. The cads! to hold their tongues and conceal who they were, when it was a debt of honour; and to trust in such a poor defence as a Statute of Limitations, and to part him from the girl he loved. He had been more curious than eager before, thinking besides the natural feeling one has not to be robbed, and to recover at all hazard that which is one's own, however wicked people should endeavour to cheat one out of it—that it would be fun to break through the secret pretences of those people, and force them to disgorge the money they had unlawfully obtained; but now Frank began to have a personal animosity against those defaulters, as his mother called them, who not only had cheated him of his money, but had made him to quarrel with Rodie, and perhaps with Rodie's sister. Confound them! they should not be let off now. He would find them, though all the world united in concealing them. He would teach them to take away his inheritance, and interfere between him and his love! It was with these sentiments hot in his heart that he hastened home.

CHAPTER XVI

THE UNJUST STEWARD ONCE MORE

Rodie Buchanan plunged into the partial darkness of his father's house, with a heart still more hot and flaming than that of Frank. He could not have told anyone why he took this so much to heart. It was not that he was unusually tender of his neighbours, or charitable beyond the ordinary rule of kindness, which was current in St. Rule's. He was one of those who would never have refused a penny to a beggar, or a bawbee to a weeping child, provided he had either the penny or the bawbee in his ill-furnished pockets, which sometimes was not the case; but, having done that by habit and natural impulse, there was no necessity in Rodie's mind to do more, or to make himself the champion of the poor, so that he really was not aware what the reason was which made him turn so hotly against Frank, in his equally natural determination to get back what was his own. The hall and staircase of Mr. Buchanan's house lay almost completely in the dark. There was one candle burning on a little table at the foot of the stair, which made the darkness visible, but above there was no light at all. Gas was not general in those days, nor were there lamps in common use, such as those which illuminate every part of our dwellings now. The dark passages and dreadful black corners of stair or corridor, which are so familiar in the stories of the period, those dreadful passages, through which the children flew with their hearts beating, not knowing what hand might grip them in the dark, or terrible thing come after them, must perplex the children of to-day, who know nothing about them, and never have any dark passages to go through. But, in those days, to get from the nursery to the drawing-room by night, unless you were preceded by the nursery-maid with a candle, was more alarming than anything a child's imagination could grasp nowadays. You thought of it for a minute or two before you undertook it; and then, with a rush, you dared the perils of the darkness, flinging yourself against the door to which you were bound, all breathless and trembling, like one escaped from nameless dangers. Rodie, nearly twenty, big and strong, and fearing nothing, had got over all those tremors. He strode up the dark stairs, three at a time, and flung open the drawing-room door, groping for it in the wall. He knew what, at that hour, he would be likely to find there. It was the hour when Mrs. Buchanan invariably went to the study "to see what papa was doing," to make sure that his fire was mended, if he meant to sit up over his sermon, or that things were comfortable for him in other ways when fires were not necessary. The summer was not far advanced, and fires were still thought necessary in the evenings at St. Rule's. Between the fire and the table was seated Elsie, with a large piece of "whiteseam," that is, plain sewing, on her knee, and two candles burning beside her. Another pair of candlesticks was on the mantelpiece, repeated in the low mirror which hung over it, but these candles were not lighted, neither were those on the writing-table at the other end of the room. When there was company, or, indeed, any visitor, in the evening they were lighted. The pair on the mantelpiece only when the visitor was unimportant, but the whole six when anybody of consequence was there, and then, you may suppose, how bright the room was, lighted al giorus, so to speak. But the household, and Elsie's little friends, when they came rushing in with some commission from their mothers, were very well contented with the two on the table. They wanted snuffing often, but still they gave, what was then supposed to be, a very good light.

Elsie looked up, pleased to see her brother, and let her work fall on her knee. Her needlework was one of the chief occupations of her life, and she considered the long hours she spent over it to be entirely a matter of course; but, by this hour of the night, she had naturally become a little tired of it, and was pleased to let it drop on her knee, and have a talk with Rodie over the fire. It was considered rather ill-bred to go on working, with your head bent over your sewing, when anyone came in. To be sure, it was only her brother, but Elsie was so glad to see him a little earlier than usual, that, though the task she had given herself for the evening was not quite completed, she was glad to let her seam drop upon her knees. "Oh, Rodie, is that you?" she said.

"Of course it's me," said Rodie. "I suppose you were not looking for anybody else at this hour?"

"I am glad you are in so soon," said Elsie. "And who was that that came with you to the door? Not Johnny Wemyss. I could tell by his foot."

"What have you to do with men's feet?" said Rodie, glad to find something to spend a little of his wrath upon. "Lassies must have tremendously little to think of. I am sure I would never think if it was one person's foot, or another, if I were sitting at home like you."

"Well," said Elsie, "you never do sit at home, so you cannot tell. I just notice them because I cannot help it. One foot is so different from another, almost as much as their voices. But what is the matter with you, Rodie? Have you been quarrelling with somebody? You look as if you were in a very ill key."

"I wonder who wouldn't be in an ill key? There is that feckless gomeril, Frank Mowbray—" ("Oh, it was Frank Mowbray?" Elsie interjected in an undertone)—"going on about debts and nonsense, and folk in the town that owe him money, and that he's coming to my father to ask him who they are; as if my father would go and split upon poor bodies that borrowed from old Anderson. I had it in my heart," cried Rodie, striking with his heel a piece of coal that was smouldering in the grate, and breaking it up into a hundred blazing fragments—"I had it in my heart to take him by the two shoulders, and fling him out like potato peelings into the road."

"Oh, Rodie, my mother's gathering coal!" cried Elsie, hastening to extinguish the fiery sparks that had fallen upon the large fur rug before the fire. "Well," she said, serenely, in a tone which would have disposed summarily, had he heard it, of poor Frank's hopes, "you are big enough to have done it: but I would not lift my hands, if I were you, on one that was not as big as myself. And what has Frank done? for he never was, that I could see, a quarrelling boy."

"Oh, not that you could see!" said Rodie, with a snort. "He's sure to keep a good face before the lassies, and especially you that he's courting, or trying to court, if he knew the way."

"He's not courting me," cried Elsie, with a blush and a laugh, giving Rodie a sisterly push, "and I wonder you will say such things to me."

"It's only because he doesna know the way then," said Rodie, picking up the pieces of blazing coal from the white hearth. "Will you let me alone, when you see I have the tongs in my hand?"

"Was it for that you quarrelled with Frank?" said Elsie, letting a little careless scorn appear in her tone, as who should say, you might quarrel with many besides Frank if that was the cause. The girls in St. Rule's, in those days, were not so disproportionate in number as they seem to be now, and she was unpopular, indeed, who had not one or two, at least, competing for her smiles.

"It was not for that!" cried Rodie, expressing, on his side, a scornful conviction that anything so unimportant was not worth quarrelling about. And then he added, "Do ye mind, Elsie, yon day in the turret-room?"

"Oh, I mind it very well," cried Elsie, with a little start; "I have always minded it. I think of it sometimes in the middle of the night when I wake up and cannot get to sleep."

"I cannot see what good it can do thinking of it then," said Rodie, always contemptuous of the ways of lassies. "But you mind how my father went on about the unjust steward. It was awfully funny the way he went on."

"It was for his sermon," said Elsie, with a little trouble in her eyes.

"It was not for his sermon. I heard him preach that sermon after, and I just listened, minding yon afternoon. But there was not a word in it about taking your bill, and writing fourscore."

"Oh, Rodie, you couldn't remember it as well as all that!"

"Why shouldn't I remember? I was a big laddie. I remember heaps of things. I mind going to Kinghorn, and crossing in the smack to Leith, years and years before."

"That was different from hearing a sermon," said Elsie, with the superiority to sermons which a minister's daughter naturally possessed.

"I did mind it, however," said Rodie, "and I knew it was not in the sermon—then where was it? and what was it for? I mind, as if it were yesterday, about taking the bill, and writing fourscore. Now, the question is," said the young man, laying down the tongs, and gazing unwinking into the glowing abyss of the fire, "what did my father mean by yon? He did not mean just nothing at all. You would not say that."

"I do not suppose," said Elsie, with a woman's quick and barely justified partisanship, "that my father ever said anything that meant just nothing at all."

"Oh yes, he does, whiles," said the more impartial boy; "but this was different. What did he mean by it? I will tell you what I have been thinking. Yon gomeril of a Frank has got it into his thick head that everybody in St. Rule's is in his debt. It is his mother that has put it into his head. Now, just supposing, for the sake of the argument, that it was true—"

"I think," said Elsie, thoughtfully, "that maybe it was true."

"Well, then," said Rodie, "we'll suppose that papa" (into this babyish title they all fell by moments, though protesting against it) "knew all about it. He generally does know about most things; people put a great deal of trust in him. They tell him things. Now, my opinion is, that old Mr. Anderson told him all about this, and who the folk were, and how they were to pay."

"Maybe," said Elsie, doubtfully.

"Maybe? I have no doubt about it; and my conviction is, this is what he was meaning yon afternoon. The old man was dead or dying, and nobody knew but papa—I mean my father. He knew what they had borrowed, and who they were. And most likely he knew that they were far from able to pay. There's a proverb about borrowed siller," said Rodie; "I cannot mind, at this moment, what it is—but it means this, that it never does you any good, and that I certainly believe." Here he made a pause. He had once borrowed a pound, and Rodie had no such harassing recollection in all his experience. He was still owing eighteenpence of that sum, and it had eaten into a whole year of his life.

Elsie said nothing; this sudden revival of the subject awakened many thoughts in her breast, but she sat with her eyes cast down, gazing, as he was, into the dazzling glow of the fire. Rodie was now kneeling on the hearth-rug in front of it, his face illuminated by the ruddy flame.

"I don't think," he said, in a steady voice, like that of a man making a statement in which was involved death or life, "that papa was right—"

"Rodie!"

"No," he repeated, solemnly, "I can't think it was right. I know you have no business to judge your own father. But I think," said the lad, slowly, "I would almost rather he had done a wrong thing like that, than one of the good things. Mind, Elsie, he had a struggle with himself. He said it over and over and over, and rampaged about the room, as you do, when you cannot make up your mind. But he knew they could not pay, the poor bodies. He knew it would be worse for them than if they had never got the money. It was an awful temptation. Then, do you mind, he said: 'the Lord commended the unjust steward.' In his sermon he explained all that, but I cannot think he was explaining it the same way yon afternoon."

"Rodie," said Elsie, with a little awe, "have you been thinking and thinking all this time, or when did you make out all that?"

"Not I," said the lad; "it just flashed out upon me when Frank was going on about his debtors, and about consulting my father. That's what made me angry as much as anything. I don't want papa to be disturbed in his mind, and made to think of that again. It was bad enough then. To be sure he will maybe refuse to speak at all, and that would be the best thing to do; and, considering what a long time has passed, he would be justified, in my opinion," said Rodie, with great gravity; "but to sit down and write fourscore when it was a hundred—I would stand up for him to the last, and I would understand him," cried the young man: "but I would rather my father did not do that."

"And of whom do you think he would be tempted to say that, Rodie?" said his sister, under her breath—Elsie had another thought very heavy at her heart.

"Oh, of the Horsburghs, and the Aitkens, and so forth, and I am not sure but Johnny Wemyss's folk would be in it," said Rodie; "and they are all dead, and it would fall upon Johnny, and break his heart. I hope my father will refuse to speak at all."

Then there was a long silence, and they sat and gazed into the fire. Elsie's idea was different. She knew some things which her brother did not know. But of these she would not breathe a word to him. They sat for some time quite silent, and there was a little stir over their heads, as if Mrs. Buchanan had risen from her chair, and was about to come down.

"Rodie, you'll have to be a W. S.," cried Elsie, "and let Jack go to India; nobody but a lawyer could have put it all out as clear as that."

Rodie sprang to his feet, and struck out a powerful arm.

"If you were not a lassie," he cried furiously, "I would just knock you down."

When Mrs. Buchanan came into the room, this was what she saw against that wavering glow in the chimney; her son's spring against an invisible foe, and Elsie demurely looking at him, with her work in her hands, from the other side of the fire.

"Eh, laddie," cried Mrs. Buchanan, "you terrify me with your boxing and your fighting. What ails you at him, and who is the enemy now? And you've broken up my gathering coal that would have lasted the whole night through."

"It's me he is fechting, mother," said Elsie, "and he says if I had not been a lassie, he would have knocked me down."

"You're never at peace, you two," said the mother, with much composure; "and we all know that Rodie had aye a great contempt for lassies. Let us just see, Elsie, if some day or other he may not meet a lassie that will give him a good setting down."

"What do I care about lassies," cried Rodie, indignant; "you're thinking of Frank Mowbray and Raaf Beaton. If ever two fellows made fools of themselves! looking as glum as the day of judgment, if Elsie turns her head the other way."

"Hold your tongue, laddie," cried Mrs. Buchanan, but with a smothered laugh. She was "weel pleased to see her bairn respected like the lave," but she was a sensible mother, and would have no such nonsense made a talk of. "Your father is not coming down-stairs again," she said; "he is busy with his sermon, so you can go to your bed when you like, Rodie. Bless me, the laddie has made the room insupportable with that great fire, and dangerous, too, to leave it burning. Elsie, my dear, I wish you were always as diligent; but you must fold up your seam now for the night."

After a little while Rodie retired to find the supper which had been waiting for him in the dining-room; for his evening hours were a little irregular, and his appetite large.

"He says Frank Mowbray is very much taken up about people that owe him debts," said Elsie, to her mother; "and that he is coming to consult my father."

"Oh, these weariful debts," said Mrs. Buchanan; "I have always said how much better it would have been to clear them off, and be done with them. It would have been all paid back before this time, and our minds at rest. But Mr. Morrison, he would not hear of it, and your father has never got it off his mind to this very day."

"Will it disturb him, mother, very much if Frank comes to talk to him?" said Elsie.

"I cannot tell why it should disturb him. The laddie has nothing to do with it, and Mr. Morrison had the old man's orders. But it will for all that. I think I will speak to Frank myself," Mrs. Buchanan said.

"Oh, no, mother," said Elsie.

"And wherefore, oh, no, mother? Many a man have I seen, and many a thing have I done to save your father. But it would be giving too much importance to this laddie. It will be his mother that sets him on. Put away your seam, Elsie, it is time that you were in your bed."

"I could not sleep a wink," said Elsie, "if I thought papa was to be troubled about this old thing."

"You had better think nothing about it," her mother replied; "for, whatever happens, you can do nothing: and what is the use of making yourself unhappy about a thing you cannot mend?"

Elsie was not so sure that she could do nothing. She thought it highly probable, indeed, that she could do much. But how was she to do it, how signify to Frank that if he disturbed her father, he had nothing to hope from her? Besides, had he anything to hope from her in any circumstances? This was very uncertain to Elsie. She was willing to believe in her own power, and that she could, if she pleased, keep him from rousing up this question; but how to do it, to condescend to allow that her father would be affected by it one way or another? And even in case Frank yielded, as she held it certain he would, to an expression of her will on the subject, was she sure that she was ready to recompense him in the only way which he would desire? While she was thinking, Mrs. Buchanan, who was moving about the room putting by her work, and arranging everything for the night, suddenly sent forth an unintentional dart, which broke down all Elsie's resolutions.

"At the same time," Mrs. Buchanan said, pursuing the tenor of the argument, as she had been, no doubt, carrying it on within herself, "I have always felt that I would like to do young Frank a good turn. Elsie, if it's true they tell me, be you kind to poor Frank. That will make up to him for anything the rest of your family may have done against him. Fain, fain, would I pay him back his siller; but be you kind to him, Elsie, if the other is not to be."

CHAPTER XVII

THE POSITION OF ELSIE

Mrs. Buchanan was a woman of great sense, yet perhaps she never made use of a more effective argument than that with which she concluded the conversation of that evening. Elsie went up to her room full of thought. It had always been impressed upon her from her earliest consciousness that her father's peace and comfort, his preservation from all unnecessary cares, from all noises and disturbing influence of every kind was one of the chiefest and most important duties of the family. It had been made the rule of her own childish conduct from the very beginning. "Oh, Miss Elsie, whatever you do, dinna make a noise, and disturb your papaw," had been the entreaty of the nursery-maid as long as she could remember. And when she was old enough to understand a reason, her mother had explained to her how papa was occupied all day long in the service of God, and for the instruction of common folk not so learned or so wise as himself. "And I think it a great privilege to mind the house and mind the doors, so that none of these small things may trouble him," her mother had said, "and you should be a proud lassie to think that you can be helpful in it, and do your part to keep everything quiet for the minister, that he may study the word of the Lord in peace." In our days, it is possible that Elsie might have been inspired by the spirit of revolt, and considered her own comfort of as much importance as her father's; but such a notion never entered her mind, and the preservation of perfect peace in that mysterious, yet so beloved and familiar study had always appeared to her the most necessary thing in the world. In their latter days, her mind had strayed away instinctively from her first early conception of papa. There had been awe to her in all his surroundings when she was a child, awe, tempered by much affection and perfect confidence, but still partaking much of that vague tremor of respect and veneration with which, but in a higher degree, she was taught to look up to God. But there is no criticism so intense, though often so unconscious, as that with which the children watch, without knowing they are watching, the development of the parent, who gradually comes out of those mists of devotion, and becomes clear and real, a being like themselves to their eyes. Elsie had soon learned in the midst of her semi-worship to be sorry for papa—poor papa who was so easily disturbed, liable to be impeded in his work, and have his composure destroyed by incidents which did not affect her mother in the least, and would not have gained herself an excuse for an imperfectly learned lesson. Why, if she was expected to learn her verbs all the same, whether there was a noise or not, should papa be unable to carry on his studies except in the most carefully preserved silence? She did not give vent to the sentiment, but it added to her reverence and devotion a strong feeling of pity for papa. Evidently he was of finer material than other people, and felt everything more keenly. Pity may be destructive of the highest reverence, but it adds to the solicitude of affection. But that scene, so well remembered in every detail, which had betrayed to her a struggle in him, had greatly heightened this effect. Poor papa! he had to be taken care of more than ever. To preserve his peace no effort was too much.

There had been a long pause in these reflections, as she herself began to be less subject to the delight of making a noise, and even Rodie expended his high spirits out of doors, and learned to respect the decorums of home. But as thought grew in Elsie's mind, a comprehension of the meaning of life grew with it, a comprehension, much aided by the philosophical remarks of Marion, and by those general views which Mrs. Buchanan was not aware were philosophy, the woman's philosophy which recognises many mysteries, and accepts many necessities in a manner quite different from the man's. The subject of her father was one of those upon which she had received much enlightenment. She had learned that the highest regard and the deepest love were quite consistent with a consciousness of certain incurable weaknesses, and a toleration that in other circumstances would have been something like contempt. Probably nobody but a woman can ever understand this extraordinary mingling of sentiment. A man is naturally indignant and angry to think that his sublime self should ever be the object of this unimpassioned consciousness of defect, though no doubt his sentiment towards his womankind is of the same mingled character: but in the woman's mind it takes away nothing from the attraction, and little from the respect with which she regards her man. Perhaps it even adds to his attraction, as making the intercourse more interesting, and bringing all the varieties of her being into play.

This gave to Elsie an almost tragic sense of the necessity of preserving her father's peace of mind at all hazards. When she came to think the whole matter over, and to realise what Rodie's view of the subject was, her mind took a new opening. She took up the Bible which was on her table, and read over the parable of the unjust steward, with this new light upon it. She had not, by some chance, heard her father's sermon on the subject, and she was not very clear as to how it was that the man was commended for his falsehood, nor did she enter upon that view of the question. Was there something good in it, as Rodie seemed to think, diminishing the burdens of the poor, trying to save those who were struggling, and could not answer for themselves? Elsie, in the silence, shook her young head with its curls over that idea. She had no pretension of knowing better than her teachers and elders. She did not think, because she did not understand, that therefore the Lord who commended the unjust steward must be wrong. She took the matter plainly, without penetrating its other meaning. Was it good, or right, or excusable, a sin that one could forgive to one's father that he should do this? Rodie seemed to think so. He said he would rather his father had done a wrong thing like that than many right things. Elsie began to cry, dropping hot tears on her Bible, all alone, not understanding, in the midst of the silence and the night. No, no, not that. It would not be so bad, perhaps, as if he had done it for himself. To save the Horsburghs and the Aitkens from ruin, even at the expense of a lie, of teaching them to lie— Oh no, no, Elsie cried, the tears pouring over her Bible. It might not be so bad in one way, but it was worse in another. It was dictating a lie to others as well as uttering it himself. Was papa guilty of that? Was that what it meant, that struggle long ago, the questioning and the self-conflict? Oh no, no, she cried to herself, oh no, no! Neither for himself, neither for others could he have done that. And yet what did it mean?

There is a point beyond which such a question cannot go. She had no way of settling it. The doubt burned her like fire, it penetrated her heart like a knife: but at last she was obliged, baffled, exhausted, and heart-broken, to leave it alone. Perhaps she never would know what the real meaning was, either of the parable in the book or the still more urgent parable of human conduct here half revealed to her. But there was at least something that she could understand, the old lesson of the house, the teaching of her childhood, to guard her father from all assault, from anything that could disturb his mind or his life. It was not the simple formula now of not making a noise lest it should disturb papa. It was something a great deal more important, not so easily understood, not so easy to perform, but still more absolute and binding. Not to disturb papa, not to allow him to be disturbed, to defend his door, if need were, with her life. To put her arm into the hoops of the bolt like Katherine Douglas in the history—that rash maiden whom every Scots girl holds high, and would emulate if she could. Elsie was faintly aware that this statement of the cause was a little nonsensical, that she would not be called upon to sacrifice her life or to break her arm in defence of her father; but she was very young, and full of passionate feeling, and her thoughts formed into the language of generous extravagance, in spite of herself. What was it really, after the outburst of that fond resolution, that she had to do?

It did not sound so great a matter after all to keep back Frank Mowbray, that was all: to prevent him from penetrating to her father's room, recalling her father's painful memories, and his struggle with himself. Her arm within the hoops! it was not so exaggerated an idea after all, it was more than breaking an arm, it might be perhaps breaking a heart: still it was a piece of actual exertion that was required of her on her father's behalf. Elsie had not given very much serious consideration to Frank Mowbray, but she knew vaguely as much as she had chosen to know, the meaning and scope of his attentions, and the possibility there was, if she did not sharply discourage him, that he would shortly demand a decision from her one way or other. Elsie had not sharply discouraged him; she had been friendly, unwilling to give pain, unwilling to act as if she believed that it could matter to him one way or another: but she had not shown him particular favour. In no way was her conscience guilty of having "led him on." Her pride sprang up in flames of indignation at the thought of having led any one on. There was Raaf Beaton too: they had both been the same to her, boys she had known, more or less, all her life, whom she liked very well to dance with, even to talk to for an idle moment, whom she would not vex for the world. Oh no, she would not vex them for the world, neither of them! nevertheless, to select one of them, to bind herself to either, to pretend to take either as the first of men? Elsie almost laughed, though her eyes were still hot with tears, at that ridiculous thought.

Yet this was the easiest way of stopping Frank from disturbing her father, oh! the easiest way! She had only to receive him a little more warmly than usual, to listen to what he said, to let him walk with her when they went out of doors, and talk to her when they were within. It is very likely that on both sides this influence also was exaggerated. There was nothing that Frank would not have done for Elsie and her smiles; but after a time no doubt his mind would have returned to his former resolutions, and he would not have felt it necessary to abandon a previously-formed and serious intention on her account. But a girl rarely understands that, nor does the man think of it, in the excitement of such a crisis. Elsie had no doubt that she had the fullest power to turn aside Frank from any attempt on her father's peace. And then came her mother's recommendation to be kind to him, to make up to him for something that was past. It was a recommendation that made her blood boil, that she should pay him for some injustice past. Be kind to him, as her mother said, to make up, make as it were money of herself to be a compensation to him! This idea was odious to the girl: but yet it was only another version of the same necessity that she should keep him from disturbing papa.

Naturally, it was not long before the opportunity came. Elsie was walking towards the East Sands with Rodie on the next day, when Frank was seen coming back from that spot, a little wet about the boots, and sandy about the trousers, which was a sign, already beginning to be understood in St. Rule's, that the wearer of these garments had been among the rocks with Johnny Wemyss, of whom, as a "character," the town had become, from its height of reprobation, half proud. Frank had been fascinated by him, as everybody else was, though he was vexed to be seen in this plight, after an hour with the naturalist, especially as Rodie, at the sight of him, had the bad breeding to show embarrassment, and even repugnance to meet his former friend.

"I'll away west," Rodie said, as soon as he was visible. "There's Mowbray. I'm not going to stay here, and see him fawning upon you. It is disgusting," Rodie said, severely. He had not yet himself begun to "fawn" upon any one, and was still intolerant of everything of this kind.

"You are not going away, just after he has seen that we saw him," cried Elsie, gripping her brother's arm, in the intensity of her feeling, "letting him see how ill you take it, and that you cannot forget! Man, Rodie, will you run away?"

"I am not running away," cried Rodie, red with wrath and shame.

"You shall not," cried Elsie, holding him with a vigorous young grip, almost as strong as his own, out of which he was still attempting to wriggle, when Frank came up, all smiling and beaming.

"Johnny Wemyss has found a new beast," he reported with a little excitement. "It is not in all the books, there has been none discovered like it. You should see his eyes just jumping out of his head."

Elsie's eyes gave a jump too; a warm flush ran over her face. Unconsciously, she held her head high.

"Oh," she said, softly, "I am not surprised! I am not surprised!"

At this Frank looked at her half alarmed, half suspicious, not quite easy in his mind, why she should take so much interest in Johnny. But after all, he was only Johnny, a fellow wrapped up in "beasts," and no competitor for anybody's favour.

Meanwhile, Rodie had twisted his elbow out of Elsie's hold, who had too much respect for appearances to continue the struggle before strangers.

"I'm away to see it," cried Rodie. "You'll come when you are ready," and off he rushed like a wild deer, with a sulky nod at Frank.

"It appears I have offended Rodie without meaning it," said Frank, taking the wise way of forestalling any reproach. "I hope he has not prejudiced you against me, Miss Elsie; for all I said that vexed him, was only that I was coming to ask your father's advice, and I have always heard that everybody asks the minister's advice. May I walk with you, and tell you about it? I don't know what he thought I meant."

"So far as I understood," said Elsie, "he thought you wanted to make my father betray some poor bodies that trusted in him." Elsie, too, thought it was wiser to forestall any other statement. But she put forth this bold statement with a high colour and a quaking heart.

"Betray!" cried Frank, growing red, too, "oh, I assure you, I had no such thought."

"You wanted my father to tell upon the poor folk that had borrowed money, and were not able to pay." Elsie averted her head for the reason that, sorely troubled by her own guesses and doubts, she could not look Frank in the face: but he interpreted this action in quite another way. He took it for a gesture of disdain, and it roused a spirit even in the bosom of Elsie's slave.

"Justice is justice," he said, "Miss Elsie, whether one is poor or rich. To hunt the poor is what I would never do; but if they are right who told me, there are others passing themselves off under the shield of the poor, that are quite well able to pay their debts—more able than we are to do without the money: and that is just what I want to ask Mr. Buchanan, who is sure to know."

It seemed to Elsie that the sands, and the rocks, and the cliffs beyond were all turning round and round, and that the solid earth sank under her feet. "Mr. Buchanan, who is sure to know," she said to herself under her breath. Oh yes, he was sure to know. He would look into the face of this careless boy, who understood nothing about it, and he would say—what would he say? It made Elsie sick and faint to think of her father—her father, the minister, the example to all men—brought face to face with this temptation, against which she had heard him struggling, which she had heard him adopting, without knowing what it meant, six years ago. No, he had not been struggling against it. He had been struggling with it, trying to convince himself that it was just and right. This came upon her like a flash of lightning, as she took a few devious steps forward. Then Frank's outcry, "You are ill, Miss Elsie!" brought her back to herself.

"No, I am not ill," she said, standing still by the rocks, and taking hold of a glistening pinnacle covered with seaweed, to support herself for a moment, till everything settled down. "I am not ill: I am just thinking," she kept her head turned away, and looked out upon the level of the sea, very blue and rippled over with wavelets in its softest summer guise, with a faint rim of white showing in the distance against the red sand and faint green banks of the Forfar coast. Of all things in this world to make the heart sick, there is nothing like facing a moral crisis, which some one you love is about to go through, without any feeling of certainty that he will meet it in the one only right way. "Oh, if it was only me!" Elsie sighed, from the bottom of her heart.

You will think it was the deepest presumption on her part, to think she could meet the emergency better than her father would. And so it was, and yet not so at all. It was only that there were no doubts in her mind, and there were doubts, she knew, inconceivable doubts, shadows, self-deceptions, on his. A great many thoughts went through her mind, as she stood thus looking across the level of the calm sea—although it was scarcely for a minute altogether, that she underwent this faintness and sickening, which was both physical and mental. The cold touch of the wet rock, the slipping tangles of dark green leathery dulse which made her grasp slip, brought her to herself, and brought her colour rushing back. She turned round to Frank with a smile, which made the young man's heart beat.

"But I am awfully anxious not to have papa disturbed," she said. "You know he is not just like other folk; and when he is interrupted at his writing it breaks the—the thread of his thoughts, and sometimes he cannot get back the particular thing he was meditating upon (it seemed to Elsie that the right words were coming to her lips, though she did not know how, like a sort of inspiration which overawed, and yet uplifted her). And then perhaps it will be his sermon that will suffer, and he always suffers himself when that is so."

"He has very little occasion to suffer in that way," cried Frank, "for every one says—and I think so myself, but I am no judge—that there is no one that preaches like him, either in the town or through all Fife. I should say more than that—for I never in London heard any sermons that I listened to as I do to his."

Elsie beamed upon her lover like the morning sun. It was strictly true to the letter, but, whether there might be anything in the fact, that none of these discredited preachers in London were father to Elsie, need not be inquired. It gave the minister's daughter a keen pang of pleasure to hear this flattering judgment. It affected her more than her mother's recommendation, or any of her own serious thoughts. She felt for a moment as if she could even love Frank Mowbray, and get to think him the first of men.

"Come and let me see the new beast," she said, with what was to Frank the most enchanting smile.

CHAPTER XVIII

JOHNNY WEMYSS

Johnny Wemyss was not perhaps at that moment a figure precisely adapted to please a maiden's eye, nor would any other lad in St. Rule's have cared to present himself before a young lady whom he regarded with interest, under his present aspect. His trousers were doubled up as far as was practicable, upon legs which were not models of shapeliness nor even of strength, being thin and wiry "shanks," capable of any amount of fatigue or exertion, but showing none of these qualities. His arms, much like these lower members, were also uncovered up to the elbow, his blue pea-jacket had a deposit of sand in every wrinkle, and the broad blue bonnet on his head had scraps of very vivid green sea-weed clinging to it, showing how Johnny's head, as well as his arms and legs, had been in contact with the recesses of the rocks. It was pushed back from his forehead, and he was holding out at the length of his hairy, sinewy arm, a thing which was calculated to call forth sentiments rather of disgust than of admiration, in persons not affected with that sympathetic interest in the researches of Johnny, which St. Rule's in general was now beginning to feel. It was a variety of that family of the Medusa, called in St. Rule's jelly fish, which fringe all the sands along that coast after a storm. Elsie had got over the repugnance to touch the clammy creatures, which is common to uninstructed persons, and was eager to have the peculiarity in its transparent structure pointed out to her, which marked it as a discovery. But Johnny was neither so animated in its exposition, nor so enthusiastic over the beauty of his prize, as he had been on many previous and less important occasions. He had been a witness of Elsie's progress, since Frank Mowbray had joined her. He had seen her pause by the rocks to recover herself from something, he could not tell what. Was it not very likely at least that it was a more full disclosure of Frank's sentiments—which, indeed, nobody in St. Rule's had any doubt about the nature of—which suddenly overcame a vigorous, healthful girl like Elsie, and made her lean against the wet rocks which were under water at full tide, and grasp the tangles of the dulse for support? Nothing could be more probable, nay, certain. And when Elsie turned towards her lover with that smile which the other half saw, and most clearly divined, and led him back with her triumphant, what other hypothesis could account for it? Johnny could follow with the most delicate nicety the conclusions that were to be drawn from the transparent lines of colour in the round clammy disc he held quivering in his hand; but he could not tell, how could he; having no data to go upon, and being quite incapable, as science will probably always continue to be of such a task, to decipher what was in a single quivering heart, though it might be of much more consequence to him. He watched them coming along together, Frank Mowbray suddenly changed from the commonplace comrade, never quite trusted as one of themselves by the young men of St. Rule's, though admitted to a certain cordiality and good fellowship—coming along transfigured, beaming all over, his very clothes, always so much more dainty than anybody else's, giving out a radiation of glory—the admired yet contemned spats upon his feet, unconsciously stepping as if to music: and altogether with a conquering hero aspect, which made Johnny long to throttle him, though Johnny was perhaps the most peaceable of all the youths of his time. An unconscious "confound him" surged up to the lips of the naturalist, himself so triumphant a minute ago in the glory of his discovery; and for one dreadful moment, Johnny felt disposed to pitch his Medusæ back into the indifferent water, which would have closed over it as calmly as though it had been the most lowly and best known of its kind. For what was the good of anything, even an original discovery, if such a thing was permitted to be under the skies, as that a girl such as Elsie Buchanan should elect out of all the world the like of Frank Mowbray, half-hearted Scot, dandy, and trifler, for her master? It was enough to disgust a man with all the courses of the earth, and even with the finest unclassed Medusæ newly voyaged out of the heart of the sea.

"Oh, Johnny," Elsie said, hurrying towards him in all that glow and splendour of triumph (as he thought). "I hear you have made a discovery, a real discovery! Let me see it! and will it be figured in all the books, and your name put to it? Wemyssea—or something of that kind."

"I had thought of a different name," said Johnny, darkly, "but I've changed my mind."

"What was that?" said Elsie, lightly taking hold of his arm in the easy intimacy of a friendship that had lasted all her life—in order that she might see more clearly the object limply held in his palm. "Tell me the difference," she said, throwing down her parcel, and putting her other hand underneath his to bring the prize more distinctly within her view. The young man turned deeply red up to his sandy hair, which curled round the edge of his blue bonnet. He shrank a little from that careless touch. And Frank, looking on with a half jealousy, quickly stifled by the more agreeable thought that it was Elsie's now distinctly identified preference of himself which made her so wholly unconscious of any feeling on the part of the other, laughed aloud out of pure delight and joy of heart.

"What are you laughing at?" said Johnny, gruffly, divining only too well why Frank laughed.

"Show me," said Elsie, "I think I can see something. You always said I was the quickest to see. Is it this, and this?" she said, bending over the hand which she held.

"Let me hold it for you," said Frank.

"I can hold up my hand myself," said Johnny; "I am wanting no assistance. As I found it myself, I hope I am able to show it myself without anybody interfering."

Elsie withdrew her hand, and looked up surprised in his face, with one of those appeals which are so much less answerable than words. She stood a little aside while he began to expound his discovery. They had all caught a few of the most superficial scientific terms from Johnny. Elsie would never have spoken of the new thing being "figured" in a book, but for those little technicalities of knowledge which he shed about him. And he had said that she was the one of all his interested society who understood best. She was the only one who knew what observation meant, the naturalist said. I think that this was a mistake myself, and that he was chiefly led away by her sympathy and by certain other sentiments of which it is unnecessary to speak.

In the meantime, he explained with a mingled gruffness and languor which Elsie did not understand.

"Oh, it's perhaps not so great a discovery after all," Johnny said. "I daresay some fellow has noted it before. That's what you always find when you take it into your head you have got something new."

"But you know all about the Medusæ," said Elsie, "and you would be sure to know if it had been discovered before."

"I'm not sure that I know anything," said Johnny, despondently. He cast the jelly fish out of his hand upon the sand. "We're just, as Newton said, like bairns picking up shells on the shore. We know nothing. It is maybe no new thing at all, but just a variety that everybody knows."

"Oh, Johnny, that is not like you!" cried Elsie, while the two young men standing by, to whom this mood on Wemyss's part was quite unknown, gaped at him, vaguely embarrassed, not knowing what to say. Rodie had a great desire to get away from a problem he could not understand, and Frank was feeling a little guilty, he could scarcely tell why. Elsie got down on her knees upon the sand, which was firm though wet, and, gathering a handful of the dulse with its great wet stalks and hollow berries, made a bed for the Medusæ, which, with some repugnance, she lifted on to the little heap.

"You will have to give me a new pair of gloves," she said, looking up with a laugh, "for I have spoilt these ones that are nearly new; and what will my mother say? But though you think it is very weak, I cannot touch a jelly fish—I am meaning a Medusa, which is certainly a far bonnier name—with my bare hands. There now, it will go easy into a basket, or I would almost carry it myself, with the dulse all about it; but to throw it away is what I will never consent to, for if you think it is a discovery, I know it must be a discovery, and it will be called after you, and a credit to us all."

"It is a discovery," cried Johnny, with a sudden change of mien. "I was a fool. I am not going to give it up, whatever happens. The less that comes to me in this world, the more I'll keep to the little I'm sure of." When he had uttered this enigmatical sentence, which was one of those mystic utterances, more imposing than wisdom, that fill every audience with confused admiration, he snapped his fingers wildly, and executed a pas of triumph. "It will make the London men stand about!" he said, "and I would just like to know what the Professor will say to it! As for the name—"

"Oh, yes, Johnny, the name?"

"It will be time enough to think of that," he said, looking at her with mingled admiration and trouble. "Anyway, it is you that have saved it for me," he said.

"Frank," said Rodie, "are you meaning to play your foursome with Raaf and Alick, or are you not?"

"I thought you had turned me out of it," said Frank.

"Oh, go away and play your game!" Elsie commanded in a tone of relief. "It is just the thing that is best for you idle laddies, with never a hand's turn to do in this world. I am going home as soon as I have seen Johnny take up his new beast like a person of sense, after taking the pet at it like a silly bairn. You are all silly, the whole tribe of you, for so much as you think of yourselves. If you're late, Alick and Raaf will just play a twosome, and leave you out."

"That's what they'll do," Rodie pronounced, authoritatively. "Come along, Frank."

And Frank followed, though torn in pieces by attractions both ways. It was hard to leave Elsie in so gracious a mood, and also with Johnny Wemyss, who had displayed a quite unexpected side to-day: but Johnny Wemyss did not, could not count, whatever he might feel: surely if there was anything a man could calculate upon, it was that. And Frank was sincerely pleased to be taken into favour again by that young despot, Rodie, who in his capacity as Elsie's brother, rode roughshod over Ralph Beaton and was more respected than he had any right to be by several more of the golf-playing community. So that it seemed a real necessity in present circumstances, with the hopes of future games in mind, to follow him docilely now.

"Why were you so petted, Johnny?" said Elsie, when reluctantly her wooer had followed her brother in a run to the links.

"I was not petted," said Johnny, with that most ineffectual reply which consists of simple contradiction. In those days petted, that is the condition of a spoilt child, was applied to all perverse moods and causeless fits of ill-temper. I do not think that in current Scots literature, of which there are so many examples, I remember the same use of the word now.

"Oh, but you were," cried Elsie, laughing, "in a pet with your new beast, and what could go further than that? I would not have been so much surprised if you had been in a pet with Rodie or me."

"There was occasion," said Johnny, relapsing a little into the clouds. "Why were you such friends with that empty-headed ass? And coming along the sands smiling at him as if—as if—"

"As if what?" said Elsie. She laughed again, the laugh of conscious power. She was not perhaps so fine a character as, considering all things, she might have been expected to be.

"Elsie," said the young man, "it's not me that shall name it. If it really turns out to be something, as I think it will, I am going to call it after you."

"A grand compliment," cried the girl, with another peel of laughter. "A jeely fish! But," she added, quickly, "I think it is awfully nice of you, Johnny; for those are the sort of things, I know, that you like best in the world."

"Not quite," said the naturalist. "There are things I care for far more than beasts, and if you don't know that, you are not so quick at the uptake as I have always thought you; but what is the good when I am nobody, and never will be anybody, if I were to howk and ferret for new beasts till I die!"

"Bide a wee, bide a wee," said Elsie, laughing, but confused; "you will be a placed minister, and as good as any of them; and what could ye have better than that?"

"I am the most unfortunate man in the world," said Johnny, "for you know that, which is the only way for a poor lad like me, it is not what I want."

"And you are not blate to say so to me that am a minister's daughter, and very proud of it," cried Elsie, with a flush of offence.

"That's just the worst of it," said Johnny, sadly, shaking his head, "for maybe you, and certainly other folk, will believe indeed I am not blate, thinking too much of myself, not to be content with a kirk if I could get one. But you should know it isn't that. I think too little of myself. Never could I be a man like your father, that is one of the excellent of the earth. It is the like of him, and not the like of me, that should be a minister. And then whatever I was, and wherever I was," he added, with a humility that was almost comic, "I would always have something inside teasing me to be after the beasts all the same."

"What are you going to do with it now?" said Elsie, looking down at the unconscious object of all this discussion, which lay semi-transparent, and a little dulled in the delicate mauve colour of its interesting markings, on the bed she had made of the tangles of the dulse at her feet.

"The first thing is, I will draw a picture of it, the best I can," said Johnny, rousing to something of his usual enthusiasm, "and then I will dissect it and get at its secrets, and I will send the drawing and the account of it to London—and then—"

"And then?" repeated Elsie.

"I will just wait," he said. His eyes which had been lighted up with eagerness and spirit sank, and he shrugged his shoulders and shook his head. "Just as likely as not I will never hear word of it more. That's been my fate already. I must just steel myself not to hope."

"Johnny, do you mean that you have sent up other things like this, and got no good of them?"

"Aye," he said, without looking up. He was not a cheerful figure, with his head bent on his breast, and his eyes fixed on the strange prize—was it a mere clammy inanimate thing, or was it progress, and fame, and fortune?—which lay at his feet. Elsie did not know what to say.

"And you standing there with wet feet, and everything damp and cold about you," she cried, with a sudden outburst. "Go home this moment, Johnny Wemyss; this time it will be different. I'm not a prophet and how should I know? But this time it will be different. How are you to get it home?"

He took his blue bonnet from his head, with a low laugh, and placed the specimen in it.

"Nobody minds," he said, smoothing down his sleeves. "I am as often without my bonnet as with it. They say it's only Johnny Wemyss: but I'm not fit to walk by the side of a bonnie princess like you."

"I am coming with you all the same," Elsie said.

They were, indeed, a very unlikely pair. The girl in all her prettiness of summer costume, the young man, damp, sandy, and bareheaded, carrying his treasure. So far as the sands extended, however, there was no one to mark the curious conjunction, and they went lightly over the firm wet sand within high-water mark, talking little, but with a perfect familiarity and kindness of companionship which was more exquisite than the heats and chills through which Frank Mowbray had passed, when Elsie for her own purposes had led him back. Elsie kept step with Johnny's large tread, she had an air of belonging to him which came from the intimate intercourse of years; and though the social distinction between the minister's daughter and the fisherman's son was very marked, externally, it was evidently quite blotted out in fact by a closer fraternity. Elsie was not ashamed of him, nor was Johnny proud of her, so far as their difference of position was concerned. He was proud of her in another sense, but she quite as much of him.

"I will call it 'Princess Elsie,'" he said at last. "I will put it in Latin: or else I will call it 'Alicia:' for Elsie and Alison and all are from Alice, which is just the bonniest name in the world."

"Nonsense," she said, "there are many that are much bonnier. I don't think Alison is very bonny, it is old-fashioned; but it was my grandmother's name, and I like it for that."

"It is just the bonniest name in all the world," he repeated, softly; but next moment they had climbed from the sands to the smooth ground near the old castle, and from thenceforward Johnny Wemyss was the centre of a moving group, made up of boys and girls, and an occasional golfer, and a fisher or two, and, in short, everybody about; for Johnny Wemyss was known to everybody, and his particular pursuits were the sport, and interest, and pride of the town.

"He has found a new beast."

"Oh, have you found a new beast? Oh Johnny, let us see it, let us see it! Oh, but it's nothing but a jeely-fish," cried, in a number of voices, the little crowd. Johnny walked calmly on, his bare head red in the sunshine, with crisp short curls surrounding a forehead which was very white in the upper part, where usually sheltered by his bonnet, and a fine red brown mahogany tint below. Johnny was quite at his ease amid the encircling, shouting little crowd, from out of which Elsie withdrew at the garden gate, with a wave of her hand. He had no objection to their questions, their jests, their cries of "Let us see it, Johnny!" It did not in the least trouble him that he was Johnny to all the world, and his "new beast" the diversion of the town.

CHAPTER XIX

A CATASTROPHE

Mrs. Mowbray was more restless than her maid, who had been with her for many years, had ever seen her before. She was not at any time a model of a tranquil woman, but ever since her arrival in St. Rule's, her activity had been incessant, and very disturbing to her household. She was neither quiet during the day nor did she sleep at night. She was out and in of the house a hundred times of a morning, and even when within doors was so continually in motion, that the maids who belonged to the house, and had been old Mr. Anderson's servants, held a meeting, and decided that if things went on like this, they would all "speak" when the appointed moment for speaking came, and leave at the next term. Mrs. Mowbray's own maid, who was specially devoted to her, had a heavier thought on her mind; for the mistress was so unlike herself, that it seemed to this good woman that she must be "off her head," or in a fair way of becoming so. There was no one to take notice of this alarming condition of affairs, for what was to be expected from Mr. Frank? He was a young man: he was taken up with his own concerns. It was not to be supposed that his mother's state would call forth any anxiety on his part, until it went much further than it yet had gone. And there were no intimate friends who could be appealed to. There was no one to exercise any control, even if it had been certain that there was occasion for exercising control. And that had not occurred as yet. But she was so restless, that she could not keep still anywhere for half-an-hour. She was constantly on the stairs, going up and down, or in the street, taking little walks, making little calls, staying only a few minutes. She could not rest. In the middle of the night, she might be seen up wandering about the house in her dressing-gown, with a candle in her hand: though when any one was startled, and awakened by the sound of her nocturnal wanderings, she was always apologetic, explaining that she had forgotten something in the drawing-room, or wanted a book.

But on the day when she had spoken to Frank, as already recorded, her restlessness was more acute than ever. She asked him each time he came in, whether he had "taken any steps;" though what step the poor boy could have taken, he did not know, nor did she, except that one step of consulting the minister, which was simple enough, but which, as has been seen, was rendered difficult to Frank on the other side. The next day, that morning on which Frank lost all his time on the East Sands, with Johnny Wemyss, and his new beast, the poor lady could not contain herself at all. She sat down at the window for a minute, and gazed out as if she were expecting some one; then she jumped up, and went over all the rooms up-stairs, looking for something, she said, which she could not find. She could not keep still. The other servants began to compare opinions and to agree with the lady's maid. At last before twelve o'clock Mrs. Mowbray put on her "things," for the third or fourth time, and sallied forth, not dressed with her usual elaborate nicety, but with a shawl too heavy for the warm day, and a bonnet which was by no means her best bonnet. Perhaps there is no greater difference between these times and ours, than the fact of the bonnet and shawl, as opposed to the easier hat and jacket, which can be put on so quickly. Mrs. Mowbray generally took a long time over the tying of her bonnet strings, which indeed was a work of art. But in the hasty irregularity of that morning she could not be troubled about the bonnet strings, but tied them anyhow, not able to give her attention to the bows. It may easily be seen what an agitation there must have been in her bosom, when she neglected so important a point in her toilet. And her shawl was not placed carefully round her shoulders, in what was supposed to be the elegant way, but fastened about her neck like the shawl of any farmer's wife. Nothing but some very great disturbance of mind could account for an outward appearance so incomplete.

"She's going to see the minister," said Hunter, her woman, to Janet, the cook. Hunter had been unable to confine her trouble altogether to her own breast. She did not indeed say what she feared, but she had confided her anxiety about her mistress's health in general to Janet, who was of a discreet age, and knew something of life.

"Weel, aweel," said Janet, soothingly, "she can never do better than speak to the minister. He will soothe down her speerits, if onybody can; but that's not the shortest gait to the minister's house."

They stood together at the window, and watched her go up the street, the morning sunshine throwing a shadow before her. At the other end of the High Street, Johnny Wemyss had almost reached his own door, with ever a new crowd following at his heels, demanding to see the new beast. And Frank had started with his foursome in high spirits and hope, with the remembrance of Elsie's smile warm around him, like internal sunshine, and the consciousness of an excellent drive over the burn, to add to his exhilaration. Elsie had gone home, and was seated in the drawing-room, at the old piano "practising," as all the household was aware: it was the only practicable time for that exercise, when it least disturbed the tranquillity of papa, who, it was generally understood, did not begin to work till twelve o'clock. And Mrs. Buchanan was busy up-stairs in a review of the family linen, the napery being almost always in need of repair. Therefore the coast was perfectly clear, and Mrs. Mowbray, reluctantly admitted by the maid, who knew her visits were not over-welcome, ran up the stairs waving her hand to Betty, who would fain have gone before her to fulfil the requirements of decorum, and because she had received "a hearing" on the subject from her mistress. "It is very ill-bred to let a visitor in, and not let me or the minister know who's coming. It is my desire you should always go up-stairs before them, and open the door." "But how could I," Betty explained afterwards, "when she just ran past me? I couldna put forth my hand, and pull her down the stairs."

Mrs. Mowbray had been walking very fast, and she ran up-stairs to the minister's study, which she knew so well, as rapidly and as softly as Elsie could have done it. In consequence, when she opened the door, and asked, breathless, "May I come in?" her words were scarcely audible in the panting of her heart. She had to sit down, using a sort of pantomime to excuse herself for nearly five minutes before she could speak.

"Oh, Mr. Buchanan! I have been so anxious to see you! I have run nearly all the way."

The minister pushed away the newspaper, which he had been caught reading. It was the Courant day, when all the bottled-up news of the week came to St. Rule's. He sighed to be obliged to give it up in the middle of his reading, and also because being found in no more serious occupation, he could not pretend to be very busy, even if he had wished to do so.

"I hope it is nothing very urgent," he said.

"Yes, it is urgent, very urgent! I thought Frank would have seen you yesterday. I thought perhaps you would have paid more attention to him, than you do to me."

"My dear Mrs. Mowbray! I hope you have not found me deficient in—in interest or in attention," the minister said.

He had still kept hold of the Courant by one corner. Now he threw it away in a sort of despair. The same old story, he said to himself grievously, with a sigh that came from the bottom of his heart.

"Do you know," said the visitor, clasping her hands and resting them on his table, "that Frank's twenty-fifth birthday is on the fifth of next month?"

She looked at him as she had never done before. Her eyes might have been anxious on previous occasions, but they were also full of other things: they had light glances aside, a desire to please and charm, always the consciousness of an effort to secure not only attention, but even admiration, a consciousness of herself, of her fine manners, and elaborate dress, finer than anything else in St. Rule's. Now there was nothing of all this about her. Her eyes seemed deepened in their sockets, as if a dozen years had passed over her since she last looked thus at the minister. And she asked him that question as if the date of her son's birthday was the most tragic of facts, a date which she anticipated with nothing less than despair.

"Is it really?" said the perplexed minister. "No, indeed, I did not know."

"And you don't seem to care either," she cried, "you don't care!"

Mr. Buchanan looked at her with a suspicious glance, as if presaging some further assault upon his peace. But he said:

"I am very glad my young friend has come to such a pleasant age. Everything has gone well with him hitherto, and he has come creditably through what may be called the most perilous portion of his youth. He has now a little experience, and power of discrimination, and I see no reason to fear but that things will go as well with him in the future, as they seem—"

"Oh," cried Mrs. Mowbray, raising her clasped hands with a gesture of despair, "is that all you have got to say, just what any old woman might say! And what about me, Mr. Buchanan, what about me?"

"You!" he cried, rather harshly, for to be called an old woman is enough to upset the patience of any man. "I don't know what there is to think of about you, except the satisfaction you must have in seeing Frank—"

She stamped her foot upon the floor; her eyes, which looked so hollow and tragic, flamed up for a moment in wrath.

"Oh, Frank, Frank! as if it were only Frank!" She paused a moment, and then began again drawing a long breath. "I came to you in my despair. If you can help me, I know not, or if any one can help me. It is that, or the pierhead, or the Spindle rock, where a poor creature might slip in, and it would be thought an accident, and she would never be heard of more."

"Mrs. Mowbray! For God's sake, what do you mean?"

"Ah, you ask me what I mean now? When I speak of the rocks and the sea, then you begin to think. That is what must come, I know that is what must come, unless," she said, "unless"—holding out her hands still convulsively clasped to him, "you can think of something. Oh, Mr. Buchanan, if you can think of something, if you can make it up with that money, if you can show me how I am to get it, how I can make it up! Oh, will you save me, will you save me!" she cried, stumbling down upon her knees on the other side of his table, holding up her hands, fixing her strained eyes upon his face.

"Mrs. Mowbray!" he cried, springing up from his chair, "what is this? rise up for Heaven's sake, do not go on your knees to me. I will do anything for you, anything I can do, surely you understand that— without this—"

"Oh, let me stay where I am! It is like asking it from God. You're God's, minister, and I'm a poor creature, a poor nervous weak woman. I never meant to do any harm. It was chiefly for my boy, that he might have everything nice, everything that he wanted like a gentleman. Oh, Mr. Buchanan! you may think I spent too much on my dress. So I did. I have been senseless and wicked all round, but I never did more than other women did. And I had no expenses besides. I never was extravagant, nor played cards, nor anything. And that was for Frank, too, that he might not be ashamed of his mother. Mr. Buchanan!"

"Rise up," he said, desperately, "for goodness' sake, don't make us both ridiculous. Sit down, and whatever it is, let us talk it over quietly. Oh, yes, yes, I am very sorry for you. I am shocked and distressed beyond words. Sit down rationally, for God's sake, and tell me what it is. It is a matter, of course," he cried, sharply, with some impatience, "that whatever I can do, I will do for you. There can be no need to implore me like this! of course I will do everything I can—of course. Mrs. Mowbray, sit down, for the love of heaven, and let me know what it is."

She had risen painfully to her feet while he was speaking. Going down on your knees may be a picturesque thing, but getting up from them, especially in petticoats, and in a large shawl, is not a graceful operation at all, and this, notwithstanding her despair, poor Mrs. Mowbray was vaguely conscious of. She stumbled to her feet, her skirts tripping her up, the corners of her shawl getting in her way. The poor woman had begun to cry. It was wonderful that she had been able to restrain herself so long; but she was old enough to be aware that a woman's tears are just as often exasperating as pathetic to a man, and had heroically restrained the impulse. But when she fell on her knees, she lost her self-control. That was begging the question altogether. She had given up her position as a tragic and dignified appellant. She was nothing but a poor suppliant now, at anybody's mercy, quite broken down, and overmastered by her trouble. It did not matter to her any longer what anyone thought. The state of mind in which she had dared to tell the minister that he spoke like an old woman, was gone from her completely. He was like God, he could save her, if he would; she could not tell how, there was no reason in her hope, but if he only would, somehow he could, save her—that was all her thought.

"Now, tell me exactly how it is," she heard him saying, confusedly, through the violent beating of her heart.

But what unfortunate, in her position, ever could tell exactly how such a thing was? She told him a long, broken, confused story, full of apology, and explanation, insisting chiefly upon the absence of any ill meaning on her part, or ill intention, and the fatality which had caught her, and compelled her actions, so often against her will. She had been led into this and that, it had been pressed upon her—even now she did not see how she could have escaped. And it was all for Frank's sake: every step she had taken was for Frank's sake, that he might want for nothing, that he might have everything the others had, and feel that everything about him—his home, his mother, his society—were such as a gentleman ought to have.

"This long minority," Mrs. Mowbray said, through her tears, "oh, what a mistake it is; instead of saving his money, it has been the destruction of his money. I thought always it was so hard upon him, that I was forced to spend more and more to make it up to him. I spent everything of my own first. Oh, Mr. Buchanan! you must not think I spared anything of my own—that went first. I sold out and sold out, till there was nothing left; and then what could I do but get into debt? And here I am, and I have not a penny, and all these dreadful men pressing and pressing! And everything will be exposed to Frank, all exposed to him on the fifth of next month. Oh, Mr. Buchanan, save me, save me. My boy will despise me. He will never trust me again. He will say it is all my fault! So it is all my fault. Oh, I do not attempt to deny it, Mr. Buchanan: but it was all for him. And then there was another thing that deceived me. I always trusted in you. I felt sure that at the end, when you found it was really so serious, you would step in, and compel all these people to pay up, and all my little debts would not matter so much at the last."

Mr. Buchanan had forgotten the personal reference in all this to himself. It did not occur to him that the money which rankled so at his own heart, and which had already cost him so much, much more than its value, was the thing upon which she depended, from which she had expected salvation. What was it she expected? thousands, he supposed, instead of fifties, a large sum sufficient to re-establish her fortunes. It was with a kind of impatient disdain that he spoke.

"Are these really little debts you are telling me of? Could a hundred pounds or two clear them off, would that be of real use?"

"Oh, a hundred pounds!" she cried, with a shriek. "Mr. Buchanan, a hundred pence would, of course, be of use, for I have no money at all, and a hundred is a nice little bit of money, and I could stop several mouths with it: but to clear them off! Oh no, no, alas, alas! It is clear that you never lived in London. A hundred pounds would be but a drop in the ocean. But when it is thousands, Mr. Buchanan, which is more like facts—thousands, I am sure, which you know of, which you could recover for Frank!"

"Mrs. Mowbray, I don't know what can have deceived you to this point. It is absolute folly: all that Mr. Anderson lent to people at St. Rule's was never above a few hundred pounds. I know of nothing more. There is nothing more. There was one of three hundred—nothing more. Be composed, be composed and listen to me. Mrs. Mowbray!"

But she neither listened nor heard him, her excitement had reached to a point beyond which flesh and blood overmastered by wild anxiety and disappointment could not go.

"It can't be true," she shrieked out. "It can't be true, it mustn't be true." And then, with a shriek that rang through the house, throwing out her arms, she fell like a mass of ruins on the floor.

Mrs. Buchanan was busy with her napery at some distance from the study. She had heard the visitor come in, and had concluded within herself that her poor husband would have an ill time of it with that woman. "But there's something more on her mind than that pickle siller," the minister's wife had said to herself, shaking her head over the darns in her napery. She had long been a student of the troubled faces that came to the minister for advice or consolation, and, having only that evidence to go upon, had formed many a conclusion that turned out true enough, sometimes more true than those which, with a more extended knowledge, from the very lips of the penitents, had been formed by the minister himself: for the face, as Mrs. Buchanan held, could not make excuses, or explain things away, but just showed what was. She was pondering over this case, half-sorry and, perhaps, half-amused that her husband should have this tangled skein to wind, which he never should have meddled with, so that it was partly his own fault—when the sound of those shrieks made her start. They were far too loud and too terrible to ignore. Mrs. Buchanan threw down the linen she was darning, seized a bottle of water from the table, and flew to her husband's room. Already there were two maids on the stairs hurrying towards the scene of the commotion, to one of whom she gave a quick order, sending the other away.

"Thank God that you've come," said Mr. Buchanan, who was feebly endeavouring to drag the unfortunate woman to her feet again.

"Oh, go away, go away, Claude, you're of no use here. Send in the doctor if you see him, he will be more use than you."

"I'll do that," cried the minister, relieved. He was too thankful to resign the patient into hands more skilful than his own.

CHAPTER XX

CONFESSION

"Then it is just debt and nothing worse," Mrs. Buchanan said. There was a slight air of disappointment in her face; not that she wished the woman to be more guilty, but that this was scarcely an adequate cause for all the dramatic excitement which had been caused in her own mind by Mrs. Mowbray's visits and the trouble in her face.

"Nothing worse! what is there that is worse?" cried the minister, turning round upon her. He had been walking up and down the study, that study which had been made a purgatory to him by the money of which she spoke so lightly. It was this that was uppermost in his mind now, and not the poor woman who had thrown herself on his mercy. To tell the truth, he had but little toleration for her. She had thrown away her son's substance in vanity, and to please herself: but what pleasure had he, the minister, had out of that three hundred pounds? Nothing! It would have been better for him a thousand times to have toiled for it in the sweat of his brow, to have lived on bread and water, and cleared it off honestly. But he had not been allowed to do this; he had been forced into the position he now held, a defaulter as she had said—an unjust steward according to the formula more familiar to his mind.

"Oh, yes, Claude, there are worse things—at least to a woman. She might have misbe— We'll not speak of that. Poor thing, she is bad enough, and sore shaken. We will leave her quiet till the laddies come home to their lunch; as likely as not Rodie will bring Frank home with him, as I hear they are playing together: and then he must just be told she had a faint. There are some women that are always fainting; it is just the sort of thing that the like of her would do. If I were you, I would see Mr. Morrison and try what could be done to keep it all quiet. I am not fond of exposing a silly woman to her own son."

"Better to her son than to strangers, surely—and to the whole world."

"I am not so sure of that," Mrs. Buchanan said, thoughtfully: but she did not pursue the argument. She sat very still in the chair which so short a time before had been occupied by poor Mrs. Mowbray in her passion and despair: while her husband walked about the room with his hands thrust into his pockets, and his shoulders up to his ears, full of restless and unquiet thoughts.

"There's one thing," he said, pausing in front of her, but not looking at her, "that money, Mary: we must get it somehow. I cannot reconcile it with my conscience, I can't endure the feeling of it: if it should ruin us, we must pay it back."

"Nothing will ruin us, Claude," she said, steadily, "so long as it is all honest and above board. Let it be paid back; I know well it has been on your mind this many a day."

"It has been a thorn in my flesh; it has been poison in my blood!"

"Lord bless us," cried Mrs. Buchanan, with a little fretfulness, "what for? and what is the use of exaggeration? It is not an impossibility that you should rave about it like that. Besides," she added, "I said the same at first—though I was always in favour of paying, at whatever cost—yet I am not sure that I would disappoint an old friend in his grave, for the sake of satisfying a fantastic woman like yon."

"I must get it clear, I must get it off my mind! Not for her sake, but for my own."

"Aweel, aweel," said Mrs. Buchanan, soothingly; and she added, "we must all set our shoulders to the wheel, and they must give us time."

"But it is just time that cannot be given us," cried her husband, almost hysterically. "The fifth of next month! and this is the twenty-fourth."

"You will have to speak to Morrison."

"Morrison, Morrison!" cried the minister. "You seem to have no idea but Morrison! and it is just to him that I cannot speak."

His wife gazed at him with surprise, and some impatience.

"Claude! you are just as foolish as that woman. Will ranting and raving, and 'I will not do that,' and 'I will not do this,' pay back the siller? It is not so easy to do always what you wish. In this world we must just do what we can."

"In another world, at least, there will be neither begging nor borrowing," he cried.

"There will maybe be some equivalent," said Mrs. Buchanan, shaking her head. "I would not lippen to anything. It would have been paid long ago if you had but stuck to the point with Morrison, and we would be free."

"Morrison, Morrison!" he cried again, "nothing but Morrison. I wish he and all his books, and his bonds, and his money, were at the bottom of the sea!"

"Claude, Claude! and you a minister!" cried Mrs. Buchanan, horrified. But she saw that the discussion had gone far enough, and that her husband could bear no more.

As for the unfortunate man himself, he continued, mechanically, to pace about the room, after she left him, muttering "Morrison, Morrison!" between his teeth. He could not himself have explained the rage he felt at the name of Morrison. He could see in his mind's eye the sleek figure of the man of business coming towards him, rubbing his hands, stopping his confession, "Not another word, sir, not another word; our late esteemed friend gave me my instructions." And then he could hear himself pretending to insist, putting forward "the fifty:" "The fifty," with the lie beneath, as if that were all: and again the lawyer's refusal to hear. Morrison had done him a good office: he had stopped the lie upon his lips, so that, formally speaking, he had never uttered it; he ought to have been grateful to Morrison: yet he was not, but hated him (for the moment) to the bottom of his heart.

Frank Mowbray came to luncheon (which was dinner) with Rodie, as Mrs. Buchanan had foreseen, and when he had got through a large meal, was taken up-stairs to see his mother, who was still lying exhausted in Elsie's bed, very hysterical, laughing and crying in a manner which was by no means unusual in those days, though we may be thankful it has practically disappeared from our experiences now—unfortunately not without leaving a deeper and more injurious deposit of the hysterical. She hid her face when he came in, with a passion of tears and outcries, and then held out her arms to him, contradictory actions which Frank took with wonderful composure, being not unaccustomed to them.

"Speak to Mr. Buchanan," she said, "oh, speak to Mr. Buchanan!" whispering these words into his ear as he bent over her, and flinging them at him as he went away. Frank was very reluctant to lose his afternoon's game, and he was aware, too, of the threatening looks of Elsie, who said, "My father's morning has been spoiled; he has had no peace all the day. You must see him another time." "Speak to Mr. Buchanan, oh, speak to Mr. Buchanan," cried his mother. Frank did not know what to do. Perhaps Mrs. Mowbray in her confused mind expected that the minister would soften the story of her own misdemeanours to Frank. But Frank thought of nothing but the previous disclosure she had made to him. And he would probably have been subdued by Elsie's threatening looks, as she stood without the door defending the passage to the study, had not Mr. Buchanan himself appeared coming slowly up-stairs. The two young people stood silent before him. Even Elsie, though she held Frank back fiercely with her eyes, could say nothing: and the minister waved his hand, as if inviting him to follow. The youth went after him a little overawed, giving Elsie an apologetic look as he passed. It was not his fault: without that tacit invitation he would certainly not have gone. He felt the situation very alarming. He was a simple young soul, going to struggle with one of the superior classes, in deadly combat, and with nobody to stand by him. Certainly he had lost his afternoon's game—almost as certainly he had lost, altogether lost, Elsie's favour. The smiles of the morning had inspired him to various strokes, which even Raaf Beaton could not despise. But that was over, and now he had to go on unaided to his fate.

"Your mother has been ill, Frank."

"I am very sorry, sir: and she has distressed and disturbed you, I fear. She sometimes has those sort of attacks: they don't mean much, I think," Frank said.

"They mean a great deal," replied Mr. Buchanan. "They mean that her mind is troubled about you and your future, Frank."

"Without any reason, I think," said Frank. "I am not very clear about money; I have always left it in my mother's hands. She thought it would be time enough to look after my affairs when I attained my Scotch majority. But I don't think I need trouble myself, for there must be plenty to go on upon. She says the Scotch estate is far less than was thought, and indeed she wanted me to come to you about some debts. She thinks half St. Rule's was owing money to old Uncle Anderson. And he kept no books, or something of that sort. I don't understand it very well; but she said you understood everything."

"There was no question of books," said Mr. Buchanan. "Mr. Anderson was kind, and helped many people, not letting his right hand know what his left hand did. Some he helped to stock a shop: some of the small farmers to buy the cattle they wanted: some of the fishers to get boats of their own. The money was a loan nominally to save their pride, but in reality it was a gift, and nobody knew how much he gave in this way. It was entered in no book, except perhaps," said the minister, with a look which struck awe into Frank, and a faint upward movement of his hand "in One above." After a minute he resumed: "I am sure, from what I know of you, you would not disturb these poor folk, who most of them are now enjoying the advantage of the charity that helped them rather to labour than to profit at first."

"No, sir, no," cried Frank, eagerly. "I am not like that, I am not a beast; and I am very glad to hear Uncle Anderson was such a good man. But," he added after a pause, with a little natural pertinacity, "there were others different from that, or else my mother had wrong information—which might well be," he continued with a little reluctance. He was open to a generous impulse, but yet he wished to reserve what might be owing to him on a less sentimental ground.

"Yes, there are others different from that. There are a few people of a different class in St. Rule's, who are just as good as anybody, as people say; you will understand I am speaking the language of the world, and not referring to any moral condition, in which, as we have the best authority for saying, none of us are good, but God alone. As good as anybody, as people say—as good blood so far as that counts, as good education or better, as good manners: but all this held in check, or indeed made into pain sometimes, by the fact that they are poor. Do you follow what I mean?"

"Yes, sir, I follow," said Frank: though without the effusiveness which he had shown when the minister's talk was of the actual poor.

"A little money to such people as these is sometimes almost a greater charity than to the shopkeepers and the fishermen. They are far poorer with their pride, and the appearance they have to keep up, than the lowest. Mind I am not defending pride nor the keeping up of appearances. I am speaking just the common language of the world. Well, there were several of these, I believe, who had loans of money from Mr. Anderson."

"I think," said Frank, respectfully, yet firmly too, "that they ought to pay, Mr. Buchanan. They have enjoyed the use of it for years, and people like that can always find means of raising a little money. If it lies much longer in their hands, it will be lost, I am told, by some Statute of—of Limitation I think it is. Well then, nobody could force them in that case; but I think, Mr. Buchanan, as between man and man, that they ought to pay."

"I think," said the minister, in a voice which trembled a little, "that you are right, Frank: they ought to pay."

"That is certainly my opinion," said Frank. "It would not ruin them, they could find the money: and though it might harass them for the moment, it would be better for them in the end to pay off a debt which they would go on thinking must be claimed some time. And especially if the estate is not going to turn out so good as was thought, I do think, Mr. Buchanan, that they should pay."

"I think you are right, Frank." The minister rose and began to walk up and down the room as was his habit. There was an air of agitation about him which the young man did not understand. "It is no case of an unjust steward," he said to himself; "if there's an unjust steward, it is—and to take the bill and write fourscore would never be the way with—Well, we have both come to the same decision, Frank, and we are both interested parties; I am, I believe, the largest of all Mr. Anderson's debtors. I owe him—"

"Mr. Buchanan!" cried Frank, springing to his feet. "Mr. Buchanan, I never thought of this. You! for goodness' sake don't say any more!"

"I owe him," the minister repeated slowly, "three hundred pounds. If you were writing that, you know," he said, with a curious sort of smile, "you would repeat it, once in figures and once in letters, £300—and three hundred pounds. You are quite right; it will be much better to pay it off, at whatever sacrifice, than to feel that it may be demanded from one at any time, as you have demanded it from me!"

"Mr. Buchanan," cried Frank, eagerly (for what would Elsie say? never, never would she look at him again!), "you may be sure I had never a notion, not an idea of this, not a thought! You were my uncle's best friend; I can't think why he didn't leave you a legacy, or something, far more than this. I remember it was thought surprising there were no legacies, to you or to others. Of course I don't know who the others may be," he added with a changed inflection in his voice (for why should he throw any money, that was justly his, to perhaps persons of no importance, unconnected with Elsie?) "but you, sir, you! It is out of the question," Frank cried.

Mr. Buchanan smiled a little. I fear it did not please him to feel that Frank's compassion was roused, or that he might be excused the payment of his debt by Frank. Indeed that view of the case changed his feelings altogether. "We need not discuss the question," he said rather coldly. "I have told you of the only money owing to your uncle's estate which I know of. I might have stated it to your mother some time since, but did not on account of something that passed between Morrison and myself, which was neither here nor there."

"What was it, Mr. Buchanan? I cannot believe that my uncle—"

"You know very little about your uncle," said the minister, testily. "Now, I think I shall keep you no longer to-day: but before your birthday I will see Morrison, and put everything right."

"It is right as it is," cried Frank; "why should we have recourse to Morrison? surely you and I are enough to settle it. Mr. Buchanan, you know this never was what was meant. You! to bring you to book! I would rather have bitten out my tongue—I would rather—"

"Come, this is all exaggerated, as my wife says," said the minister with a laugh. "It is too late to go back upon it. Bring a carriage for your mother, Frank, she will be better at home. You can tell her this if you please: and then let us hear no more of it, my boy. I will see Morrison, and settle with him, and there is no need that any one should think of it more."

"Only that it is impossible not to think of it," cried Frank. "Mr. Buchanan—"

"Not another word," the minister said. He came back to his table and sat down, and took his pen into his fingers. "Your foursome will be broken up for want of you," he said with a chilly smile. The poor young fellow tried to say something more, but he was stopped remorselessly. "Really, you must let me get to my work," said the minister. "Everything I think has been said between us that there is to say."

And it was Elsie's father whom he had thus offended! Frank's heart sank to his boots, as he went down-stairs. He did not go near his mother, but left her to be watched over and taken home by her maid, who had now appeared. He felt as if he could never forgive her for having forced him to this encounter with the minister. Oh! if he had but known! He would rather have bitten out his tongue, he repeated to himself. The drawing-room was empty, neither Elsie nor her mother being visible, and there was no Rodie kicking his heels down-stairs. A maid came out of the kitchen, while he loitered in the hall to give him that worthy's message. "Mr. Rodie said he couldna wait, and you were just to follow after him: but you were not to be surprised if they started without waiting for you, for it would never do to keep all the gentlemen waiting for their game." Poor Frank strolled forth with a countenance dark as night; sweetheart and game, and self-respect and everything—he had lost them all.

CHAPTER XXI

HOW TO SET IT RIGHT

"What is the matter, mother?" Elsie said, drawing close to her mother's side. The minister had come to dinner, looking ill and pale. He had scarcely spoken all through the meal. He had said to his wife that he was not to be disturbed that evening, for there was a great deal to settle and to think of. Mrs. Buchanan, too, bore an anxious countenance. She went up to the drawing-room without a word, with her basket of things to mend in her arms. She had always things to mend, and her patches were a pleasure to behold. She lighted the two candles on the mantelpiece, but said with a sigh that it was a great extravagance, and that she had no right to do it: only the night was dark, and her eyes were beginning to fail. Now the night was no darker than usual, and Mrs. Buchanan had made a brag only the other evening, that with her new glasses she could see to do the finest work, as well as when she was a girl.

"What is the matter, mother?" Elsie said. She came very close to her mother, putting a timid arm round her waist. They were, as belonged to their country, shy of caresses, and Elsie was half afraid of being thrown off with an injunction not to be silly; but this evening Mrs. Buchanan seemed to be pleased with the warm clasp of the young arm.

"Nothing that was not yesterday, and for years before that. You and me, Elsie, will have to put our shoulders to the wheel."

"What is it, mother?" The idea of putting her shoulder to the wheel was comforting and invigorating, far better than the vague something wrong that clouded the parents' faces. Mrs. Buchanan permitted herself to give her child a kiss, and then she drew her chair to the table and put on her spectacles for her evening's work.

"Women are such fools," she said. "I am not sure that your father's saying that he was not to be disturbed to-night, you heard him?—which means that I am not to go up to him as I always do—has cast me down more than the real trouble. For why should he shut himself up from me? He might know by this time that it is not brooding by himself that will pay off that three hundred pounds."

"Three hundred pounds!"

"It is an old story, it is nothing new," said the minister's wife. "It is a grand rule, Elsie, not to let your right hand know what your left doeth in the way of charity; but when it's such a modern thing as a loan of money, oh, I'm afraid the worldly way is maybe the best way. If Mr. Anderson had written it down in his books, The Rev. Claude Buchanan, Dr—as they do, you know, in the tradesmen's bills—to loan £300—well, then, it might have been disagreeable, but we should have known the worst of it, and it would have been paid off by this time. But the good old man kept no books; and when he died, it was just left on our consciences to pay it or not. Oh, Elsie, siller is a terrible burden on your conscience when you have not got it to pay! God forgive us! what with excuses and explanations, and trying to make out that it was just an accident and so forth, I am not sure that I have always been quite truthful myself."

"You never told lies, mother," said Elsie.

"Maybe not, if you put it like that; but there's many a lee that is not a lee, in the way of excuses for not paying a bill. You'll say, perhaps, 'Dear me, I am very sorry; I have just paid away the last I set aside for bills, till next term comes round;' when, in fact, you had nothing set aside, but just paid what you had, and as little as you could, to keep things going! It's not a lee, so to speak, and yet it is a lee, Elsie! A poor woman, with a limited income, has just many, many things like that on her mind. We've never wronged any man of a penny."

"No, mother, I'm sure of that."

"But they have waited long for their siller, and maybe as much in want of it as we were," Mrs. Buchanan said, shaking her head. "Anyway, if it's clear put down in black and white, there is an end of it. You know you have to pay, and you just make up your mind to it. But, when it is just left to your conscience, and you to be the one to tell that you are owing—oh, Elsie! Lead us not into temptation. I hope you never forget that prayer, morning nor evening. If you marry a man that is not rich, you will have muckle need of it day by day."

Elsie seemed to see, as you will sometimes see by a gleam of summer lightning, a momentary glimpse of a whole country-side—a panorama of many past years. The scene was the study up-stairs, where her father was sitting, often pausing in his work, laying down his pen, giving himself up to sombre thoughts. "Take now thy bill, and sit down quickly, and write fourscore," she said to herself, under her breath.

"What are you saying, Elsie? Fourscore? Oh, much more than fourscore. It is three hundred pounds," said Mrs. Buchanan. "Three hundred pounds," she repeated deliberately, as if the enormity of the sum gave her, under the pain, a certain pleasure. "I have told you about it before. It was for Willie's outfit, and Marion's plenishing, and a few other things that were pressing upon us. Old Mr. Anderson was a very kind old man. He said: 'Take enough—take enough while you are about it: put yourself at your ease while you are about it!' And so we did, Elsie. I will never forget the feeling I had when I paid off Aitken and the rest who had just been very patient waiting. I felt like Christian in the Pilgrim's Progress, when the burden rolled off his back. Oh, my dear! a poor woman with a family to provide, thinks more of her bills than her sins, I am sore afraid!"

"Well, mother, those that have to judge know best all about it," said Elsie, with tears in her voice.

"My bonnie dear! You'll have to give up the ball, Elsie, and your new frock."

"What about that, mother?" cried Elsie, tossing her young head.

"Oh, there's a great deal about it! You think it is nothing now: but when you hear the coaches all driving past, and not a word said among all the young lassies but who was there and what they wore, and who they danced with: and, maybe, even you may hear a sough of music on the air, if the wind's from the south: it will not be easy then, though your mind's exalted, and you think it matters little now."

"It will be, maybe—a little—hard," Elsie assented, nodding her head; "but, if that's all, mother?"

"It will not be all," said Mrs. Buchanan, once more shaking her head. "It will be day by day, and hour by hour. We will have to do without everything, you and me. Your father, he must not be disturbed, more than we can help; or how is he to do his work? which is work far more important than yours or mine. And Rodie is a growing laddie, wanting much meat, and nothing must interfere with his learning either, or how could we put him out creditably in the world? I tell you it is you and me that will have to put our sheulders to the wheel. Janet is a good, sensible woman, I will take her into my confidence, and she'll not mind a little more work; but, Betty—oh, my dear, I think we'll have to give up Betty: and you know what that means."

"It means just the right thing to mean!" cried Elsie, with her countenance glowing. "I am nearly as old as Betty, and I have never done a hand's turn in my life. It would be strange if I couldn't do as much for love, as Betty does for wages."

"Ten pounds a year and her keep, which will count, maybe, for fifteen more. Oh Elsie, my dear, to think that I should make a drudge of my own bairn for no more saving than that."

"It is a pity it is not a hundred pounds," cried Elsie, half-laughing, half-crying; "but in four years, mother, it would make up a hundred pounds. Fancy me making up a hundred pounds! There will be no living with me for pride."

Mrs. Buchanan shook her head, and put her handkerchief to her eyes, but joined in, too, with a tremulous laugh to this wonderful thought.

"And there's your father all his lane up the stair," she said, regretfully, "with nobody to speak to! when you and me are here together taking comfort, and making a laugh at it. There's many things, after all, in which we are better off than men, Elsie. But why he should debar himself from just the only comfort there is, talking it over with me—what's that?"

It was a noise up-stairs, in the direction of Mr. Buchanan's study, and they both sprang to their feet: though, after all, it was not a very dreadful noise, only the hasty opening of a window, and the fall of a chair, as if knocked down by some sudden movement. They stood for a moment, looking into each other's suddenly blanched faces, an awful suggestion leaping from eye to eye. Had it been too much for his brain? Had he fallen? Had something dreadful happened? Elsie moved to open the door, while her mother still stood holding by the table; but the momentary horror was quieted by the sound of his steps overhead. They heard him come out of his room to the head of the stairs, and held their breath. Then there was a cry, "Mary! Mary!" Mrs. Buchanan turned upon her daughter, with a sparkle in her eye.

"You see he couldna do without me after all," she said.

When Elsie sat down alone she did not take her work again all at once, but sat thinking, thoughts that, perhaps, were not so sweet as they had been in the first enthusiasm of self-sacrifice. Her mother had left her for a still more intimate conference and sharing of the burden, which, when two people looked at it together, holding by each other, seemed so much lighter than when one was left to look at it alone. There swept across Elsie's mind for a moment, in the chill of this desertion, the thought that it was all very well for mamma. She had outgrown the love of balls and other such enjoyments; and, though she liked to be well dressed, she had the sustaining conviction that she was always well dressed in her black silk; which, one year with another, if it was the most enduring, was also one of the most becoming garments in St. Rule's. And she had her partner by her side always, no need to be wondering and fancying what might happen, or whom she might see at the ball, perhaps at the next street corner. But at nineteen it is very different; and, it must be owned, that the prospect of the four years which it would take for Elsie, by all manner of labours and endurances, to make up the hundred pounds, which, after all, was only a third part of what was wanted—was not so exhilarating when looked at alone, as it was when the proud consciousness of such power to help had first thrilled her bosom. Elsie looked at her own nice little hands, which were smooth, soft, and reasonably white—not uselessly white like those of the people who never did a hand's turn—but white enough to proclaim them a lady's hands, though with scars of needlework on the fingers. She looked at her hands, and wondered what they would look like at the end of these four years? And she thought of the four balls, the yearly golf balls, at not one of which was she likely to appear, and at all the other things which she would have to give up. "What about that?" she said to herself, with indignation, meaning, what did it matter, of what consequence was it? But it did matter after all, it was of consequence. Whatever amount of generous sophistry there may be in a girl's mind, it does not go so far as to convince her that four years out of her life, spent in being housemaid, in working with her hands for her family, does not matter. It did matter, and a tear or two dropped over her work. It would be hard, but Elsie knew, all the same, that she had it in her to go through with it. Oh, to go through with it! however hard it might be.

She was drying away her tears indignantly, angry with herself and ashamed, and resolute that no such weakness should ever occur again, when she became aware of several small crackling sounds that came from the direction of the turret, the lower story of which formed an appendage to the drawing-room, as the higher did to the study. Elsie was not alarmed by these sounds. It was, no doubt, some friend either of Rodie's or her own, who was desirous of making a private communication without disturbing the minister's house by an untimely visit, and calling attention by flinging gravel at the window. She could not think who it was, but any incident was good to break the current of her thoughts. There was a little pale moonlight, of that misty, milky kind, which is more like a lingering of fantastic day than a fine white night with black shadows, and there was a figure standing underneath, which she did not recognise till she had opened the window. Then she saw it was Johnny Wemyss. He had a packet in his hand.

"I thought," he said, "that I would just come and tell you before I sent it off by the night-coach. Elsie! I am sure—that is to say, I am near sure, as sure as you dare to think you are, when it's only you—"

"What?" she cried, leaning out of the window.

"That yon is a new beast," said the young man. His voice was a little tremulous. "I never lifted my head till I had it all out with it," he said, with a nervous laugh; "and I'm just as near sure—oh, well, some other idiot may have found it out yesterday! but, barring that—I'm sure—I mean as near sure—"

"Oh, you and your beasts!" cried Elsie. Her heart had given a jump in her breast, and she had become gay and saucy in a moment; "and you never were more than near sure all your life. I knew it was, all the time."

They laughed together under the gray wall, the girl lightly triumphant, the boy thrilling in every nerve with the certainty which he dared not acknowledge even to himself.

"I have called it 'Princess Elsie,'" he said, "in Latin, you know: that is, if it is really a new beast."

"There is nine striking," said she; "you will have to run if you are to catch the night-coach."

"I will—but I had to come and tell you," he cried over his shoulder.

"As if there was any need! when I knew it all the time."

This was enough, I am glad to say, to turn entirely the tide of Elsie's thoughts. She stood listening to the sound of his heavy shoes, as he dashed along the rough cobbles of the pavement, towards the centre of the town from which the coach started. And then she came in with a delightful, soft illumination on her face, laughing to herself, and sat down at the table and took up her seam. Four years! four strokes of the clock, four stitches with the needle! That was about all it would come to in the long stretching, far panorama of endless and joyous life.

CHAPTER XXII

IN THE STUDY

The hour was heavier to the parents up-stairs, where the minister was so despondent and depressed that his wife had hard ado to cheer him. The window which down-stairs they had heard him throw open, stood wide to the night, admitting a breeze which blew about the flame of the candles, threatening every moment to extinguish them; for the air, though soft and warm, blew in almost violently fresh from the sea. Mrs. Buchanan put down the window, and drew the blind, restoring the continuity and protecting enclosure of the walls; for there are times and moods when an opening upon infinite air and space is too much for the soul travailing among the elements of earth. She went to his side and stood by him, with her hand on his shoulder.

"Dinna be so down-hearted, Claude, my man," she said, with her soft voice. Her touch, her tone, the contact of her warm, soft person, the caressing of her hand came on him like dew.

"Mary," he said, leaning his head back upon her, "you don't know what I have done. I did it in meaning, if not in fact. The thought of you kept me back, my dear, more than the thought of my Maker. I am a miserable and blood-guilty man."

"Whisht, whisht," she said, trembling all over, but putting now a quivering arm round him; "you are not thinking what you say."

"Well am I thinking, well am I knowing it. Me, His body-servant, His man—not merely because He is my Saviour, as of all men, but my Master to serve hand and foot, night and day. For the sake of a little pain, a little miserable money, I had well-nigh deserted His service, Mary. Oh, speak not to me, for I am a lost soul—"

"Whisht, Claude! You are a fevered bairn. Do you think He is less understanding, oh, my man, than me? What have you done?"

He looked up at her with large, wild eyes. Then she suddenly perceived his hand clenched upon something, and darting at it with a cry forced it open, showing a small bottle clasped in the hollow of his palm. She gripped his shoulder violently, with a low shriek of horror.

"Claude, Claude! you have not—you did not—"

"I poured it out before the Lord," he said, putting the phial on the table; "but the sin is no less, for I did it in meaning, if not in deed. How can I ever lift my head or my hand before His presence again?"

"Oh, my laddie! my man!" cried his wife, who was the mother of every soul in trouble, "oh, my Claude! Are you so little a father, you with your many bairns, that you do not know in your heart how He is looking at you? 'Such pity as a father hath unto His children dear.' You are just fevered and sick with trouble. You shut out your wife from you, and now you would shut out your Lord from you."

"No," he said, grasping her hand, "never again, Mary, never again. I am weak as water, I cannot stand alone. I have judged others for less, far less, than I myself have done."

"Well, let it be so," said his wife, "you will know better another time. Claude, you are just my bairn to-night. You will say your prayers and go to your bed, and the Lord in heaven and me at your bedside, like a dream it will all pass away."

He dropped down heavily upon his knees, and bent his head upon the table.

"Mary, I feel as if I could say nought but this: Depart from me, for I am a sinful man, oh Lord."

"You know well," she said, "the hasty man that Peter was, if ever he had been taken at his word. And do you mind what was the answer? It was just 'Follow me.'"

"Father, forgive me. Master, forgive me," he breathed through the hands that covered his face, and then his voice broke out in the words of an older faith, words which she understood but dimly, and which frightened her with the mystery of an appeal into the unknown. Kyrie Eleison, Christ Eleison, the man said, humbled to the very depths.

The woman stood trembling over him not knowing how to follow. His voice rolled forth low and intense, like the sound of an organ into the silent room; hers faltered after in sobs inarticulate, terrified, exalted, understanding nothing, comprehending all.

This scene was scarcely ended when Elsie burst out singing over her work, forgetting that there was any trouble in the world: to each its time, and love through all.

Mr. Buchanan was very much shaken with physical illness and weakness next morning, than where there is nothing more healing for a spirit that has been put to the question, as in the old days of the Inquisition, but by rack and thumbscrew still more potent than these. His head ached, his pulses fluttered. He felt as if he had been beaten, he said, not a nerve in him but tingled; he could scarcely stand on his feet. His wife had her way with him, which was sweet to her. She kept him sheltered and protected in his study under her large and soft maternal wing. It was to her as when one of her children was ill, but not too ill—rather convalescent—in her hands to be soothed and caressed into recovery. This was an immense and characteristic happiness to herself even in the midst of her pain. In the afternoon after she had fed him with nourishing meats, appropriate to his weakness, a visitor was announced who startled them both. Mr. Morrison, the writer, sent up his name and a request to have speech of Mr. Buchanan, if the minister were well enough to receive him. There was a rapid consultation between the husband and wife.

"Are you fit for it, Claude?"

"Yes, yes, let us get it over: but stay with me," he said.

Mrs. Buchanan went down to meet the man of business, and warn him of her husband's invalid condition.

"He is a little low," she said. "You will give no particular importance, Mr. Morrison, to any despondent thing he may say."

"Not I, not I," cried the cheerful man of business. "The minister has his ill turns like the rest of us: but with less occasion than most of us, I'm well aware."

Mrs. Buchanan stayed only long enough in the room to see that her husband had drawn himself together, and was equal to the interview. She had a fine sense of the proprieties, and perception, though she was so little of a sensitive, of what was befitting. Morrison perceived with a little surprise the minister's alarmed glance after his wife, but for his part was exceedingly glad to get rid of the feminine auditor.

"I am glad," he said, "to see you alone, if you are equal to business, Mr. Buchanan, for I've something which is really not business to talk to you about: that is to say, it's a very bad business, just the mishap of a silly woman if you'll permit me to say so. She tells me she has confided them to you already."

"Mrs. Mowbray?" said the minister.

"Just Mrs. Mowbray. The day of Frank's majority is coming on when all must come to light, and in desperation, poor body, she sent for me. Yon's a silly business if you like—a foolish laddie without an idea in his head—and a lightheaded woman with nothing but vanity and folly in hers."

"Stop a little," said Mr. Buchanan, in the voice which his rôle of invalid had made, half artificially, wavering, and weak; "we must not judge so harshly. Frank, if he is not clever, is full of good feeling, and as for his mother—it is easy for the wisest of us to deceive ourselves about things we like and wish for— she thought, poor woman, it was for the benefit of her boy."

"You are just too charitable," said Morrison, with a laugh. "But let us say it was that. It makes no difference to the result. A good many thousands to the bad, that is all about it, and nothing but poverty before them, if it were not for what she calls the Scotch property. The Scotch property was to bear the brunt of everything: and now some idiot or other has told her that the Scotch property is little to lippen to: and that half St. Rule's was in old Anderson's debt—"

"I have heard all that—I told her that at the utmost there were but a few hundreds—"

"Not a penny—not a penny," said Morrison. "I had my full instructions: and now here is the situation. She has been more foolish than it's allowable even for a lightheaded woman to be."

"You have no warrant for calling her lightheaded; so far as I know she is an irreproachable woman as free of speck or stain—"

"Bless us," said the man of business, "you are awfully particular to-day, Buchanan. I am not saying a word against her character: but lightheaded, that is thoughtless and reckless, and fond of her pleasure, the woman undoubtedly is: nothing but a parcel of vanities, and ostentations, and show. Well, well! how it comes about is one thing, how to mend it is another. We cannot let the poor creature be overwhelmed if we can help it. She spent all her own money first, which, though the height of folly, was still a sign of grace. And now she has been spending Frank's, and, according to all that appears, his English money is very nearly gone, and there is nothing but the Scotch remaining."

"And the Scotch but little to lippen to, as you say, and everybody says."

"That's as it may be," said Morrison, with a twinkle in his eye. "It's better than the English, anyway. She deserves to be punished for her folly, but I have not the heart to leave her in the lurch. She's sorry enough now, though whether that is because she's feared for exposure or really penitent, I would not like to say. Anyway, when a woman trusts in you to pull her out of the ditch, it's hard just to steel your heart and refuse: though maybe, in a moral point of view, the last would be well justified and really the right thing to do. But I thought you and I might lay our heads together and see which was best."

"There is that money of mine, Morrison."

"Hoots!" said the man of business, "what nonsense is that ye have got in your head? There is no money of yours."

"Forgive me, but you must not put me down so," said the minister. "I have done wrong in not insisting before. The arrangement was that it should be repaid, and I ought not to have allowed myself to be persuaded out of it, I owed Mr. Anderson—"

"Not a penny, not a penny. All cancelled by his special instructions at his death."

"Morrison, this has been upon my mind for years. I must be quit of it now." He raised his voice with a shrill weakness in it. "My wife knows. Where is my wife? I wish my wife to be present when we settle this account finally. Open the door and call her. I must have Mary here."

"Well, she is a very sensible woman," said Mr. Morrison, shrugging his shoulders. He disapproved on principle, he said always, of the introduction of women to matters they had nothing to do with, which was the conviction of his period. But he reflected that Buchanan in his present state was little better than a woman, and that the presence of his wife might be a correction. He opened the door accordingly, and she came out of her room in a moment, ready evidently for any call.

"Mary, I wish you to be here while I tell Morrison, once for all, that I must pay this money. I perhaps gave you a false idea when we talked of it before. I made you believe it was a smaller sum than it was. I—I was like the unjust steward—I took my bill and wrote fourscore."

"What is he meaning now, I wonder?" said Morrison to Mrs. Buchanan, with a half-comic glance aside. "He is just a wee off his head with diseased conscientiousness. I've met with the malady before, but it's rare, I must say, very rare. Well, come, out with it, Buchanan. What is this about fourscore?"

"You misunderstand me," he cried. "I must demand seriousness and your attention."

"Bless us, man, we're not at the kirk," Morrison said.

The minister was very impatient. He dealt the table a weak blow, as he sometimes did to the cushion of his pulpit.

"Perhaps I did it on purpose," he said, "perhaps it was half-unconscious, I cannot tell; but I gave you to believe that my debt was smaller than it really was. Morrison, I owed Mr. Anderson three hundred pounds."

The tone of solemnity with which he spoke could scarcely have been more impressive had he been reasoning, like St. Paul, of mercy, temperance, and judgment to come. And he felt as if he were doing so: it was the most solemn of truths he was telling against himself; the statement as of a dying man. His wife felt it so, too, in a sympathy that disturbed her reason, standing with her hand upon the back of his chair. Morrison stood for a moment, overcome by the intensity of the atmosphere, opening his mouth in an amazed gasp.

"Three hundred pounds!" the minister repeated, deliberately, with a weight of meaning calculated to strike awe into every heart.

But the impression made upon his audience unfortunately did not last. The writer stared and gasped, and then he burst into a loud guffaw. It was irresistible. The intense gravity of the speaker, the exaltation of his tone, the sympathy of his wife's restrained excitement, and then the words that came out of it all, so commonplace, so little conformable to that intense and tragic sentiment—overwhelmed the man of common sense. Morrison laughed till the tremulous gravity of the two discomposed him, and made him ashamed of himself, though their look of strained and painful seriousness almost brought back the fit when it was over. He stopped all of a sudden, silenced by this, and holding his hand to his side.

"I beg your pardon, Mrs. Buchanan. It was just beyond me. Lord's sake, man, dinna look so awesome. I was prepared to hear it was thirty thousand at the least."

"Thirty thousand," said the minister, "to some people is probably less than three hundred to me: but we cannot expect you to feel with us in respect to that. Morrison, you must help us somehow to pay this money, for we cannot raise it in a moment; but with time every penny shall be paid."

"To whom?" said Morrison, quietly.

"To whom? Are not you the man of business? To the estate, of course—to the heir."

"Not to me, certainly," said the lawyer. "I would be worthy to lose my trust if I acted in contradiction to my client's wishes in any such way. I will not take your money, Buchanan. No! man, though you are the minister, you are not a Pope, and we're not priest-ridden in this country. I'll be hanged if you shall ride rough shod over my head. I have my instructions, and if you were to preach at me till doomsday, you'll not change my clear duty. Pay away, if it's any pleasure to you. Yon wild woman, I dare to say, would snatch it up, or any siller you would put within reach of her; but deil a receipt or acquittance or any lawful document will you get from auld John Anderson's estate, to which you owe not a penny. Bless me, Mrs. Buchanan, you're a sensible woman. Can you not make him see this? You cannot want him to make ducks and drakes of your bairns' revenue. John Anderson was his leal friend, do you think it likely he would leave him to be harried at a lawyer's mercy? Do you not see, with the instincts of my race, I would have put you all to the horn years ago if it had been in my power?" he cried, jumping suddenly up. "Bless me, I never made so long a speech in my life. For goodsake, Buchanan, draw yourself together and give up this nonsense, like a man."

"It is nonsense," said the minister, who, during all this long speech, had gone through an entire drama of emotions, "that has taken all the pleasure for five long years and more out of my life."

"Oh, but, Claude, my man! you will mind I always said—"

"Ye hear her? That's a woman's consolation," said the minister, with a short laugh, in which it need not be said he was extremely unjust.

"It's sound sense, anyway," said Mr. Morrison, "so far as this fable of yours is concerned. Are you satisfied now? Well, now that we've got clear of that, I'll tell you my news. The Scotch property—as they call it, those two—has come out fine from all its troubles. What with good investments and feus, and a variety of favourable circumstances, for which credit to whom credit is due—I am not the person to speak—John Anderson's estate has nearly doubled itself since the good man was taken away. He was just a simpleton in his neglect of all his chances, saying, as he did—you must have heard him many a day—'there will aye be enough to serve my time.' I am not saying it was wonderful—seeing the laddie was all but a stranger—but he thought very, very little of his heir. But you see it has been my business to see to the advantage of his heir."

"Your behaviour to-day is not very like it, Morrison."

"Hoots!" said the man of business, "that's nothing but your nonsense. I can give myself the credit for never having neglected a real honest opening. To rob or to fleece a neighbour was not in that line. I am telling you I've neglected no real opening, and I will not say but that the result is worth the trouble, and Frank Mowbray is a lucky lad. And what has brought me here to-day—for I knew nothing of all this nonsense of yours that has taken up our time—was just to ask your advice if certain expedients were lawful for covering up this daft mother's shortcomings—certain expedients which I have been turning over in my head."

"What is lawful I am little judge of," said the minister, mournfully. "I have shown you how very little I am to be trusted even for what is right."

"Toots!" was the impatient reply. "I am not meaning the law of Scotland. If I do not know that, the more shame to me." It is another law I am thinking of. When I'm in with the King in the house of Rimmon, and him leaning on my shoulder, and the King bows down in the house of Rimmon, and me to be neighbourlike I bow with him, is this permitted to thy servant? You mind the text? That's what I've come to ask. There may be an intent to deceive that has no ill motive, and there may be things that the rigid would call lies. I've no respect for her to speak of, but she's a woman: and if a man could shield a creature like that—"

"I'm thinking," said Mrs. Buchanan, "now that your own business is over, Claude, and Mr. Morrison with his business to talk to you about, you will want me no longer. Are you really as sure as you say, Mr. Morrison, about the siller? You would not deceive him and me? It is not a lee as you say, with the best of motives? for that I could not bide any more than the minister. Give me your word before I go away."

"It is God's truth," said the lawyer, taking her hand. "As sure as death, which is a solemn word, though it's in every callant's mouth."

"Then I take it as such," she said, grasping his hand. "And, Claude, ye have no more need of me."

But what the further discussion was between the two men, which Mrs. Buchanan was so high-minded as not to wait to hear, I can tell no more than she did. They had a long consultation; and when the lawyer took his leave, Mr. Buchanan, with a strong step as if nothing had ever ailed him, not only conducted him to the door but went out with him, walking briskly up the street with a head as high as any man's; which perhaps was the consequence of his release, by Morrison's energetic refusal, from the burden which he had bound on his shoulders and hugged to his bosom for so long; and certainly was the happy result of having his thoughts directed towards another's troubles, and thus finally diverted from his own.

CHAPTER XXIII

THE LAST

"Elsie," said Mrs. Buchanan in the evening, when they were seated again together at their work, at the same hour in which they had discussed and settled on the previous night the necessary economies by which three hundred pounds were to be scraped together in as many years.

"Elsie, you will think I am going back of my word. But we are now seeing clearer, papa and I. There will be no need for what we were thinking of. I will keep on Betty who is a good lass on the whole, if she would get sweethearts and nonsense out of her head—and my dear there will be no reason why you should not go to the ball."

"Mother," said Elsie, "is it Willie?"

"No, it's not Willie—it's just the nature of events—Mr. Morrison he will not hear a word of it. He says Mr. Anderson, who was a good man, and a leal friend, and well I know would never have let harm come to your father, had left full instructions. Mr. Morrison is a fine honest man, but he is a little rough in his ways. He just insulted papa—and said he might throw away his siller if he liked, but not to him, for he would not receive it. And what is to be said after that? I always thought—"

"I would rather, far rather it had been paid! What am I caring about balls or white hands. I would rather have worked them to the bone and got it paid," Elsie cried.

"To whom," replied her mother, with an unconscious copy of the lawyer's tone, "to yon silly woman that has nothing to do with it, to throw away on her feathers and her millinery, and shame the auld man's settled plan? Your father was hard to move, but he was convinced at the last. And what do you think," she added, quickly, eager to abandon so dangerous a subject in view of Elsie's sudden excitement and glowing eyes, "Frank Mowbray turns out to be a very lucky laddie—and Mr. Morrison has as good as doubled his estate. What do you think of that? He will be a rich man."

"Oh, I am glad to hear it," cried Elsie with great indifference, "but, mother, about this money. Oh would you not rather pay it and be done with it, and wipe it out for ever and ever? What am I caring about balls? It will be years and years before you need take any thought for me. I would rather be of some use than go to the Queen's balls, let alone the Golf—and nobody that I am heeding would care a pin the less for me if my hands were as red as Betty's." She looked at them with a toss of her head, as she spoke, stretching them out in their smoothness and softness. This was the point at which Elsie's pride was touched. She did not like to think of these small members becoming as red as Betty's, who, for her part, was perfectly pleased with her hands.

"What were you meaning if I might ask about it being years and years before we need take any thought for you?"

Elsie was much startled by this question. She knew what she meant very well, but she had not intended to betray to her mother, or any one, what that hidden meaning was, and the words had come to her lips in the tide of feeling without thought. She gave one hurried glance at her mother's face, herself crimson red from chin to brow.

"I was meaning nothing," she said.

"That is not the way folk look when they mean nothing," her mother said.

"But it's true. I meant just nothing, nothing! I meant I would want no plenishing like Marion. I meant—that you need not take account of me, or say, as I've heard you saying, 'I must put this by for'—it used always to be for Marion. You are not to think of me like that," Elsie cried.

"And wherefore no? If I were not to think of you like that, I would be an ill mother: and why you less than another? You are taking no whimsies into your head, I hope, Elsie—for that is a thing I could not put up with at all."

"I have no whimsies in my head, mother," cried Elsie bending low over her work.

"You have something in it, whimsey or no," said her mother severely, "that is not known to me."

And there was a little relapse into silence and sewing for both. Elsie's breath came quick over her lengthened seam, the needle stumbled in her hold and pricked her fingers. She cast about all around her desperately for something to say. Indeed no—she had not meant anything, not anything that could be taken hold of and discussed: though it was equally true that she knew what she meant. How to reconcile these things! but they were both true.

"Mother," she said, after five dreadful moments of silence, and assuming a light tone which was very unlike her feelings. "Do you mind you told me that if there was any way I could make it up to Frank—but now that he's to be so well off there will be no need of that any more."

"Were you ever disposed to make it up to Frank?" her mother said quickly, taking the girl by surprise.

"I never thought about it—I—might never have had any occasion—I—don't know what I could have—done," Elsie replied, faltering.

"Because," said Mrs. Buchanan in the same rapid tone, "it would just be better than ever now. He will have a very good estate, and he's a very nice callant—kind and true, and not so silly as you might expect from his upbringing. If that was your thought, Elsie, it would be far wiser than I ever gave you credit for—and your father and me, we would never have a word but good and blessing to say—"

"Oh, mother," cried Elsie, "you to say the like of that to me—because a person was to have a good estate!"

"And wherefore no? A good estate is a very good thing: and plenty of siller, if it is not the salt of life—oh, my dear, many a time it gives savour to the dish. Wersh, wersh without it is often the household bread."

"It is not me," cried Elsie, flinging high her head, "that would ever take a man for his siller: I would rather have no bread at all. Just a mouthful of cake,[A] and my freedom to myself."

[A] It may here be explained for the benefit of the Souther that cake in the phraseology of old Scotland meant oat cake, in distinction from the greater luxury of "loaf-bread:" so that the little princess who suggested that the poor people who had no bread might eat cake, might have been a reasonable and wise Scot, instead of the silly little person we have all taken her to be.

"I said there were whimsies in the lassie's head," said Mrs. Buchanan, "it's the new-fangled thing I hear that they are setting up themselves against their natural lot. And what would you do with your freedom if you had it, I would like to know? Freedom, quotha! and she a lassie, and little over twenty. If you were not all fools at that age!"

"I was meaning just my freedom—to bide at home, and make no change," said Elsie, a little abashed.

"'Deed there are plenty," said Mrs. Buchanan, "that get that without praying for't. There are your aunties, two of them, Alison and Kirsteen—the old Miss Buchanans, very respectable, well-living women. Would you like to be like them? And Lizzie Aitken, she has let pass her prime, and the Miss Wemysses that are settling down in their father's old house, just very respectable. If that is what you would like, Elsie, you will maybe get it, and that without any force on Providence. They say there are always more women than men in every country-side."

Elsie felt herself insulted by these ironical suggestions. She made no answer, but went on at her work with a flying needle, as if it were a matter of life and death.

"But if that's not to your mind," Mrs. Buchanan added, "I would not take a scorn at Frank. There is nothing to object to in him. If there was anything to make up to him for, I would say again—make it up to him, Elsie: but being just very well off as he is, there is another way of looking at it. I never saw you object to him dangling after you when nothing was meant. But in serious earnest he well just be a very good match, and I would be easy in my mind about your future, if I saw you—"

"That you will never see me, mother," cried Elsie, with hot tears, "for his siller! I would rather die—"

"It need not be altogether for his siller," Mrs. Buchanan said, "and, oh! if you but knew what a difference that makes. To marry a poor man is just often like this. Your youth flies away fighting, and you grow old before your time, with nothing but bills on every hand, bills for your man, and bills for your bairns, hosen and shoes, meat and meal—and then to put the lads and lassies out in the world when all's done. Oh, Elsie, the like of you! how little you know!"

"You married a poor man yourself, mother," the girl cried.

"The better I'm fitted to speak," said Mrs. Buchanan. "But," she said, putting down her work, and rising from her chair, "I married your father, Elsie! and that makes all the difference," she said with dignity, as she went away.

What was the difference it made? Elsie asked herself the question, shaking back her hair from her face, and the tears from her eyes. Her cheeks were so hot and flushed with this argument, that the drops from her eyes boiled as they touched them. What made the difference? If ever she married a man, she said to herself, he should be a man of whom she would think as her mother did, that being him was what made all the difference. The image that rose before her mind was not, alas! of a man like her father, handsome and dignified and suave, a man of whom either girl or woman might be proud. She was not proud of his appearance, if truth must be told: there were many things in him that did not please her. Sometimes she was impatient, even vexed at his inaptitudes, the unconscious failures of a man who was not by birth or even by early breeding a gentleman. This thought stung her very sorely. Upon the sands ploutering, as she said, in the salt water, his bonnet pushed back, his shirt open at the neck, his coat hanging loosely on his shoulders! Elsie would have liked to re-dress that apparition, to dust the yellow sand from him and the little ridges of shattered shells which showed on his rough clothes as they did on the sea-shore. But no hand could keep that figure in order, even in a dream. And alas! he would be no placed minister like her father, or like Marion's husband, with a pleasant manse and a kirk in which all men would do him honour. Alas, alas, no! They did not reverence Johnny. They came plucking at him, crowding about him, calling to him, the very littlest of them, the very poorest of them, Elsie said to herself, to let them see the new beast! But at this thought her heart melted into the infinite softness of that approval, which is perhaps the most delightful sentiment of humanity, the approval of those we love—our approval of them more exquisite still than their approval of us. Elsie did not care the least for the new beast. She was altogether unscientific. She did not see the good of it, any more than the most ignorant. But when she thought of his genial countenance beaming over the small, the poor, the ignorant, her heart swelled, and she approved of him with all her soul.

Elsie had no easy life during the remaining months of the summer. After Frank Mowbray's birthday, when all was settled, and he had begun to trim up and brighten Mr. Anderson's old house, which was to be his future home, she had a great deal to bear from the members of her family, who one and all supported Frank's suit, which the young man lost no time in making. He for himself would take no refusal, but came back and back with a determination to be successful, which everybody said would eventually carry the day: and each one in succession took up his cause. All St. Rule's indeed, it may be said, were partisans of Frank. What ailed her at him, her friends said indignantly? who was Elsie Buchanan that she should look for better than that? A fine fellow, a good income, a nice house, and so near her mother! Girls who were going to India, or other outlandish places, asked, with tears in their eyes, what she could desire more? It was not as if there was any one else to disturb her mind, they said: for by this time Ralph Beaton and the rest were all drifting away to India and the Colonies to fulfil their fate: and to think of Johnny Wemyss as lifting his eyes to the minister's daughter, was such a thing as no one could have believed. Marion came in expressly from the country, with her three babies, to speak powerfully to the heart of her sister. "You will regret but once, and that will be all your life," she said solemnly. And it has already been seen how her mother addressed her on the subject. Rodie, too, made his wishes distinctly known.

"Why will you not take him?" he said; "he is as decent a chap as any in the town. If you scorn him, very likely you will never get another: and you must mind you will not always have me to take you about everywhere, and to get your partners at the balls."

"You to get me partners!" cried Elsie, wildly indignant; "you are a bonnie one! You just hang for your own partners on me; and as for taking me to places, where do you ever take me? That was all ended long ago."

But things became still more serious for Elsie, when her father himself came to a pause in front of her one day, with a grave face.

"Elsie," he said, "I hear it is in your power to make a young man's life, or to mar it; at least that is what he says to me."

"You will not put any faith in that, father. Who am I, that I should either make or mar?"

"I am tempted to think so myself," he said, with a smile; "but at your age people are seldom so wise. You are like your mother, my dear, and, I doubt not, would be a tower of strength to your husband, as I have good reason to say she has been; but that is not to say that any man has a right to put the responsibility of his being to another's charge. No, no; I would not say that. But there is no harm in the lad, Elsie. He has good dispositions. I would be at ease in my mind about your future, if you could find it in your heart to trust it to him."

"Father," cried Elsie, very earnestly, "I care no more about him than I do for old Adam, your old caddie. Just the same, neither more nor less."

Her father laughed, and said that was not encouraging for Frank.

"But, my dear," he said, "they say a lassie's mind is as light as air, and blows this way and that way, like the turn of the tide."

"They may say what they like, father," cried Elsie, with some indignation. "If you think my mother is like that, then your daughter can have no reason to complain."

"Bless me, no," cried Mr. Buchanan; "your mother! that makes all the difference."

These were the same words that Mrs. Buchanan had said. "As if because she was my mother she was not a woman, and because he was my father he was not a man," said Elsie to herself; "and where is the difference?" But she understood all the same.

"I will not say another word," said the minister. "If you care for him no more than for old Adam, there is not another word to say; but I would have been glad, on my own account, if you could have liked him, Elsie. It would have been a compensation. No matter, no matter, we'll say no more."

Elsie would have been more touched if her father had not alluded to that compensation. She had within herself a moment of indignation. "Me, a compensation," she cried to herself, "for your weary three hundred pounds. It is clear to me papa does not think his daughter very muckle worth, though he makes a difference for his wife!"

While all this was going on in the front of affairs, another little drama was proceeding underneath, in which Elsie was a far more interested performer, though she had no acknowledged title to take part in it at all.

For great and astonishing things followed the discovery of the new beast. Letters addressed to John Wemyss, Esq., letters franked by great names, which the people in the post-office wondered over, and which were the strangest things in the world to be sent to one of the student's lodgings, near the West Port, that region of humility—kept coming and going all the summer through, and when the time approached for the next College Session, and red gowns began to appear about the streets, Johnny Wemyss in his best clothes appeared one day in the minister's study, whither most people in St. Rule's found their way one time or other: for Mr. Buchanan, though, as we have seen, not quite able always to guide himself, was considered a famous adviser in most of the difficulties of life. Johnny was shamefaced and diffident, blushing like a girl, and squeezing his hat so tightly between his hands, that it presented strange peculiarities of shape when it appeared in the open air once more. Johnny, too, was by way of asking the minister's advice—that is to say, he had come to tell him what he meant to do, with some anxiety to know what impression the remarks he was about to make might have upon Elsie's father, but no thought of changing his resolutions for anything the minister might say. Johnny told how his discovery had brought him into communication with great scientific authorities in London, and that he had been advised to go there, where he would find books and instruction that might be of great use to him, and where he was told that his interests would be looked after by some persons of great influence and power. Mr. Buchanan listened with a smile, much amused to hear that the discovery of an unknown kind of "jeely fish" could give a man a claim for promotion: but when he heard that Johnny intended to go to London, he looked grave and shook his head.

"I am afraid that will very much interfere," he said, "with what seems to me far more important, your studies for your profession."

"Sir," said Johnny, "I'm afraid I have not made myself very clear. I never was very much set on the Church. I never thought myself good enough. And then I have no interest with any patron, and I would have little hope of a kirk."

The minister frowned a little, and then he smiled. "That mood of mind," he said, "is more promising than any other. I would far rather see a young lad that thought himself not good enough, than one that was over sure. And as for interest, an ardent student and a steady character, especially when he has brains, as you have, will always find interest to push him on."

"You are very kind to say so, Mr. Buchanan," said Johnny; "but," he added, "I have just a passion for the beasts."

"Sir," said the minister, looking grave, "no earthly passion should come in the way of the service of God."

"Unless, as I was thinking," said Johnny, "that might maybe be for the service of God too."

But this the minister was so doubtful of—and perhaps with some reason, for the discoverers of jelly fishes are not perhaps distinguished as devout men—that the interview ended in a very cool parting, Mr. Buchanan even hinting that this was a desertion of his Master's standard, and that the love of beasts was an unhallowed passion. And Johnny disappeared from St. Rule's shortly after, and was long absent, and silence closed over his name. In those days perhaps people were less accustomed to frequent letters than we are, and could live without them, for the most anxious heart has to acknowledge the claim of the impossible. Johnny Wemyss, however, wrote to Rodie now and then, and Elsie had the advantage of many things which Rodie never understood at all in these epistles. And sometimes a newspaper came containing an account of some of Mr. Wemyss's experiments, or of distinctions won by him, which electrified his old friends. For one thing, he went upon a great scientific voyage, and came home laden with discoveries, which were, it appeared, though no one in St. Rule's could well understand how, considered of great importance in the scientific world. And from that time his future was secure. It was just after his return from this expedition, that one day there came a letter franked by a great man, whose name on the outside of an envelope was of value as an autograph, openly and boldly addressed to Miss Elsie Buchanan, The Manse, St. Rule's. It was written very small, on a sheet of paper as long as your arm, and it poured out into Elsie's heart the confidences of all those silent years. She showed it to her mother, and Mrs. Buchanan gasped and could say no word. She took it to her father, and the minister cried "Johnny Wemyss!" in a voice like a roar of astonishment and fury.

"Do you mean this has been going on all the time," he cried, "and not a word said?"

"Nothing has been going on," said Elsie, pale but firm.

"Oh, it was settled, I suppose, before he went away."

"Never word was spoken either by him or me," said Elsie; "but I will not say but what we knew each other's meaning, I his, and he mine," she added, softly, after a pause.

There was a good deal of trouble about it one way and another, but you may believe that neither father nor mother, much less Rodie and John, though the one was a W. S., and the other an advocate, could interfere long with a wooing like this.

Margaret Oliphant – A Short Biography

Margaret Oliphant Wilson was born on April 4th, 1828 to Francis W. Wilson, a clerk, and Margaret Oliphant, at Wallyford, near Musselburgh, East Lothian.

She spent her childhood at Lasswade, near Dalkeith, Glasgow before moving to Liverpool.

Her youth was spent in establishing a writing style so much so that, in 1849, she had her first novel published: Passages in the Life of Mrs. Margaret Maitland based on the Scottish Free Church movement. It met with some success and was a good start to her career.

Two years later, in 1851, her third book Caleb Field was published. It was also now that she met the publisher William Blackwood in Edinburgh and was asked to contribute to his well-received Blackwood's Magazine. It was to be a lifetimes endeavor. Over the course of the relationship she would have well over 100 articles published.

In May 1852, Margaret married her cousin, Frank Wilson Oliphant, at Birkenhead, and they settled at Harrington Square, Camden, London. He was an artist working primarily in stained glass. With the marriage she became Margaret Oliphant Wilson Oliphant.

Their marriage produced six children but three tragically died in infancy.

When her husband developed signs of the dreaded consumption (tuberculosis) they moved, on the advice of doctors, to warmer climes. In January 1859 it was to Florence, and then to Rome where, sadly, he died.

Margaret was naturally devastated but was also now left without support and only her income from her writing. She returned to England and took up the task of supporting her three remaining children by her literary activity.

By now she was being published both as an established novelist and regularly in Blackwood's Magazine, amongst others. Her incredible and prolific work rate increased both her commercial reputation and the size of her reading audience.

Against this her domestic life continued to be tragic, full of sorrow and disappointment.

In January 1864 her only remaining daughter Maggie died and was buried in her father's grave in Rome. Her brother, who had emigrated to Canada, was shortly afterwards involved in financial ruin. Margaret generously offered a home to him and his children, adding another demand to her already heavy responsibilities.

In 1866 she settled at Windsor to be closer to her sons, who were being educated at near-by Eton School. That year, her second cousin, Annie Louisa Walker, came to live with her as a companion-housekeeper. Windsor was now to be her home for the rest of her life.

Her literary career for three decades was one of constant delivery and success. Whether she wrote historical works or across several genres in fiction: domestic realism, historical, romance or supernatural she was successful.

For more than thirty years she pursued a varied literary career but family life continued to bring problems.

The literary ambitions she wished for her sons were unfulfilled. Cyril Francis, the eldest, died in 1890, leaving a Life of Alfred de Musset, incorporated in his mother's Foreign Classics for English Readers. The younger, Francis, who she nicknamed 'Cecco', collaborated with her in the Victorian Age of English

Literature and won a position at the British Museum, but was rejected by Sir Andrew Clark, a famous physician. Cecco died in 1894.

With the last of her children now lost to her, she had but little further interest in life. Her health steadily and inexorably declined.

Margaret Oliphant Wilson Oliphant died at the age of 69 in Wimbledon on 20th June 1897. She is buried in Eton beside her sons.

At her death, Margaret was still working on Annals of a Publishing House, a record of Blackwood's Magazine with which she had enjoyed such a successful relationship.

Her Autobiography and Letters, which present a thoughtful picture of her domestic anxieties, was published in 1899. Only parts were written with a wider audience in mind: she had originally intended the Autobiography for her son, but he died before she could finish it.

Opinions on Oliphant's work are split, with some critics seeing her as a 'domestic novelist', while others recognize her work as influential and important to the Victorian literature canon. Critical reception from her contemporaries is also divided. John Skelton took the view that Oliphant wrote too much and too quickly. Writing a Blackwood's article called 'A Little Chat About Mrs. Oliphant', he asked, "Had Mrs. Oliphant concentrated her powers, what might she not have done? We might have had another Charlotte Brontë or another George Eliot." However not all of the contemporary reception was negative. The esteemed M. R. James admired Oliphant's supernatural fiction, concluding that "the religious ghost story, as it may be called, was never done better than by Mrs. Oliphant in 'The Open Door' and 'A Beleaguered City'. Mary Butts lavished praise on Oliphant's ghost story 'The Library Window', describing it as "one masterpiece of sober loveliness".

More modern critics of Oliphant's work include Virginia Woolf, who asked in Three Guineas whether Oliphant's autobiography does not lead the reader "to deplore the fact that Mrs. Oliphant sold her brain, her very admirable brain, prostituted her culture and enslaved her intellectual liberty in order that she might earn her living and educate her children."

Whatever the merits of their cases Margaret Oliphant has been shamefully neglected in modern years. She is now becoming more widely recognised as a leading writer of her day.

Margaret Oliphant – A Concise Bibliography

A canon of more than 120 works, including novels, travel books, histories, and volumes of literary criticism.

Novels

Margaret Maitland (1849)
Merkland (1850)
Caleb Field (1851)
John Drayton (1851)

Adam Graeme (1852)
The Melvilles (1852)
Katie Stewart (1852)
Harry Muir (1853)
Ailieford (1853)
The Quiet Heart (1854)
Magdalen Hepburn (1854)
Zaidee (1855)
Lilliesleaf (1855)
Christian Melville (1855)
The Athelings (1857)
The Days of My Life (1857)
Orphans (1858)
The Laird of Norlaw (1858)
Agnes Hopetoun's Schools and Holidays (1859)
Lucy Crofton (1860)
The House on the Moor (1861)
The Last of the Mortimers (1862)
Heart and Cross (1863)
Salem Chapel (1863)
The Rector (1863)
Doctor's Family (1863)
The Perpetual Curate (1864)
Miss Marjoribanks (1866)
Phoebe Junior (1876)
A Son of the Soil (1865)
Agnes (1866)
Madonna Mary (1867)
Brownlows (1868)
The Minister's Wife (1869)
The Three Brothers (1870)
John: A Love Story (1870)
Squire Arden (1871)
At his Gates (1872)
Ombra (1872
May (1873)
Innocent (1873)
The Story of Valentine and his Brother (1875)
A Rose in June (1874)
For Love and Life (1874)
Whiteladies (1875)
An Odd Couple (1875)
The Curate in Charge (1876)
Carità (1877)
Young Musgrave (1877)
Mrs. Arthur (1877)
The Primrose Path (1878)
Within the Precincts (1879)

The Fugitives (1879)
A Beleaguered City (1879)
The Greatest Heiress in England (1880)
He That Will Not When He May (1880)
In Trust (1881)
Harry Joscelyn (1881)
Lady Jane (1882)
A Little Pilgrim in the Unseen (1882)
The Lady Lindores (1883)
Sir Tom (1883)
Hester (1883)
It Was a Lover and his Lass (1883)
The Lady's Walk (1883)
The Wizard's Son (1884)
Madam (1884)
The Prodigals and their Inheritance (1885)
Oliver's Bride (1885)
A Country Gentleman and his Family (1886)
A House Divided Against Itself (1886)
Effie Ogilvie (1886)
A Poor Gentleman (1886)
The Son of his Father (1886)
Joyce (1888)
Cousin Mary (1888)
The Land of Darkness (1888)
Lady Car (1889)
Kirsteen (1890)
The Mystery of Mrs. Biencarrow (1890)
Sons and Daughters (1890)
The Railway Man and his Children (1891)
The Heir Presumptive and the Heir Apparent (1891)
The Marriage of Elinor (1891)
Janet (1891)
The Cuckoo in the Nest (1892)
Diana Trelawny (1892)
The Sorceress (1893)
A House in Bloomsbury (1894)
Sir Robert's Fortune (1894)
Who Was Lost and is Found (1894)
Lady William (1894)
Two Strangers (1895)
Old Mr. Tredgold (1895)
The Unjust Steward (1896)
The Ways of Life (1897)

Short stories
Neighbours on the Green (1889)

A Widow's Tale and Other Stories (1898)
That Little Cutty (1898)
The Open Door (1918)

Selected Articles

Mary Russel Mitford (Blackwood's Magazine, Vol. 75, 1854)
Evelin and Pepys (Blackwood's Magazine, Vol. 76, 1854)
The Holy Land (Blackwood's Magazine, Vol. 76, 1854)
Mr. Thackeray and his Novels (Blackwood's Magazine, Vol. 77, 1855)
Bulwer (Blackwood's Magazine, Vol. 77, 1855)
Charles Dickens (Blackwood's Magazine, Vol. 77, 1855)
Modern Novelists—Great and Small (Blackwood's Magazine, Vol. 77, 1855)
Modern Light Literature: Poetry (Blackwood's Magazine, Vol. 79, 1856)
Religion in Common Life (Blackwood's Magazine, Vol. 79, 1856)
Sydney Smith (Blackwood's Magazine, Vol. 79, 1856)
The Laws Concerning Women (Blackwood's Magazine, Vol. 79, 1856)
The Art of Caviling (Blackwood's Magazine, Vol. 80, 1856)
Béranger (Blackwood's Magazine, Vol. 83, 1858)
The Condition of Women (Blackwood's Magazine, Vol. 83, 1858)
The Missionary Explorer (Blackwood's Magazine, Vol. 83, 1858)
Religious Memoirs (Blackwood's Magazine, Vol. 83, 1858)
Social Science (Blackwood's Magazine, Vol. 88, 1860)
Scotland and her Accusers (Blackwood's Magazine, Vol. 90, 1861)
The Chronicles of Carlingford (Blackwood's Magazine 1862–1865)
Girolamo Savonarola (Blackwood's Magazine, Vol. 93, 1863)
The Life of Jesus (Blackwood's Magazine, Vol. 96, 1864)
Giacomo Leopardi (Blackwood's Magazine, Vol. 98, 1865)
The Great Unrepresented (Blackwood's Magazine, Vol. 100, 1866)
Mill on the Subjection of Women (The Edinburgh Review, Vol. 130, 1869)
The Opium-Eater (Blackwood's Magazine, Vol. 122, 1877)
Russian and Nihilism in the Novels of I. Tourgeniéf (Blackwood's Magazine, Vol. 127, 1880)
School and College (Blackwood's Magazine, Vol. 128, 1880)
The Grievances of Women (Fraser's Magazine, New Series, Vol. 21, 1880)
Mrs. Carlyle (The Contemporary Review, Vol. 43, May 1883)
The Ethics of Biography (The Contemporary Review, July 1883)
Victor Hugo (The Contemporary Review, Vol. 48, July/December 1885)
A Venetian Dynasty (The Contemporary Review, Vol. 50, August 1886)
Laurence Oliphant (Blackwood's Magazine, Vol. 145, 1889)
Tennyson (Blackwood's Magazine, Vol. 152, 1892)
Addison, the Humorist (Century Magazine, Vol. 48, 1894)
The Anti-Marriage League (Blackwood's Magazine, Vol. 159, 1896)

Biographies

Edward Irving (1862)

Francis of Assisi (1871)
Count de Montalembert (1872)
Dante (1877)
Cervantes (1880)
Life of Sheridan in the English Men of Letters series (1883)
John Tulloch (1888)
Laurence Oliphant (1892)

Historical & Critical Works

Historical Sketches of the Reign of George II (1869)
The Makers of Florence (1876)
A Literary History of England from 1760 to 1825 (1882)
The Makers of Venice (1887)
Royal Edinburgh (1890)
Jerusalem (1891)
The Makers of Modern Rome (1895)
William Blackwood and his Sons (1897)
The Sisters Brontë. In: Women Novelists of Queen Victoria's Reign (1897)

www.ingramcontent.com/pod-product-compliance
Lightning Source LLC
Chambersburg PA
CBHW071401170626
46811CB00003B/1221